I pulled a Dead End Dating card from my purse and handed it to Ash. He stuffed it into his pocket.

"I'll be in touch if I find anything."

"That, or if you get lonely."

A grin split his face and my heart gave a tiny little pitter-patter. "That's the worst pickup line I've ever heard."

I tossed a major *shut up!* at my hormones and frowned. "I'm not trying to pick you up. I'm a matchmaker. It's my job to help lonely men and women the world over. So," I eyed him, "are you?"

"Am I what?"

"Lonely?"

"No."

"Are you married?"

"No."

"Do you have a girlfriend?"

"No."

"Boyfriend?"

"No."

"A blow-up doll named Ginger?"

He shook his head. "You do talk a lot."

Love was definitely in the air.

Also by Kimberly Raye
published by Ballantine Books

Dead End Dating
Dead and Dateless

Your Coffin or Mine?

A Novel of Vampire Love

KIMBERLY RAYE

BALLANTINE BOOKS • NEW YORK

A Ballantine Books Mass Market Original

Copyright © 2007 by Kimberly Groff
Excerpt from *Just One Bite* copyright © 2007 by Kimberly Groff.

Published in the United States by Ballantine Books, an imprint of The Random House Publishing Group, a division of Random House, Inc., New York.

BALLANTINE BOOKS and colophon are trademarks of Random House, Inc.

This book contains an excerpt from the forthcoming mass market edition of *Just One Bite* by Kimberly Raye. This excerpt has been set for this edition only and may not reflect the final content of the forthcoming novel.

ISBN 978-0-345-49218-0

Cover illustration: Marcin Baranski

Printed in the United States of America

www.ballantinebooks.com

OPM 9 8 7 6 5 4 3 2 1

For Debbie Villanueva,
for always being supportive and understanding,
and for never, *ever* bitching when I drag you to the
bookstore to buy my latest book!

Acknowledgments

Writing is hard work, and I couldn't do it without the help of several key people: my wonderful editor, Charlotte Herscher, who makes me feel like I can actually write a good book; my agent, Natasha Kern, who calms me down when I'm frantic and also makes me feel like I can write a good book; my loving husband, who doesn't mind eating take-out when I'm on a deadline; my writing buds, Nina Bangs and Gerry Bartlett, who are always supportive and eager to dish about the ins and outs of the publishing business. My heartfelt thanks to all of you!

And many, *many* thanks to my readers who send notes and e-mails, and visit me on MySpace. Your encouragement means everything to me!

One
♥ ♥ ♥

I was being followed.

If that wasn't creepy enough, it was dark out, I was all alone, and I was standing in a smelly alley near Times Square.

Talk about a Wes Craven flick.

For me, however, it was just another day in the life of a fantabulous five-hundred-year-old (and holding) born vampire. My name? Countess Lilliana Arrabella Guinevere du Marchette, but my best buds call me Lil.

Because of my BV heritage, I ooze sex appeal, and since it's oozing out of a totally hot package (great body, great face, kickin' highlights), I've had more than my share of stalkers. Like the rest of my kind, I attract the opposite sex en masse.

Okay. So maybe en masse might be stretching things

a *teensy* bit. Particularly since I haven't had an official date in . . .

Well, I can't actually remember the last time. (Fix ups DO NOT count, Ma.) To make matters worse, I was sorta, kinda dumped recently by a megahot bounty hunter after our one and only night together (sniffle).

But neither of those is due to a lack of hotness on my part. The Dating Deficit? My choice. No, really. I've given up meaningless flings in favor of finding my eternity mate, settling down, and propagating the species.

As for the bounty hunter . . . I'm sure (fingers crossed) he'll soon realize what a vampilicious babe I am and come begging my forgiveness. I, of course, will tell him—as would any female who'd been dumped with not so much as a *Later* scribbled on a Post-it—to go bite himself.

At least that was the revenge fantasy I was currently tuning into. In between numero uno—I rip off all of his clothes and we make like jackrabbits—and three—he rips off all of mine and we make like jackrabbits.

I know, right? It was one measly night. I should get a life (or an afterlife in my case) and forget all about him. And the way he kissed. And touched. And tasted.

Yes, I've tasted him, too, but not during sex. I'm weak, but not *that* weak. The tasting occurred before the sex.

I'd been staked and he'd been trying to help me recoup my strength. I'd drank from him and since then we've had this mental connection thing going on. He can send me thoughts and vice versa.

Not that he's sent me anything in the past months.

No desperate apologies. No sweet nothings. No flowers. Not even a measly *IOU for a night of hot, wild, primo mattress dancing.*

All the more reason to push him completely out of my mind and get back on track, right? Right.

So, um, where was I?

Oh, yeah. Dark, creepy alley. My being followed. No huge deal.

Until now.

Wedge heels tapped the pavement behind me and thundered through my head as I rounded a corner and started down another alley. The sharp aroma of cheap hair spray mingled with generic body spray burned my nostrils. I turned and caught a glimpse of a chipped manicure clutching a tiny disposable camera before my stalker realized I was looking and ducked behind a Dumpster.

A man I'd expected (see the long rambling above), but a *woman*?

While I knew chicks got off to really hot chicks everyday (I could appreciate the latest Angelina Jolie pic as much as the next mature, sexually confident, semilonely woman), I couldn't shake the gut feeling that there was more to this than a love-struck groupie eager to feed her own private fantasies.

I kept staring at the Dumpster until she stole another glance at me. My gaze collided with hers for a nanosecond and her stats rolled through my head like movie credits (another perk of being a vampire is that I can look into someone's eyes and read their mind).

Gwen Rowley. Thirty-nine years old. Italian. Full-time fourth-grade teacher and part-time private investigator. Divorced mother of three. Hated men. Even more, she hated her mother, who'd put her up to following a small-time matchmaker when she could have been (a) grading tomorrow's math assignment, and then, (b) tailing her ex and his new girlfriend. They were going bowling. Gwen hated bowling, too.

She retreated behind the massive metal monster and the connection ended before I could find out the really good stuff.

Like who in Damien's name was her mother and why would she want me followed?

And, more important, had Gwen started dating again?

FYI: In addition to being a hot, happening *vampere,* I'm also Manhattan's newest primo matchmaker.

Gwen peeked around the corner once more, camera poised, and my instincts screamed for me to shift into Super Vamp mode, make like my last client fee, and—*poof*—disappear.

Fast.

Our species, and the dozens of Others out there, hadn't survived thousands of years by keeping a high profile. We exercised caution and kept to ourselves and avoided cameras at all cost.

I paused and made a show of adjusting my shoe (snakeskin Prada stiletto for the record), and gave her my best profile.

Hey, we're talking *stiletto*. As in mucho P-A-I-N. I simply *had* to stop and wiggle my toes.

And ease my own conscience. What can I say? I've got a soft spot for potential clients. Even more, I'm a jumbo marshmallow when it comes to potential clients with bossy, overbearing mothers (DO NOT get me started).

The camera clicked a few times. Finally, I ceased with the hamming it up and shifted into action mode. I stepped forward, my feet moving so fast that I emerged from my back alley route a half a block away, walked into the massive high-rise near the heart of Times Square, and sailed onto the elevator before Gwen had a chance to blink, much less follow.

Did I mention that born vamps are superfast in addition to being total mind-reading hotties?

While I wasn't opposed to giving the woman a few pics so she didn't go back empty-handed, I hadn't taken a back alley route for the great scenery. The last thing—the very *last* thing—I needed was to be caught dead (or undead) in a place like *this*.

I stepped off the elevator on the eighth floor and walked into the lobby of KNYC, a local cable network near the NBC studios. KNYC was responsible for several homegrown news programs, a handful of talk shows, and the recent reality smash *Manhattan's Most Wanted.*

MMW was a local version of *The Bachelor* that paired up one of the city's most sought after males with fifty marriage-minded, crème de la crème females, and let him weed them down to The One.

At least that was the idea. The last guy—a Wall Street financier—had narrowed his bevy of bombshells down to The One Who'd Taken the Rock and Hauled Ass. She'd pocketed the cash, headed for Mexico, and the financier had ended up on Dr. Phil.

This year's bachelor? Some heartthrob weather guy at one of the local stations. Since I don't really watch much television (except *Date My Mom* and *I Love New York,* both purely for research), I couldn't say exactly which one. But being a super-intuitive vampere, I didn't have to see him to know the really important stuff. Namely, he actually had a job and decent looks, otherwise he'd be telling fortunes on Coney Island instead of on television.

Inside the lobby of the station, plush gold carpeting cushioned my stance and eased the pressure on my tootsies. Pale yellow walls decorated with gold Art Deco mirrors surrounded me. Cinnamon-colored leather chairs traced the perimeter. Several tables overflowed with magazines. A man stood near a glass doorway marked STUDIO A, a headset hooked around his neck and a clipboard in his hands.

The only man in a room that otherwise overflowed with single, successful, smart, attractive, *desperate* women.

Talk about a target-rich environment.

I'd taken on several vamps and weres over the past few months, but Others were much harder to pair up than your average human. For vamps, there was too much emphasis on Orgasm Quotients (the number of times a female vamp sang "Oh Happy Day" during any one sexual encounter) and Fertility Ratings (a little digit that reflected how likely a male was to hit a bulls-eye when it came to procreation). Likewise, weres were obsessed with alpha males and lunar cycles. Since I'm an equal opportunity matchmaker with enough credit card bills to make the national deficit look like chump change, I'd decided to take the easy route and beef up my human client list.

I smiled, reached into my leather Prada clutch for a stack of business cards, and stepped toward the first cluster of females.

I was just about to slide a card into an attractive woman's hand—twenty-five, nurse, fed up with losers with great big egos and tiny penises—when I heard the deep, familiar voice.

"Help me."

T𝔀O
❤ ❤ ❤

My entire body went rigid and my heart paused mid-beat. (Yep, I've got one and it keeps time like everyone else's.) If I wasn't a vampire with a royal heritage to uphold and a Christian Dior skirt and jacket to keep wrinkle-free, I would have fainted dead away.

It couldn't be . . . Ty?

It wasn't, I realized a few frantic heartbeats later when I heard the voice again. Higher pitched this time, and not nearly as stirring.

"I could use some help here. I think my boobs are crooked."

My heart started beating again and I turned to see the female who'd come up behind me.

She (and I use the term loosely) had long, flowing red hair. She wore a pale beige lip gloss (MAC Spring

Sunset) and a faint shimmer of bronzing blush. My attention shifted downward, over a clingy crimson dress, shapely calves, to a pair of strappy red suede high heels.

Not bad.

I might have bought the whole XX act if I hadn't been gifted with the deluxe benefits package that comes with my kind at birth.

Super-hearing? *Check.*

Night vision? *Check.*

Mind-reading ability? *Check.*

Unsurpassed beauty? *Check, check.*

Big brown eyes rimmed with kohl collided with mine.

John Schumacker. Forty-two years old. Insurance adjuster. Divorced. No children. Wife had an affair. But not because John had driven her to it or anything like that. So what if he'd worked a lot of hours? He'd wanted to give her nice things. He hadn't been desperate to avoid intimate contact because of a certain erectile dysfunction and even if he had, it was no big deal. Men the world over had the same problem. He was just a little fast on the draw, that was all. Nothing major. Certainly not enough to send Melba running into the arms of some Latino lover named Julio with a big bank account and an even bigger—

I tore my gaze away and concentrated on his perfectly lined mouth. Gender aside, the man knew how to use a lip pencil.

"What do you think?" The question came out soft

and breathy, as if he were doing his best to convince me that he was more Jane than John. He wiggled his shoulders as if to adjust an uncomfortable bra strap.

"I think you need a personal shopper."

"What?" He glanced down. "I bought this off the mannequin at Macy's just yesterday. It's the latest for this season. And it all matches."

"The dress is great. But it's a *dress*."

"So?" He frowned at me. "A chick can't have a nice dress or what?"

"I hate to break it to you, but you're not a chick."

His gaze narrowed. "I'm one hundred percent, prime, Grade A chick. I'm chick to the bone. I'm—"

"Chicks don't say *chicks*," I cut in. "When I refer to one of my same sex sistahs, I say *woman*. Or *lady*. Maybe the occasional *you dumb bee-yotch*. *Chick* is a guy term. Like *broad* or *hot mama*. The shoes are a nice touch, though." I hadn't read cross-dresser in his mental repertoire and I couldn't help but wonder. "Enzo Angiolini?"

"What?"

Cross-dresser my ass. "Enzo is a who, not a what, and you are definitely NOT a chick." I eyed him, my gaze sweeping him from head to toe—oooh, nice pedicure—and back up. "You're not even close."

"Am, too." Panic chased desperation across his face and I suddenly felt like the IRS agent given the lucky task of auditing Mother Teresa.

"Come with me," I said before I could stop myself. "I grabbed his hand. When he didn't budge, I exerted a little vamp strength and hauled him along after me.

"Come on, lady," he muttered, his voice deeper now. "Don't turn me in. I'm just trying to make a living." He tried to dig in his heels but only succeeded in stumbling after me. His voice lowered a notch. "I'm undercover, okay? I'm working an insurance fraud case. See that blonde over there?"

I stopped. My head swiveled to a group of women. All blond.

"The tall one. Blue dress. Nice legs. She's currently collecting a check for a debilitating back injury."

"She looks all right to me."

"Exactly." His voice lowered as if he were about to tell me something I didn't know. "She's lying."

"You think?"

He nodded. "She's milking the insurance company. I've been following her for two weeks now."

I glanced at her shoes. Three-inch pumps. "So what are you waiting for? Take her down." If the height wasn't cause for an arrest, the fact that they were white and we weren't even close to Memorial Day would have been reason enough.

"I can't. Yes, the shoes are a direct violation of her doctor's orders, but it isn't enough ammunition to hold up in court. She's just standing there. She hasn't really *done* anything. Yet. But if she sets one foot on the dance floor, goes waterskiing, bungee jumping, or any of the other crap they do on those group dates, her butt is mine. That's why you can't blow the whistle on me. I'm tailing her." He held up a maroon clutch purse. "And I'm getting it all on tape."

"Won't it be on tape anyway because the show is being taped?"

"*If* she makes it that far. But what if she doesn't? She might not make it past the applicant phase, and I need to crack this case regardless. I'm filming everything in the meantime. My promotion is riding on it."

A promotion he desperately needed since his wife had taken him to the cleaners and he was now living in a one-room efficiency eating SpaghettiOs every night.

My chest hitched.

Excitement, I told myself. Divorced? Lonely? Smacked of potential client to me. I certainly didn't *care* that he was divorced and lonely.

All right, already. So maybe I cared a little. Have you ever smelled a can of SpaghettiOs?

"Come." I hauled him through the glass doors and out into the hallway.

"Wait." His voice fell several octaves as he struggled to keep up. "Stop. Please don't do this, lady. You can't blow the whistle on me. I need this. I need—"

"—a better bra," I finished for him as I jerked him into the ladies' room.

The door rocked shut behind us. I leaned over and checked to make sure the stalls were empty before I turned back to him.

"My best piece of advice: underwire. Otherwise, you're liable to lose the stuffing. What's in there anyway?" I stepped back and eyed the uneven lumps.

"My gym socks."

No wonder he was lonely.

I rummaged in my purse, pulled out a Dead End Dating business card and scribbled on the back. "First thing tomorrow morning, head over to La Perla." I handed him the card. "Here's the address. Go to the counter and ask for a pair of silicone inserts, *then* ask for the bra."

He stared down at the card. "You're helping me?"

I shrugged. "You're a poor schmuck in need of a little guidance and I *do* own a dating service. The best in Manhattan, as a matter of fact. Lil Marchette," I held out a hand, "at your service."

"I'm John." As if I didn't already know. He gripped my fingers for a small shake before shifting his gaze back to the card. "Thanks, but I don't need a date."

My gaze collided with his, but I didn't vamp him. I didn't have to. Realization sparked and he nodded.

"Then again, if I got my promotion, I could afford to date again. A good service would certainly come in handy to help me get back into the game."

"Exactly. In the meantime," I eyed his chest. "Let's see what we can do to help you out right now." I reached out and cupped John's gym socks.

"I need you."

The words echoed through my head and I stiffened. "Listen, buster. This is strictly professional." I squeezed and juggled. "Don't take my interest personally. I just can't stand to see a pair of decent sling backs go to waste. When it comes to footwear, you're not doing half bad. It's all the rest. You need to stand up straighter, hold your chest out more. You're loud, you're proud, you're a *woman*. Carry yourself like one."

"*I really need you.*"

"I mean it." I frowned at John. "Just because I'm adjusting your boobs doesn't mean I have any romantic interest in you. I have my own boobs if I want to cop a feel. And if I want more, I have a significant other." Okay, so I'd *had* a significant other. For about six hours—six and a half, tops. That still didn't mean I was desperate enough to jump the first guy who let me feel his boobs. Particularly since he was human. Sure, humans were great for sex and feeding, but it wasn't as if you could take them home to the folks. At least not my folks. Already, my mother was debating between arsenic and a sharp-shooter to take out my youngest brother's human fiancée—

"*Dammit, would you listen?*"

The deep, stirring voice cut into my thoughts again and drew my undivided attention. My hands froze mid-squeeze and my heart stalled.

"*I don't have much time, Lil. You have to listen to me. I need you. I'm in . . .*"

The words faded before the sentence ended, but it didn't matter. My gut clenched and my throat went tight and I *knew.*

I hadn't been hallucinating before when I'd heard the first unmistakable *"Help me."*

It was his voice, right?

The one and only Ty Bonner. *The* jerk-off-made-vampire who'd given me the brush-off.

And he was in trouble.

Deep, deep trouble.

Three
❤ ❤ ❤

You shouldn't be doing this.

The warning echoed in my head for the trillionth time since I'd left the television station, but I was too busy breaking and entering to pay much attention.

I stood mid-block on Washington Street in the heart of the meatpacking district. While the rest of the area had fallen into the hands of New York's trendsetters, the art galleries and the chic restaurants hadn't crept this far south.

It was early evening, barely eight o'clock, but the large warehouse that housed Ty's third-floor loft loomed dark and quiet against the moonlit sky. Shadows clung to the large steel door. The surrounding motif was classic gangsta. Orange and blue graffiti cut across the fading red metal and splattered the surrounding brick. The remains of a lightbulb hung overhead and tiny particles of glass shimmered from the cracks in the sidewalk.

The only light drifted from the apartments across the street. Not that I needed any. My gaze sliced through the darkness and zeroed in on the small buzzer that sat next to the massive door.

Back when I'd been wanted for murder, Ty had aided and abetted and we'd been roommates. I knew firsthand that he had neighbors on the first and second floors, so I pressed the button and waited.

And waited.

Then again, maybe the neighbors had moved out. Particularly the guy on the second floor. I know I would have taken a hike if two vamps (one of them wanted for slicing and dicing) had dropped through my ceiling while I was doing the nasty.

My fingers closed around the door latch and turned. Hardware groaned and the lock soon gave. I flattened my palm against the metal and pushed. Wood cracked and splintered. The door swung inward. I stepped into the narrow hallway and made my way to the freight elevator at the far end.

I hooked one finger under the massive gate and pushed. The iron mesh slid upward like nails grating on a chalkboard. Stepping inside, I punched the button for the third floor. The engine groaned, wheels turned, and the contraption started to move north.

I wasn't sure what I was going to accomplish by coming here. I just knew I had to *do* something. It had been two hours since I'd heard Ty's silent message.

Since then?

Nada.

While I'd handed out cards at the MMV studio and given my own ten-minute video interview (not that I was even remotely interested in being on the show—my mother would DIE—but I'd had to go through the motions), I'd tried to convince myself that the silent message had been a mistake. Ty had obviously dialed a wrong number. He'd been trying to contact the slut he'd left me for and had inadvertently sent the message to *moi*.

"You have to listen to me. I need you. I'm in . . . "

In what?

In the middle of slapping the salami? And he'd needed a booty call to keep from going blind?

Or maybe he'd been in the shower and he'd needed someone to bend over and pick up the soap?

Or maybe he'd been in the mood for a little AB negative and he'd needed a warm, willing donor?

Really, who knew how many women Ty was currently playing? He probably let everyone with a vagina and a pair of fangs sip away at him. He could be telepathically linked to every female vampire in Manhattan.

Or he could be in serious trouble.

My mind voted for the first explanation. My hormones chanted for number two. And my heart?

Girlfriend, pu-lease.

I was saving that particular piece of anatomy for Count Right. Since Ty's a made vampire and I'm born, settling down, squeezing out a few baby vamps, and living eternally ever after are not in the realm of possibility for us. Made vamps can't procreate. I need one of my own kind for that. Someone as mega-licious as Ty, but with the appropriate born vamp DNA. Someone like, say, Remy Tremaine.

Remy was the chief of the Fairfield police department, and owned a megabucks security company on the side. I hadn't really liked him at first. We'd been friends forever and I'd seen him wear knickers back in the old country. Nuff said.

Recently, however, he'd helped me in a desperate fight for my life with a vengeful female vamp. Funny how kicking royal ass can make a man oodles more attractive.

Then again, Ty kicked ass for a living. Day in. Day out. He faced danger with a capital D. Which meant that I couldn't get him or his naked badass bod off my mind.

It also meant that he'd probably pissed off his fair share of people and made a great deal of enemies. People who might want to hurt him. Or worse . . .

The elevator car came to a jarring stop. I stepped into another small hallway. The gangsta theme continued. More blue and orange with a little purple, and a few four-letter words thrown in.

I reached his door and grabbed the knob. With any luck, the place would be a train wreck and ripe with clues as to his whereabouts.

Metal ground and snapped. The door creaked open.

My preternatural gaze sliced through the darkness

and swept the inside of the large loft. Ditto on the train wreck. Furniture had been overturned. Pillows had been slashed. Drawers upended. Trash littered the floor. I was fairly certain there were dozens of possibilities for fingerprints and DNA.

Unfortunately, my Super Vamp benefits package didn't include crime scene analysis and I didn't have a friggin' clue what to do or where to start looking.

I concentrated on breathing instead. Not a requirement for my kind, but it comes in handy when I get a little freaked.

Just breathe. In. Out. In . . .

I stepped inside the loft and a sick feeling started in the pit of my stomach. Instead of drinking in the whole scene in one large gulp, I decided to sip slowly, one small section at a time.

Moonlight filtered through the floor-to-ceiling windows that filled one wall and illuminated what had once been a dark blue leather couch. It had been shredded, along with a nearby black leather chair. The chrome and glass coffee table had been upended. A matching entertainment center lay on its side. Shards of glass littered the floor and mingled with broken bits of electronics. The big-screen television sat like a huge cave filled with dangling wires and broken components.

My throat burned as my attention shifted to the kitchen. Once upon a time, that is.

The refrigerator looked as if someone had taken a baseball bat to it. More glass littered the floor courtesy of several shattered bottles of O positive. The rich smell still lingered in the air. Dark, dried splotches stained the wood where the liquid had pooled.

I know, I know. I'm such a bitch. Here I'd been accusing the guy of slipping his fangs into any and everything in a thong when he'd really been bottling it.

Because he couldn't stand the thought of drinking from another woman who's name didn't start with an *L* and end with an *il*? Well, yeah. That's what my heart chanted and hope blossomed in my chest. Guilt nipped at my heels as I made my way over to the far corner where the bedroom had once been.

The bed frame lay in a broken heap on the floor, the wood splintered. One of the mattresses had been flung against a nearby wall; the other sagged against the dresser. A deep sapphire-blue comforter lay in a shredded pile on the floor next to several dark red stains.

Hope and guilt disintegrated into a rush of fear.

Crazy, I know. I'm a vamp. I shouldn't be afraid of anything, right?

At the same time, I shouldn't have a mad, bad crush on Brad Pitt (he's a human, for Damien's sake) or get calls from bill collectors I can't pay (all born vamps are loaded), or do half the things I do on a daily basis, such as bring my human assistant Evie her favorite latte, slip five bucks to the local homeless guy, or rank a male BV's smile higher than his fertility rating (it's a vamp thing.)

Word up, I'm not your average *vampere*.

My hands trembled and my skin prickled as I toed my way through a pile of scattered clothes toward one of the dried puddles.

I knew even before I drank in the rich aroma that it wasn't the imported stuff splattered all over the kitchen. The stains were much larger, the color richer. And the smell . . .

The smell was too ripe.

Too potent.

Too *Ty*.

I tried to swallow, but suddenly my throat refused to work. My heart stalled. The air lodged in my chest (not a good feeling since it wasn't supposed to be there in the first place) and my primo blood ran cold.

As cold as the tip of the gun that was suddenly pressed between my shoulder blades.

"Fair's fair," came the equally frosty voice. "He's dead now, and so are you."

Four

♥ ♥ ♥

Don't panic. Do. Not. *Panic.*

It was just a man with a gun making death threats. No biggie.

At least when it came to the gun and the death threats. I *am* a vampire. Translation: I can dodge bullets and leap tall buildings in a single bound. Wait a second; that's Superman. Oh, well, you get the idea.

Gun? No problemo.

Death? Technically, been there, done that.

It was the *man* part that was making my head spin and my nerves tingle.

He stood directly behind me, a solid mass of muscle and warm flesh that made my undead heart skip its next beat. He pressed closer, and his body seemed to grow hotter, until I felt like a marshmallow dangling over an open campfire.

I know, I know. What kind of a ho am I to even think of melting over this guy? I'm standing in the middle of Ty's apartment, smack-dab in the middle of what could only be a major crime scene, and I'm getting all ooey gooey over another man.

A human on top of that.

At least I was pretty certain he had the whole living, breathing thing going on. My nostrils flared and I drank in his scent. Definitely more Ivory soap than Krispy Kremes.

FYI: Born vamps give off a rich, sugary-sweet scent detectable only by other born vampires. The scent was unique to each individual vampire, and ran the gamut from cinnamon rolls to Key lime pie, crème brûlée to cherries jubilee. The fantabulous *moi*? Cotton candy.

No sweet scent meant either human, made vampire, or an Other. Others included the whole *were* nation—from werewolves to *were*-poodles—as well as any other being that didn't qualify as human.

I concentrated on taking another whiff, searching for a hint of Alpo or cat litter. Nada. His fingertips burned into my arm. Definitely too warm for a made vampire.

Not that made vamps were ice cold, as Hollywood would have us think. They were more lukewarm. Except, of course, when they were panting and sweating and having incredible sex. Then they warmed right up like anyone else.

My thoughts shifted to Ty, who'd definitely undergone a significant rise in body temp the last time we were together.

The only time.

The Captain Ho morphed into Protective Vamp. I bitch-slapped my hormones into submission and stiffened.

"Let's hope that's not a gun in your hand and you're just extremely glad to see me," I told the guy. "Otherwise, if you don't back off, things are going to get really ugly in here."

Several seconds ticked by before a soft chuckle vibrated the hair on the back of my neck.

"Go ahead and laugh, buddy. You won't be doing it for very long," I said.

"Your name wouldn't be Lil, would it?"

"Do I know you?"

"No, but I know you. I've heard all about you. You're one of a kind."

A smile tugged at my lips. "I do have a fabulous sense of style."

"I don't know about that, but you've definitely got a big mouth." The gun fell away and I turned to get my first glimpse of my attacker.

My gaze collided with his and . . . nothing. Which nixed the human theory. I could read humans faster than the latest edition of *InStyle*. Lose the *were* theory as well. I wasn't getting any vibes off this guy other than the sexual variety.

He was yummy-looking with his cropped black hair and tanned complexion. He had the darkest eyes I'd ever seen—so dark that I could see my own reflection mirrored in their depths—and kissable lips. (Not that I was thinking about kissing him, mind you, but if I had been a ho-ho and looking to get lucky, I would definitely say his lips scored a big fat ten on the Kiss-O-Meter.) He wore a black button-up DKNY shirt and Levi's. Not enough style to make me salivate, but enough to satisfy my internal fashionista.

"You're the vampire who was wanted for murder a few months back," he went on. "You drove Ty nuts while he was trying to save your ass."

"I saved my own ass, thank you very much." When he gave me a knowing look, I added, "Yes, Ty helped a little. But he was busy being in a garlic-induced coma when I really needed him, so I had to step up to the plate and save us both." My gaze narrowed. "Who are you?"

"Ash," he said, walking toward the floor-to-ceiling, wall-to-wall windows. He glanced out as if looking for someone. Or something. "Ash Prince."

One down. One to go. "*What* are you?"

His eyes twinkled as his gaze swiveled to me. "A homicide detective with the New York Police Department."

"That's not what I meant and you know it."

His eyes brightened, lightening into a liquid gold before fading again. "I could tell you, but then I'd have to kill you."

"I'm a vampire. You could try, but it's not going to happen."

He winked. "Oh, it could happen, all right. Faster than you think."

"Go on." I held out my hands. "Just try to stake me. I could turn you into a popsicle faster than you could say grape or cherry."

"I don't have to stake you. I have other ways."

Because he wasn't an ordinary Other. At least none that I'd encountered. Which didn't really mean anything because I'm not exactly the most worldly vamp. Sure, I'm five hundred years old (and holding), but I've led a fairly sheltered afterlife up until opening Dead End Dating.

Since then, however, I'd gotten up close and personal with several werewolves (twenty-eight to be exact), oodles of made vampires and even a were-Chihuahua named Rachel. I'd definitely expanded my horizons.

As I stared at Ash, I was fairly certain I hadn't expanded quite that much. I decided to change my line of questioning before I became privy to his *other ways*. "Where's Ty?"

His gaze collided with mine again. "I was going to ask you the same thing."

"I don't know. That's why I'm here. I'm looking for him."

"Ditto," he told me. Another glance out the window and he turned to survey the room.

"How do you know him?"

"He helps me out on the occasional case, and I help him out." He eyed the chaos before running a hand over his face. "We had a meeting yesterday. He didn't show. When he didn't call, I thought I would swing by and see why he got held up." His gaze lingered on the sticky pools of blood. "Something bad happened here."

"Ya think?" He flashed me a glare, but I was unmoved.

He walked toward the kitchen and knelt down to examine the shards of glass. He dabbed a finger into the splattered blood and took a sniff, proof beyond a doubt (if there'd been one) that he wasn't a made vampire. Otherwise, he would be tasting rather than smelling.

I could feel my own hunger stir and tamped it down.

"This looks pretty fresh. No coagulation. Which says that whoever did this was here pretty recently."

Which meant that Ty hadn't been unable to pick up a phone these past few months to call me. He simply hadn't wanted to. So much for soothing my ego.

"Ty, on the other hand, hasn't been here for a pretty long while." He knelt near the dark stain. He touched his fingertips to it and took a whiff. "This smells like him and there's definite coagulation.

I hate to admit that this bit of news brightened my otherwise gloomy day, but it brightened my otherwise gloomy day. "You think so?"

"This is what I do." He examined the stain. "I know so."

"Or maybe you're the reason he's missing." My brain started to piece things together and my suspicion stirred. Anger roiled in the pit of my stomach and I felt my jaw tighten. The sharp end of my fangs grazed my tongue. "How do I know you didn't do this and now you're trying to cover it up?" I took an intimidating step toward him. At least, it would have been intimidating to anyone else—human, vamp, or Other.

But Ash . . . There was something about him that seemed almost invincible. Crazy, I know. While there were some powerful creatures in the world—yours truly included—none were invincible. Superman had his Kryptonite, vamps had wooden stakes, and weres had silver bullets. Whatever Ash was, I felt fairly certain that he had weaknesses as well.

No, really.

He stared at me, his gaze pushing into mine, but that didn't stop me from taking another step forward. "How do I know," I went on, "that you didn't pull a Jeffrey Dahmer and stuff Ty into the fridge?" *Because you're mentally linked to him, bozo, and he couldn't very well call out to you if he'd been dismembered.*

That, and the fact that the fridge door was hanging on for dear life, revealing an empty refrigerator, the light busted, the shelves demolished.

I took one more menacing step before I stalled. (Okay, so my courage gave out, but we're talking *invincible.*) I waited for an answer and used the ticking silence to mentally calculate how far up Ash's ass I could actually stick my primo shoe before he turned on me.

If he turned out to be a vamp killer.

"You're right," he finally said after carefully sizing me up. "I could be lying through my teeth." That dark gaze found mine and again I saw his eyes brighten from a bleak obsidian to a blinding tequila sunrise. Then they cooled. "But I'm not."

I believed him. Hey, I had Super Vamp senses. Even more, he had spotless clothes. If he had, indeed, been responsible, there would have been some telltale sign.

I started to tell him about my mental link with Ty, but then thought better of it. Hey, I knew absolutely zip about this guy except that he had mucho sex appeal and wore really cool clothes.

Yikes, what was I *thinking*?

In my book, mucho sex appeal and cool clothes ranked numbers one and two on my Must Have in an Eternity Mate list. As opposed to the usual (1) astronomical fertility rating, and (2) astronomical fertility rating. Forget talking to him. I should be jumping him on the spot.

The notion stirred a very vivid image, followed by a rush of guilt. Misplaced guilt, I reminded myself. *I* was not the one who'd bailed on Ty without so much as a *see ya*.

Except that he might not have bailed. He might have been kidnapped after our night of hot, wild sex. Which would have made it impossible for any sort of goodbye, or even a note. He could be being beaten and tortured at this very moment.

Or worse. My gaze zeroed in on the dark stain. "You don't think he's—"

"—permanently dead? Staked through the heart? Head chopped off? Body cut into little pieces?"

Ewww. "Uh," I swallowed, "something like that."

He shook his head. "Not enough blood. No arterial matter. No flayed skin."

Double ewww.

"But wherever he's at," Ash went on, "I don't think he's in good shape. Judging by the size of the puddle, he lost quite a bit of blood."

Loss of blood meant he was weak. Probably drifting in and out of consciousness, barely coherent, which would totally explain why he hadn't contacted me again.

I glanced around at the chaos again and my chest tightened. Ty's words replayed in my head and I got this sinking feeling in the pit of my stomach. A feeling usually reserved for the stack of credit card bills currently taking up half of my desk.

"We have to help him," I said, letting go of the last of my vengeful thoughts. Hey, I'm female and we're entitled to change our minds. Judging by this latest info, I was firmly convinced Ty wasn't a total jerk-off and I was willing to give him the benefit of the doubt.

Ash was right. Something bad *had* happened.

He glanced at the mess and then at me. "Any ideas what we should do?"

"You're the detective. You tell me."

"We start with the girlfriend."

"Girlfriend? Are you telling me that he has a *girlfriend*?" And to think I'd actually forgiven him in the last five seconds. What an idiot. I gave myself a massive mental head slap. I was *so* going to find him and decapitate him myself. I fought down a wave of anger and tried to sound disinterested. "So, who's his girlfriend?"

"I'm looking at her."

I glanced behind me before the truth struck. I whirled and blond hair slapped me in the face. "Me?"

"Yeah," he said as if he'd just pointed out that I also had two eyes, a nose, and a mouth. Duh.

"Wait a second. You think *I'm* his girlfriend? Did he say that? And if he did, when did he say it? And how? Did he seem happy about it? Angry? Suicidal?" The questions poured out before I could stop them. Not that I would have. I wanted to know *everything*. Every minute detail of every super sweet thing Ty Bonner had ever said about me. "Do you think he meant it? Did he mention anything else—"

"Whoa." He signaled with his hands. "Time out. I think you're getting a little carried away. He didn't actually say it. I just assumed."

"Why?"

"Because." He shrugged. "I could just tell."

"How?"

"Because he said you had a big mouth."

My mind rifled back to our night together and my eyes narrowed. "That dirty rat fink. I can't believe he told you that we—"

"He didn't," Ash cut in. "He didn't say a word about you personally. Just that you like to talk a lot."

"And this translates to girlfriend how?"

"Guys talk about their current squeeze or their latest blow job: 'I boffed this girl or gave it to that one.' You know the spiel."

No, but I was quickly finding out.

"They don't talk about wives or girlfriends," Ash added. "That would just be weird."

Okay, it sort of made sense. (Was my ego hanging on by a thread or what?) "So he said I like to talk a lot and that's it?"

He nodded. "But I think he liked it. The talking, I mean. He looked aggravated. At the same time, I think he thought you were funny."

"Okay, now that could go either way."

"Funny in a good way."

I drew a deep breath and let my lungs fill to calm my nerves. Okay, I was the funny girlfriend. It wasn't exactly the hot, delicious, irresistable GF, but it would do. "So how can I help?"

"Well," he smiled, "For starters, you can tell me what he said when he contacted you telepathically."

Five

♥ ♥ ♥

After some mega-shock, I spent the next five seconds filling Ash in on my mental dish with Ty.

"That's it?" he asked when I finished.

I shrugged. "What can I say? I'm a sucker for tall, dark, and silent." Literally.

The notion stirred a memory of me and Ty and *yum,* and I quickly snapped my mind closed to it. Particularly since I hadn't eaten yet and Ash had more sex appeal than Brad Pitt, Toby Keith, and that guy from Nickelback all rolled into one. My hormones, bless their traitorous little souls, were obviously having a major yowza fest.

"He must have said something about his whereabouts. An address. A building description. A fucking weather update. *Something.*"

I shook my head. "He didn't say anything else."

"Didn't you get some sort of mental picture? A visual of the place? A face?"

"Can I do that?"

He shrugged. "I don't know. You're the one with the telepathic connection. You tell me."

"I never have. But then we've never really done it that much. When I hear him, I don't see anything." Well, maybe a few pics of Ty naked that lingered in my head whenever I heard his deep, seductive voice. "It's all just black."

"Yeah." He stared at me knowingly, as if he could see the thoughts flying around. "Sure it is."

I thought about using my convincing vampness on him, but I had the gut feeling it wouldn't work.

"I wish I'd gotten more, but I didn't. He just stopped sending."

Ash seemed to think. "Maybe he didn't stop. Maybe someone else stopped him."

That's what I'd thought. Well, that and that he was simply too busy doing the bump and hump with a megalicious stripper vamp named Bambi. Or Bubbles. Or Colette. (Did I ever mention the slut countess who stole my very first boyfriend?)

Not that it mattered. Ty and I didn't have an actual commitment. Sure, we'd spent time together and he'd saved me from spending eternity at Riker's Island. But really, when you peeled away all the life and death stuff, it amounted to one measly fantabulous night of sex.

But the thing was, I *liked* him and I thought he liked me. Not that he couldn't go out and have crazy, outrageous monkey sex with someone else and still like me. But it did sort of kill my whole happily ever after fantasy.

A secret fantasy, I might add.

See, born vampires aren't exactly die-hard romantics. Rather, the entire race centers around sex. BVs stop aging when they lose their virginity. Their search for an eternity mate is based entirely on Fertility Ratings and Orgasm Quotients. Love, if there is such a thing, or even like, simply doesn't figure in.

So you can understand why Ty and I riding off into the sunset (me wearing a killer pair of Sergio Rossi leather stiletto boots) is not something I can actually admit to anyone. Not without them thinking I'd drank one too many glasses of the bottled stuff. Bottled blood equaled slower reflexes, which equaled cuckoo to a born vampire.

At least that's what my father said.

He was also the vampire who'd almost decapitated himself with a pair of hedge clippers in an all-out battle with his werewolf neighbor over azalea bushes (I am so not touching that one).

Anyhow, I wasn't in any hurry to see myself starring in the next episode of *Intervention,* so I kept my mouth shut about the fantasy. Besides, my mother was already slipping valium into her AB negative thanks to my youngest brother, Jack, and his impending nuptials to a human. Why ruin a good thing and shift all that motherly disapproval back to moi?

"Have *you* tried contacting *him*?"

I nodded. "He's not responding. That, or I'm not doing it right."

"Are you focusing? Projecting?"

I nodded. "Yes. I think." When he flashed me an exasperated look, I added, "I've never been mentally linked to anyone before. I'm still on the learning curve."

"Keep trying. In the meantime, I'll see what I can come up with here." He pulled a card from his back pocket. "Here's my cell number. Call me if he contacts you again."

I pulled a Dead End Dating card from my purse and handed it to him. He stuffed it into his pocket.

"I'll be in touch if I find anything," he told me.

"That, or if you get lonely."

A grin split his face and my heart gave a tiny little pitter-patter. "That's the worst pickup line I've ever heard."

I tossed a major *shut up!* at my hormones and frowned. "I'm not trying to pick you up. I'm a matchmaker. It's my job to help lonely men and women the world over. So," I eyed him, "are you?"

"Am I what?"

"Lonely?"

"No."

"Are you married?"

"No."

"Do you have a girlfriend?"

"No."

"Boyfriend?"

"No."

"A blow-up doll named Ginger?"

He shook his head. "You do talk a lot."

"It's part of the job. Surely you don't just work all the time."

"Actually, I do."

"You really should get out more. Think of all the wonderful life experiences that are passing you by." He gave me a get-outa-here look. "Okay, fine. But think of all the really hot women who are passing you by. Don't tell me you don't like women."

"I do. Occasionally. But I'm not interested in dating one."

"That's what they all say. But sooner or later, the lonely bug bites everyone and then you do something desperate. One minute you're watching television by yourself and the next you're cruising the Internet, surfing chat rooms and viewing profiles on MySpace. You wind up talking dirty to a hot little Swedish number named Inga." I made a tsk-tsk sound. "Tragic."

"How's that?"

"Because Inga is really a five-hundred-pound Japanese guy with a pot belly and bunions. But you don't know this because he's got all of these great pics posted and so you fall into a deep, meaningful back and forth exchange, only to have your heart broken into a thousand pieces when you find out the truth. Then you're scarred for life, afraid to trust anyone. You turn into a hermit, invest in a couple dozen cats. They find you one day, facedown in the kitty litter. Dead. Alone."

He eyed me for a long moment. "Does that story usually work?"

"Usually. Sometimes I tell it with dogs instead of cats. Or even Chia Pets. But you didn't really look like the gardening type."

He grinned and shook his head. "Call me if you hear from him again, okay?"

I nodded. Not that I was going to sit around waiting on Ty and worrying. I didn't do worry very well. Rather, I was going to be proactive. I would send out a message to him every hour on the hour, and the rest of the time I would spend working.

I had bills to pay, after all, and as ominous as things seemed (Ty was missing and there was still the little issue of me being followed), I'd still had an extremely productive evening. I'd met John-the-insurance-fraud-investigator, who obviously needed some serious help in the soul mate department. I'd also passed out a ton of cards and even gotten several in return.

Love was definitely in the air.

Unfortunately, love wasn't the only thing. The realization hit me, along with the smell, when I left Ty's building and started down the street toward the corner. My nostrils flared and the foul scent grew stronger with each step and— Ugh.

I glanced down at the brown mess squishing out from beneath the toe of my snakeskin Prada. I twisted and started scraping my shoe on the concrete to clean the mess. I'd just about gotten everything off when I heard the faint sound.

The *meow* echoed through my head and my first instinct was to run the other way.

I know cats are cute and snuggly, but I'm just not into them. Most vampires aren't, and the ones who are keep them around from pure necessity. Like my great uncle Pierre who still lives a zillion kilometers from civilization (aka the nearest shopping mecca) in the remote French countryside. While he has a huge staff of servants to help him out with the need to feed, sometimes he gets tired of the same old, same old. He likes a little variety, and since the nearest village is home to a pack of werewolves, he turns to whatever's handy, i.e., his cat. I *know.* Talk about a flossing nightmare. But to each his own.

The sound kept blaring in my head as I neared the corner. Louder. More desperate.

Meow.

It wasn't like I cared. No cats. That was my motto. Not only because of the hair issue, but because I was determined not to wind up facedown in the kitty litter.

At the same time, it *was* my civic duty to ensure that the streets of New York City remained free of piles of stray-cat poop. Talk about a fast way to kill a pair of killer shoes.

My Pradas, the poor things, would never be the same.

I took a few more steps before turning down a narrow alley that wound down the side of the building and around the back. My vision cut through the darkness, skating this way and that as I searched for the source. I caught a whiff of damp fur and more poop. The sound grew louder.

I bypassed garbage cans and a Dumpster and there it was. The Prada killer in the flesh.

Not that there was much flesh on it. It looked like a full-grown cat, yet it was so scrawny and malnourished that it couldn't have weighed more than the small bag of MAC necessities I kept in my purse. The black fur was matted. Big, bright green eyes glittered back at me and my chest hitched.

I stiffened against the feeling and put on my best you-are-so-busted look. "You owe me six hundred bucks," I told the cat. "Since you can't possibly pay me back, I'm calling the animal shelter. They'll pick you up and the streets will once again be safe for designer shoes."

He blinked and shivered.

"Don't look at me like that. I *am* calling the animal shelter."

Another blink and more shivering.

"You can't just stay here, pooping and starving. The animal shelter will feed you and find you a home." *And put you out of your misery if no one wants you.* The thought struck and guilt spiraled through me.

Wait a second. I don't even like cats. Never have. Never will. They shed and they shit and I don't even want to think what they taste like.

Meow.

"You're not coming home with me." Excuse me?

Back the Ferrari up. I was not—repeat NOT—thinking about taking this shoe destroyer home with me.

Was I?

My brain did a quick scrambling before the right answer popped up.

No. Definitely not. Sure, they allowed pets in my building, but we're talking the cute, fuzzy kind. Not an over-the-hill, shriveled-up excuse for a feline.

To my left, I saw a rat big enough to saddle and mount scurry under a stack of cardboard boxes.

"There you go," I told the cat. "You can feast on Mickey and I'm off the hook."

Unless Mickey decided to feast on Killer, here. The rat was certainly big enough for a knock-down, drag-out. And who knew? It might win and then I wouldn't just be guilty of animal neglect. I'd be a murderer.

Like I know the word vampire is synonymous with the big M for the most part, but I'm not really as bloodthirsty as most of my brethren. No, really. It's true. My dirty little secret.

Which wouldn't be so secret if I snatched up Killer, took him home, and gave him a bath and a saucer of milk. And cuddled up with him on the couch.

He meowed and did more of the I'm-alone-and-I'm-scared-and-you-are-so-wonderful-for-saving-me blinking.

"It won't work. You wouldn't last five seconds at my place. Trust me. I'm ruthless."

Yeah, right, the cat seemed to say.

"Really, I am. You don't want to make me mad." I

flashed him a little fang for show, which would have sent most animals running the other way. But the cat simply sat there. Looking at me. Begging me. "I don't like cuddling."

Whadayaknow? Neither do I. Cuddling is for kittens. I'm old. Temperamental. Grouchy.

"And I don't like a lot of noise during the day when I'm trying to sleep."

As weak as I am, I can barely hold up my head much less make a lot of racket.

"And keep your hair to yourself because I'm NOT vacuuming up after you." If there was one thing I hated more than cats and pushy Visa collectors, it was vacuuming. Don't do it. Don't like it. Not happening. End of story.

Sheesh, I'm nearly bald as it is. How much shedding could I actually do?

"And don't even think about peeing on any of my rugs."

I'm old, not incontinent.

"Or clawing at the furniture. I don't actually have a lot of furniture—I only recently moved out of my parents' place—but what I do have, I cherish."

I can barely clean myself, much less scratch. I'm weak. Starving.

"And," I added as I stepped forward and scooped up the poor, pathetic thing, "if we're going to be roommates, you can't do any pooping on the floor. It's the litter box or, I swear, I'm shipping you to my uncle Paul."

Six
❤ ❤ ❤

By the time I walked into Dead End Dating a half hour later (after a stop at the nearby grocery for a carton of milk), it was after ten o'clock and Evie had already left.

That or she'd grown a zillion zits, a bad haircut, a size twelve foot, and a penis.

I stopped and eyed the young man sitting at her desk. "Hello?"

"Yo." He looked to be about nineteen or twenty. Human. He had dark hair that curled down around his ears and stuck out every which way, a piercing in his right eyebrow, and a pair of wire-rimmed glasses with black electrical tape wrapped around the nose-piece. He had a headset hooked in his ears. An iPod blasted Disturbed.

"I'm Lil."

He didn't so much as glance up, his gaze fixed on Evie's computer terminal. A small set of tools lay open on the desk. "Cool."

I motioned around me to the small outer office. "I own this tribute to fabulous decorating skill."

"Phat."

"Do you have a name?"

Die Slut had been tattooed on the back of his left hand and *Kill the Whore* on his right. His fingernails, painted with black nail polish, flew over the keyboard of Evie's computer. A display of numbers and letters scrolled across the screen. "Word."

O-kay. "That, um, wasn't a comment. See question mark on the end."

"Word."

"No, really, could you tell me your name?" If he looked up, I could see for myself, but his attention stayed riveted on the computer.

"*Word*," he said, pulling off the earphones. He still didn't look at me as he shifted his attention to the tool set. He retrieved a tiny screwdriver and reached for a small box that I recognized as a Flash drive. "That's my name. It blows, doesn't it?" He started unscrewing the front panel of the drive. "I was named after some old guy that I can't even remember. My great uncle something or other. I dunno. Never met him." He set the screwdriver aside and reached for another that was even smaller.

I set the scrawny cat down on his wobbly legs. He wrapped himself around my ankles and stayed put. One paw rested on the toe of my shoe and my chest hitched. While he was a pain in the ass, he *was* sort of cute, in a scrawny, half-starved way. And he obviously had superb taste.

I shifted my attention from the skinny cat to the skinny young man. "What's your last name?"

"Dalton."

"Ah, so you're related to Evie." Evie was my loyal assistant. She could handle five phone lines, an extra large latte, a temperamental computer, and a tube of MAC's Morning Sunrise all at the same time, and without breaking a sweat. If Evie hadn't been human, I would have sworn we were Siamese twins separated at birth. The girl definitely had it going on in a major way.

"She's my third cousin. I keep hoping she'll go out with me since we're so far removed, but she says the idea creeps her out."

I had a hunch it was Word himself who creeped her out, but I kept this thought to myself.

"A rip, isn't it?" he went on. "What with her being so fine and me being such a genius, we could make one hot match."

"Or an interesting episode of Dr. Phil."

He turned back to the drive. "You're funny. You're pretty hot, too."

I already knew that, but what I really wanted to know was how he knew it since he hadn't so much as glanced my way.

Look at me. I sent out the silent thought, but he didn't glance up. *Hell-o? Look. At. Me.*

His head wobbled. *Atta boy.* He slid a look my

way. *Come on, you can do it.* Our eyes connected. *Bingo!*

Word Dalton. Nineteen and three quarters. He liked listening to music—particularly the undeniably nonPC "Die Slut" and "Kill the Whore." He liked chugging beer and playing his PSP and chugging beer and working on computers and chugging beer. He wasn't technically a virgin, but he was close. For reasons completely unknown to him, of course, on account of *he* thought he was a pretty hot guy and he aimed to please, which was why he'd gotten his penis pierced—

Ugh. I soooo didn't need *that* visual.

"You want to go out sometime?" He shifted his attention back to his work, grabbed a cord, and plugged the flash drive into the main computer as he waited for my answer.

"Let me guess. Chug some beer and maybe catch a Die Slut show?"

He stared at me with the same awe men used when I vamped them. "You like Die Slut?"

Not in this eternity. I smiled. "Doesn't everybody?"

"Rad." He grinned. "So you wanna go?"

Uh, no. I was a vampire. He was food. I should rip his throat out or something equally vicious.

I contemplated the murderous thought for a nanosecond before a shudder ripped through me.

Oh, all right. I'll admit it. I'm only batting two out of three when it comes to Super Vamp must-haves. I stared at his hopeful expression, his desperate eyes. Just like the cat.

Not that I was taking him home, mind you. One stray was one too many. But I couldn't squash his hopes and dreams just like that.

I smiled. "Obviously, I would love to, if I didn't already have a boyfriend." Well, I *did*. Ash had referred to me as the closest thing to Tag's girlfriend, which would make him the closest thing to my boyfriend. Sort of. "But if a date is what you're interested in, you're certainly in the right place."

"I don't pay for dates."

I didn't have to be a mind-reading ultra vamp to know *that* was a load of bull. "So what are you doing?"

"Installing a flash drive. After that, I'll be upgrading and then you're good to go."

"Thanks."

"Don't thank me until you've seen the bill. I take all major credit cards and cash. Or we can talk alternative payment solutions."

I smiled. "Perfect. I'm definitely up for a little trade."

His head whipped around so fast that I felt certain he'd given himself whiplash. "Really?" His eyes bugged out and his Adam's apple bobbed.

"Absolutely." I smiled. "I'll give you a free profile complete with two potential matches."

The eyes retreated back into his head. "I'd rather have sex with you."

"You and the rest of the heterosexual male population." I leveled a stare at him. "You're sweet, in a pierced, tattooed sort of way. And I'm sure you're brilliant. But it's not happening." I smiled again. "Not with me, that is. But I'll make sure your two matches are die-hard Die Slut fans." He seemed to think. "I'll even make it three matches if you'll hook up a docking station for my iPod." I *did* have an entire stack of cards from *Manhattan's Most Wanted* (not that any of them had probably heard of Die Slut, but I would cross that bridge later). Since they were all women, I needed to find an equal number of men.

I eyed Word.

He wasn't exactly my ideal in the testosterone department, but with a good shampoo and some acne cream, he just might do.

"*Three* real dates?"

I nodded.

"In the same year?"

"In the same month," I told him. "*This* month."

"You're shittin' me, right?"

"Not at all. I'm Manhattan's latest and greatest when it comes to matchmakers. I'm also a personal hygiene consultant and part-time wardrobe specialist, both of which," I quickly added, "come with the profile."

He shook his head in amazement. "I haven't had three dates in a single year, let alone the same month."

Why didn't this surprise me? I smiled. "Consider it done." I reached into Evie's top drawer and pulled out a new client packet. "Just fill out this question-

naire when you finish up and we'll get started right
away."

He shoved his glasses back up on his nose and his
gaze swiveled to the Krispy Kreme station set up a
few feet away.

I'd started offering free doughnuts with every profile several months ago as a temporary promotion.
I'd tried at least a dozen others since—breath mints,
pens, mugs, condoms—but nothing had gone over
quite as well. The doughnuts were now a permanent
fixture, along with coffee, tea, and the occasional in-
sulin injection.

"Can I have a doughnut, too?" Word asked.

"If you hook up the speakers that go with the
docking station, you can have the entire box." Do I
know how to bargain or what?

I picked up Killer, left Word to his computer work,
and walked into my office. I set the cat on the floor,
opened the small latte I'd picked up, and gave it to
the scrawny animal.

Killer sniffed the lukewarm liquid and wiggled his
whiskers before dipping his black head. He started
lapping up the goody.

A sliver of warmth went through me, followed by
a grumble of hunger. I retrieved what looked like a
wine bottle from my minifridge, settled at my desk,
and popped the cork. The ripe scent spiraled through
the air and slid into my nostrils and I closed my eyes.
The aroma stirred my nerve endings and made my
body tingle. I took a long drink, the cold liquid gliding down my throat. I don't normally like my dinner

cold (what vampire did?), but I was having trouble finding a microwave to go with my office decor.

Lame, huh? But it's all I had at the moment and it was a thousand times better than the truth: that I was desperately hoping I would eventually get used to the cold stuff. Then maybe, just maybe I could forget the warm, sweet taste of Ty's blood and stop craving it.

Stop craving *him*.

Geez, I'd been doing just fine before I'd met the guy. I'd been the bottle queen. No playing *Name That Blood Type* as I passed cute guys on the street. I'd been happy. Or at least content. I'd had the utmost confidence that my own Count Right would come around someday.

But then Ty had walked into my life and now all I could think about was sinking my fangs into him again. And having sex with him. And sinking my fangs into him *while* I was having sex with him.

Not that I would. No. I was *so* over him.

Or I would be just as soon as I reassured myself that he was okay. I needed closure. Then I could totally and completely forget him. I could enjoy my dinner again, and my afterlife would be back to normal.

Hey, it could happen.

I turned my attention to my computer, opened my e-mail account, and stared at my overflowing in-box. I'd just clicked on my first message when the phone rang. My eyes snagged on the latest Victoria's Secret offer—ten dollars off *and* free body butter—as I snatched up the phone.

"Thank you for calling Dead End Dating, where your perfect match is just a Visa, Mastercard, or Discover swipe away." It wasn't the greatest slogan, but my business was still fairly new and I was testing the waters.

"What about American Express?" A familiar female voice asked, and my heart jumped into my throat.

My gaze swiveled to the caller ID display. My mother's phone number blazed back at me and dread rolled through me.

Uh-oh.

Seven

♥ ♥ ♥

*W*ay to go, Lil.

I gave myself a mental kick in the ass for not checking the caller ID *before* picking up the phone and then fought down a wave of guilt.

She *was* my mother. She hadn't endured hours and hours of labor to bring me into this world so that I could avoid her—which I did whenever possible because she drove me nuts. The woman gave me an afterlife. The least—the very least—I could do was talk to her. Especially since I couldn't exactly hang up without her knowing it and heaping more misery on me later.

I pasted on a smile (just in case Big Brother turned out to be Big Mama) and remembered my game plan for just this type of situation. *Single syllable answers.*

Do not engage. She would get frustrated and hang up and I'd be home free.

"Um, hi, Mom."

"So do you take American Express or not?"

"No." Definitely one syllable. "Not yet."

"Oh, well, it makes no never mind."

"Uh-huh."

"I just thought I would ask since your father prefers I use the American Express to avoid the monthly percentages of our other credit cards, but he'll just have to deal with it."

"Deal with what?" Wait. Did I just engage?

"I want to hire you, dear."

I'd engaged, all right. What's worse, I heard myself do it again. "You want to hire *me*?" I remembered the Moe's uniform currently doing time in my hall closet—lime-green polo shirt, beige Dockers—and cringed.

Moe's is the family business. We're talking copy machines. We're talking printing services. We're talking major yuck.

"I already told you, I'm not working for Dad. I know it's hard for you to understand, but I have bigger aspirations than replacing the toner in a copy machine or collating some guy's thesis paper."

"While I can't imagine a more successful enterprise than Moe's—your brothers are all managers and they adore it—that's not what I'm calling about."

Phew, that was close.

"I need a matchmaker."

What?

My heart gave a panicked *ka-thumpety-thump*. "But you already have Dad." I opened my mouth and the words poured out, tumbling over each other as anxiety washed over me. "You've been committed for five hundred and twenty-two years. I'm sure that whatever he did, you can work it out. You can't just throw away half a millennium because he squeezes the toothpaste from the middle or pops open a beer can with his fangs. It's the quirky things that make him special—"

"Lilliana," my mother tried to cut in, but I was already on a roll, freaked with the possibility that my mother might actually be leaving my father. Breaking things off. Moving in with *me*.

"You can't," I blurted. "I know Dad can be a pain, but he doesn't mean to be. He's just eccentric. And pompous. And maybe a little snotty. But he can't help it on account of how he was raised and—"

"Lilliana Arabella Guinevere du Marchette," she snapped and just like that I morphed from a fantabulous, well-dressed businesswoman into a fantabulous, well-dressed five-year-old.

"Yes, ma'am?"

"I'm not leaving your father, though I can't say I haven't thought about it. Since Viola stole his chainsaw—the one he usually uses to cut down the azalea bushes—he's been a man possessed. He's hired a former Navy SEAL for a search and rescue. They're meeting out in the pool house as we speak."

"They're going to break into Viola's house?"

"The SEAL, not your father. At least, I think he's a SEAL. Maybe your father said veal, and I just misheard him."

"Why would Dad hire a small calf to go up against a werewolf?"

"Who knows? I told you. He's possessed. I wouldn't put anything past him."

"Why doesn't he just buy another chainsaw?" A majorly stupid question to which I already knew the answer. My dad was a born vampire and Viola wasn't. The reputation of the entire race—as fearless, superior, condescending bloodsuckers—depended on his recovery of that one power tool.

"It isn't the chainsaw. It's the principle of the thing." What'd I tell ya? "She waltzed right in and took it out from under him. Speaking of which, he's checked every entrance, every security camera, and he still can't figure out how she got into the garage."

"She *is* a werewolf."

"That means she's hairy, not invisible. Your father has spent hours staring at the video surveillance and there's nothing. Just the normal comings and goings of you and your brothers. Our friends."

I.e., bats. In particular, a pink one.

Guilt rifled through me.

See, Viola didn't actually *steal* my father's chainsaw.

I might have let her borrow it a few months back when I was finding mates for her and twenty-seven other female werewolves. They'd needed alpha males in time for the lunar eclipse and a major mating fest, and I'd needed the hefty check Viola had doled out. I'd handed over the chainsaw as a bonus when one of the alpha males hadn't met the exact criteria. Viola had welcomed a negotiating tool to get my father to stop cutting down her hedges.

Or his.

No one really knew which side of the property line the azalea bushes actually fell on, which was why my father and Viola had been going at it in court as well as at home. One judge had sided with my father, while another had ruled in Viola's favor. The battle was still on, and I'd obviously managed to land myself right in the middle.

"So your relationship with Dad is all good?"

"Of course."

Phew.

Now that I'd gotten over my initial fears, something wonderful occurred to me. My mother actually wanted to *hire* me. Translation: She had finally realized that I wasn't wasting my life doing something frivolous. She'd recognized my talent and she was now taking me seriously. A lump jumped in my throat and I barely managed to croak, "So, um, what can I do for you?"

"You can find an appropriate match for your brother."

"No problem. I've got just the vampire for Max—"

"Not Max, dear." Max was my oldest brother. He was hot and hunky and single, and totally full of himself.

"Isn't Rob already living with someone?" Rob was

next in line to Max, also hot and hunky and single, and equally full of himself.

"It's not Rob. I want you to find someone for Jack." Jack was the third brother, ditto on the hot and hunky and full of himself, but he wasn't single. Not for long, anyhow.

"Isn't Jack marrying Mandy?"

"Of course not. Vampires don't get married. They commit. And only to other born vampires. He's just infatuated right now. Once he sees that she is far from an appropriate match, he'll forget all about Mindy and this marriage nonsense."

"Her name is Mandy and they've already booked the hotel." Jack had been, by far, the worst of all my brothers when it came to being an egotistical, self-centered, do-me-and-get-lost player. Until he'd met Mandy. Now he actually passed for decent, and I didn't have to kick his ass every time he opened his mouth.

"I think three matches will be sufficient," my mother went on as if I hadn't said a word. "I want the crème of the crop. Nothing less than a double-digit Orgasm Quotient."

Quick FYI: The current OQ record sat at sixteen (an impressive baker's dozen for yours truly), while the average lingered somewhere around seven or eight. Why the big deal? Each time a BV female orgasmed, she released an egg. No orgasm meant no egg, which meant no flitter-flutter of little bat wings.

What'd I tell ya? It's all about sex.

"And I need them in two weeks," my mother

added. "Your father and I are having a dinner party—just family and a few close friends—and we thought it would be the perfect opportunity to show them off to Jack."

Just say no.

But if I did, she would undoubtedly think it was because I couldn't produce and I'd be back to wasting my life on something frivolous.

At the same time, I couldn't find matches for Jack. He already had Mandy and (I never thought I'd say this) he was in love. Sure, she was human. But she was also smart and pretty and, more important, *nice.*

Say yes, find a few bogus matches, and you're off the hook.

Right, genius. If I didn't produce quality females, my mother would think I wasn't any good at my job. Hence the whole wasted life thing again. Short of falling on the sharp end of a pencil or dancing naked in broad daylight on a beach in Costa Rica, I was stuck.

A sick feeling washed over me, the same feeling I'd had earlier at Ty's place. A feeling that told me the next two weeks were going to be the worst of my life.

"Just tell me how much I owe you and I'll give you my Visa number."

I quoted the usual amount, plus a little bonus for pain and suffering (mine, of course). My mom didn't so much as gasp, so I added, "I usually work a profile for at least a month, which means I'll also have to charge a rush fee since you want me to do it in half that time."

"Whatever, dear. Just add it to the card."

I smiled. Two weeks *was* an awful long time. Scientists could invent a cure for meddling mothers. Brad Pitt could fall madly in love with me and whisk me away to his island in the Caribbean. My mother could fall head over heels in love with her new human daughter-in-law and, for once in her afterlife, butt the hell out.

News flash: In addition to being a closet romantic, I'm also a hopeless optimist.

The possibilities suddenly seemed endless as I took down the card number, said goodbye, and went to my laptop to open up an account for my brother. I'd just keyed in his name and stats when the phone rang again. One glance at caller ID confirmed that it was not my mother. I snatched up the receiver.

"Dead End Dating, where the women are beautiful, the men sexy, and the pockets deep."

"Thank God you finally picked up. I left three messages on your cell."

"Hey, Mandy." Dr. Mandy Dupree was a resident in forensic pathology and my youngest brother's fiancée. She was a petite redhead with a cute figure and the misguided notion that my mother actually liked her.

I know, right? The woman could barely stand me and I was the fruit of her loins.

The *matchmaking* fruit of her loins.

I stared at my brother's name on the screen and guilt rolled through me. Not that I was going to pair him up. Not with anyone viable. I would come up with a few decent people and parade them in front of my parents for show. Jack would refuse to bite (he was in love, after all), and he and Mandy would never be the wiser. I'd still get my fee and my mother would face the inevitable.

"You didn't forget, did you?"

"Of course, I didn't forget." My mind started to race. I had agreed to be the official maid of honor, which meant I'd already gotten roped into interviewing harpists and flute players. (Can you say disc jockey?)

Not that I'd admitted as much to my mother. Jacqueline Marchette would find out soon enough when Jack and Mandy marched down the aisle.

If she showed.

Max was betting she would see the light and be at the wedding. Rob had a few g's riding on her staying home and sulking. I, who knew our madre better than anyone, had put my money on her showing up and raising such a stink that we would all wish she'd stayed home.

"I knew you wouldn't forget."

"You bet your ass I wouldn't."

"What about your mother? I left two messages on her cell to remind her." Her voice took on a desperate quality. "You do think she'll come, don't you?"

Never in a million years. "I'm sure she wouldn't miss it for the world." I know. My bad. But she sounded so hopeful that I couldn't bring myself to break the news. "The only way she would miss something of this magnitude is if she were kidnapped and bound with ropes of garlic."

"You're so funny, Lil. I'm so glad we're going to be sisters. I always wanted a sister. Someone I could talk to about boys and do makeup with and try out new hairdos with."

"If you ask to borrow my clothes, I'm hanging up." A girl had to have her boundaries.

She laughed. "Hurry over, okay? I don't know where to start. This is like the most important thing *ever*."

"The biggie," I agreed. "Top of the mountain."

She went silent for a long moment. "You forgot, didn't you?"

"How could I forget the most important thing *ever*?" Unless, of course, I was stressed out of my head with an MIA made vampire, a meddling mother, and a struggling business. "But let's just say—in theory— that I *did* forget. What would it be that actually slipped my mind?"

"The bridal shop. I left the address on your cell. I'm picking out the wedding dress tonight."

"Now?"

"Right now, and I really need your advice."

I eyed the stack of profiles that begged for my un-divided attention. I also had an in-box full of e-mail. I had to proof the newest ad for the local newspaper. I'd promised to help Word with his profile when he finished up with the computer. I needed to get a bag of kitty litter and a bed for Killer. *And*—and this was the biggie—I had to find Ty before something really bad happened.

I didn't have time to lounge around at Vera Wang, a glass of champagne in hand, and spend someone else's money on a ridiculously expensive dress that would only be worn—

Wait a second. Was I insane?

Free drinks?

Shopping?

Someone else's green?

"I'm on my way."

Eight
♥ ♥ ♥

They say confession is good for the soul. Being a denizen of the dark (and because I mowed down that lady at Barney's last week trying to get to a half-off BCBG bag), I need all the help I can get. So here goes . . .

I've had the fantasy.

No, I'm not talking the one about winning the lottery or being Brad Pitt's one and only or being a rock star/supermodel/Dallas Cowboys cheerleader.

I'm talking *the* fantasy.

The (big sigh) wedding fantasy.

The one with the white doves and sprays of pink roses and the ice sculpture shaped like my favorite Salvatore Ferragamo hobo bag. The MAC Super Luster lip gloss favors for the women, mini-bottles of Ralph Lauren for the men. A horse-drawn carriage. A multitiered cake done in the palest pink with edible silver bows and French piping.

I know, I know. I'm a vampire who can't eat solid food. What the hell am I doing envisioning a wedding cake? But they smell scrumptious and you can't have a wedding without a cake.

Since I was someday hoping for my own *dum, dum, da-dum,* I couldn't help but be excited for Mandy. I dropped Killer off at home—with a saucer of milk and several newspapers—and took a cab to the address my soon-to-be sister-in-law had left on my cell.

"But this is Queens," I told the driver when he finally pulled up in front of the small shop located between a Vietnamese bakery and a pizza parlor, far, far away from Vera or Lazaro or Jim Hjelm, or any of the other prominent designers of bridal couture.

"This is the address, lady. That'll be fifteen bucks." He glanced in the rearview mirror and wiggled his eyebrows suggestively. "That is, unless you want to take it out in trade."

No, really. Such is the life of a vampire with mucho sex appeal and really great accessories.

"Here's a twenty." I handed him the money.

His face fell. "You sure?"

I stared into his eyes and saw more than I ever wanted to know about Wally Gillespie aka Minnie Me.

"Keep the change." I slid from the backseat. "And if you do decide to go through with the penis enlargement," I handed him a Dead End Dating card, "give me a call. I can definitely hook you up."

His mouth dropped open, but I turned away before he could say anything.

I walked the two feet to a glass storefront with the words *Wedding Wonderland* done in white neon script. Pulling open the door, I quickly found myself surrounded by big, poofy dresses, fake flowers, and the smell of potpourri. An instrumental version of "You Light Up My Life" flowed from a CD player in the corner.

Mandy and an older looking woman with the same red hair and giddy expression sat on a white velvet sofa in front of a coffee table overflowing with bridal magazines.

"Oh, good," Mandy squealed. "You're here. Mom, she's here!"

I'd met Harriet Dupree once before when I'd been planning a baby shower for Viola and the other twenty-seven pregnant werewolves I'd hooked up for the lunar eclipse. Mandy had volunteered to help and her mother had dropped off several serving platters (and oodles of chicken wings) for the big occasion. She'd also stood around oohing and gooing over all the baby gifts and telling me how positively darling I was—and precious *and* gorgeous—and that she just could not, repeat, COULD NOT, understand how some man had not snatched me up a long, long time ago.

I know. Me, too.

Anyhow, I've liked her ever since.

"Lil!" The older Dupree threw her arms around me and smothered me in a big hug. "So good to see you."

"You, too."

"All right, ladies." *Clap, clap.* "Since everybody's here, let's get started. While I don't mind staying late, I've got two poodles and a pit bull waiting at home for their supper."

I turned to see the store's proprietor. She had bright bleached-blond hair, enough eye makeup to impress Marilyn Manson, and bloodred nails about three inches long. She wore gold-rimmed glasses that hung from a chain around her neck and bright red lipstick. Black spandex pants hugged her thighs and a red, white, and gold abstract top hugged the biggest pair of breasts I've ever seen (which speaks volumes since I've been around for more than five hundred years). She smelled of hair spray and Italian sausage. Her accent dripped Jersey.

Our gazes locked and I got the down low. Shirley Cannoli. Born and raised in—where else?—Jersey. Still lived there. Newly divorced from her husband, Norman, of twenty-five years. Two grown daughters, one of whom went to NYU while the other did nails at a small shop in Hoboken. She didn't normally stay after hours because of her "babies," i.e., pets, but she was on a mission to beef up her customer base. She'd had three boob jobs and was now planning a facelift. Provided, of course, that she impressed this par-

ticular bride. She was certain this would be her stepping stone to more hoity-toity weddings like the ones
splattered all over the pages of the Life Styles section
every Sunday. Which was why she'd agreed to a private showing so frickin' late when she should be at
home watching Leno. Not that she was complaining.
Hell, no. She was grateful that she was standing here
in her latest pair of Do Me shoes instead of sitting at
home with her feet propped up and her bunions free.
She was also eternally grateful that her cousin
Michael had married Harriet's half-sister. Otherwise,
she wouldn't be getting this chance. All she needed
was one good mention.

I, personally, figured she needed a lot more than
that. But she looked so excited and I couldn't help
but give props to a fellow entrepreneur. I smiled and
sank down on the sofa between Mandy and her mom.

"Before we get started, can I interest anyone in a
little refreshment?"

I slid my hand into the air. "I'll have champagne."
Another glance around the room. "Make that two
glasses."

"I've got Jell-O shots," Shirley announced with a
hopeful expression. "See, the whole point of the alcohol is to relax, so I figured I'd get the most bang for
my buck. One shot and you're as loose as a goose."

"That's so clever, Shirley," Harriet said. "I'll have
one."

"I have to work tomorrow, so I'll pass," Mandy
said. "Lil?"

"I think I'll pass." While I could enjoy the occasional glass of champagne, one shot and I wouldn't just be sitting here, suffering in silence. No, I'd be trying on dresses with Mandy and, worse, probably liking them. "On second thought, go ahead and hit me."

"Atta girl," Shirley said, giving me a wink.

A few seconds later, I was sucking down a watermelon whiz and praying that Jell-O didn't count as a solid. (See the whole vampire liquid-diet issue.)

"We can't start yet," Mandy told Shirley when she turned to a rack of dresses that lined a nearby wall. "We're still waiting for Jack's mother."

"Um, why don't you go ahead and show us what you have?" I motioned to Jersey.

"She's not coming, is she?" Mandy asked once the woman had turned to rifle through one of the wall racks.

"She wanted to." In an alternate reality where born vampires loved and respected their human brethren. "It's just that she was feeding the piranha in the swimming pool and one of them took a hand off, so she had to go to bed early so she could rest and regrow." Can I improvise or what? "She didn't want to spurt blood all over the dresses, but she told me to tell you to have fun."

"How awful." Mrs. Dupree patted my hand. "She should try aloe vera, oatmeal, and mayonnaise. My own mother swore by it for cuts and things. Just mix it up, pack it on, oh, and cover it with a piece of raw bacon. Twenty-four hours and you're as good as new."

"Mom, she doesn't need a home remedy." Mandy lowered her voice to a conspiratorial level. "She's a vampire."

"Oh, yes." Harriet waved a hand as if she'd just remembered. "Well, tell her we send our best and wish her a speedy recovery."

Yes, Mrs. Dupree was privy to the family gene pool. Other than passing out and overdosing on cream puffs from the Dupree family bakery, she'd been as accepting as the next mother who's daughter was about to hit the jackpot.

"Now this is my number-one seller," Shirley announced when she turned, a dress overflowing her arms.

It was white.

It was beaded.

It was lacy.

It was scary.

"Number one, huh?" I asked, eyeballing the busy confection. The taste of watermelon lingered on my tongue and my head felt a little fuzzy.

"It's great," Mandy said, her eager eyes filled with excitement.

"Lovely," Mrs. Dupree declared. "Positively lovely." She reached for a tissue and dabbed at an overflow of tears. "Sorry. This is just a really emotional time for me, what with my only daughter finally getting married."

The word *finally* had enough emphasis to launch a small missile. Mrs. Dupree had been married since the age of seventeen and the fact that her only daughter was pushing twenty-seven was an uncomfortable situation she'd had to explain at more than one of her weekly book club meetings.

Humph. If Harriet thought twenty-seven was bad, she would surely have kicked the bucket ages ago if she'd been in my mother's shoes. The woman had been making excuses for yours truly for four hundred and eighty years, and she was still going strong every month at her Connecticut Huntress meeting.

I had a rush of guilt, which I quickly traded in in favor of good, old-fashioned abject horror. We're talking *taffeta*.

"Can we see a few more before she starts trying anything on?" I asked Jersey.

"Um, sure." Shirley went back to the rack and I turned to Mandy.

"Just pick out the ones you like that you absolutely don't think you can live without. We'll decide on a few favorites and then you can try them on."

"Oh, absolutely." She nodded vigorously, looking like a premenstrual woman in a Godiva store. Not a good sign for someone who processes dead bodies for a living. But the wedding bug could bite even the most serious, levelheaded individual.

I'd seen it firsthand when one of my best friends, Nina Two of the infamous Ninas, had married a born vampire named Wilson just last year. Always sane and levelheaded, Nina had morphed into a raving lunatic weeks before the commitment ceremony. She'd gone on a binge to find the perfect blue napkins. That would be cerulean, not indigo or cornflower or any other shade out there. Personally, I would have gone with silver and called it a day. But not Nina. She'd been determined. Excited. Obsessed.

My gaze swiveled to Mandy and the crazed light in her eyes. Ditto. "Now remember," I told her, "look at all the details of the dress, picture yourself in it. We'll ex the losers and try on the keepers."

"Got it," she told me, giving another vigorous nod.

Shirley turned back to us and the fashion show continued.

"It's great," Mandy said when the woman held up prospect number two. "Definitely a keeper."

Harriet Dupree nodded. "Positively lovely."

Shirley added it to the first one to be tried on, and then held up number three.

"Oh. My. God. Gotta have it," Mandy declared.

"Yep, that one's really lovely."

Enter number four.

"Have you ever seen so much beading? I adore beads. That's definitely a keeper."

"Yes, beads are truly lovely."

"Oh, and tulle. I LOVE tulle. I need that one, too."

"Yes, we must try that, as well."

Mandy and her mother continued to salivate while I reached for another Jell-O shot.

It was going to be a long night.

Nine

❤ ❤ ❤

Mandy tried on forty-eight dresses. No, really. In fact, she would have tried on forty-nine or even one hundred and forty-nine, but Shirley's Back to the 1980s collection tipped the scales at forty-eight, so that's where Mandy stopped. Needless to say, she hadn't picked one in particular. They were all beautiful. Perfect.

Meanwhile, I had sucked down six Jell-O shots, which explained the blurry doorknob and the moving keyhole when I arrived home a good hour before daybreak.

I jabbed at the hole once, twice, three times before closing my eyes and giving myself a mental pep talk.

Easy. Take your time. You can do it. Just concentrate. And whatever you do, don't throw up.

Yes, vampires could blow chunks like anyone else.

Actually, we could do it better than everyone else because our metabolism is extremely delicate and if our bodies don't like something, then step aside Old Faithful.

Alcohol, like other fluids, doesn't bother us so much. But green apple Jell-O? And grape? And cherry? That seemed to be a different story entirely. I was dangerously close to tossing right then and there. That, or passing out if I didn't get to sit down sometime before the New Year.

CNN blasted from my neighbor's television and blared in my ears, making my head throb that much more. Reality check: The whole afterlife experience for vamps is magnified tenfold. When we're hungry, we're ravenous. When we're sad (a rarity for most vamps with the exception of yours truly), we could cry enough to hydrate a *From Fat to Fit* camp. When we're angry, we're talking remember the Alamo. And when we have a massive headache from too many Jell-O shots? Move over Tylenol and pass the Vicodin.

I narrowed my eyes and stabbed at the keyhole again. Bingo. A few seconds later, I kicked off my shoes as I walked the few feet to my bedroom. I contemplated checking my cell messages (I'd turned off the phone while at Wedding Wonderland), but quickly decided against it. I'd barely managed to fit the key in my front door. Punching itty-bitty buttons on my Razor was out of the question. I had peeled off my clothes during the last few steps. I didn't bother with lights (it's not like I really needed them) and I didn't bother with lingerie. I chanced a glance at the blinds to make sure they were tight and secure and then crawled into bed in my undies. I closed my eyes and begged the room to stop spinning long enough for me to conk out. A few seconds, and sleep would come like it always did. Thankfully. One. Two. Three—

"Lil?"

The deep voice pushed into my ears and my eyes popped open.

I bolted upright and my gaze made a beeline for the six foot plus of beefcake standing in the open bedroom doorway.

Ash Prince stared back at me, a half grin crooking his lips and cracking open the shadow of his face. His gaze glittered like twin beams of light in the darkness. He still wore the same jeans and button-up shirt that he'd worn earlier that evening, and the same sexy expression.

I nixed the last thought and focused on summoning my outrage. "What are you doing in here?"

"Waiting for you. Do you usually stumble in this late?"

"Haven't you ever heard of a cellphone?"

"You didn't answer yours."

Oh, yeah.

He arched one dark brow. "Too busy getting sloshed?"

"I'm not sloshed." I swallowed and tasted green apple and liquor. "I'm semisloshed. So what's with the breaking and entering?"

"We lifted a set of prints that didn't belong to Ty. I've put it through the database, but we can't find a match. I need prints from you so that we can make sure they belong to a third party. If they're yours, we can toss them. But if they're not, then they might eventually lead us to Ty."

"Uh, yeah. Sure. What do I do?"

"Nothing." He held up the half-full bottle of O positive I'd opened yesterday evening. "I'll just take this with me."

"And what exactly are you going to do with the contents?" I asked him. "Toss or drink?"

He grinned. "I'm not really thirsty right now."

"But if you were . . . AB negative or a Bud Lite?" When he just smiled, I added, "Give already. I know you're not a vampire. So what exactly are you?"

"Late," he announced, glancing at his watch. "It's almost sunrise."

"And you have to hurry because the sun might cause you to burst into flames? Or change into a were lizard and do a little basking?"

His grin widened. "I've got a breakfast date at a diner on Fifth."

"Oh."

"Nice try, though."

"Thanks."

"Call me." He winked and then he turned. I listened to his footsteps as he headed toward the door. Metal creaked and clicked and then he was gone.

And I was half-naked.

The truth struck as I glanced down to see my favorite Egyptian cotton sheet bunched in my lap. My semi-impressive Cs stood at attention, clad in my favorite Swedish lace bra from La Perla. It was wispy and pink and practically see-through.

Now I totally understood the wink.

Call him? I had half a mind to call the rat fink, all right. And chew him a new one. At the same time, he had been grinning. As opposed to frowning. Which meant I still had it going on in the eye candy department.

Funny, but the knowledge didn't make me feel half as euphoric as it should have. Because as fine as Ash was, he wasn't Ty. I didn't feel the same rush of heat from my head to my toes. No tingling nipples or stirring hunger.

Okay, so maybe my hunger stirred a little. But that was a pretty regular occurrence for me since I bottled it 24/7.

Bottom line, I didn't have the same intense *Do me now or I'll spontaneously combust* reaction to ultrahot Ash that I did to Ty. A fact that worried me as much as it pissed me off.

"Where are you?" I sent out the mental question as I collapsed back on the bed and stared at the ceiling. *"Are you hurt? Bleeding? Shacked up with a vamp named Juicy Lucy?"*

I waited, listening, hoping, but the only thing I heard was the sound of a toaster dinging, followed by the weather update coming from next door.

Sunshine. Cool temperatures. Breezy.

The last thought stuck as I closed my eyes.

Instead of picturing myself doing a Marilyn on the streets of New York in my favorite white halter dress, I saw myself on a beach in Maui wearing the coolest Dior bikini with a gold mesh miniwrap. It was broad daylight and the sun was shining. The wind blew in off the water, lifting the edges of my wrap and tickling over my skin.

"I've been waiting for you." Ty's voice slid into my ears as he came up behind me. And then it was his fingers that lifted the edges of the silky, weblike material from around my waist and tickled over my belly button.

Mmm . . .

I wasn't sure if it was the endless string of wedding dresses, the stress my mother had just heaped on me, or the Jell-O shots (probably the shots), but one minute I was lost in a hot and heavy embrace and the next, I was standing barefoot, wearing a grass skirt and a pair of coconut shells, and saying *I do* while a group of half-naked islanders played an ancient Hawaiian love song.

What?

I mean, sure, I wouldn't mind a wedding in Hawaii. But not barefoot (at the very least, I needed a pair of rhinestone Zsa Zsa flip-flops) and not looking like a hula girl. And—and this was the biggie—not to Ty.

Born. Made. It *so* wasn't going to happen.

At least not the wedding part. But the fingers slipping under my wrap . . . That I hadn't completely ruled out.

Let's say I find him and he's really sorry and desperate to make it up to me for saving his hide. What sort of person would I be if I turned him away? I can accept a token of appreciation as graciously as the next vamp.

Yeah, yeah, gracious and vamp don't usually go together in the same sentence, but we're fantasizing here.

He'd be appreciative. I'd be gracious (and fashionably dressed in the latest designer beachwear). Sex would be a given.

At least that's what I told myself as I rewound my erotic thoughts to the post–*I do* phase and hit play.

Ty slid his arms around me and I leaned into him. We spent the next several minutes engaged in a very heated reunion until I conked out completely.

Ten

♥ ♥ ♥

"**Y**ou're never going to guess what just happened." Evie's voice carried over the line later that afternoon when I finally managed to wake up and answer the blaring phone.

"Good or bad?" I mumbled, blinking away the last fuzzies of sleep.

"Think fabulous."

"I won a free shopping trip to Donna Karan?"

"Better."

"I won the lottery?"

"Even better."

"My mom called to say she's sorry for the guilt and manipulation and wants to buy me a Mercedes to make up for the pain and anguish she's heaped on me for most of my life?"

"I said fabulous. Not miraculous. You got a callback."

"A what?" I asked as I forced my legs over the side of the bed. Something soft squished between my toes. *Killer.*

"*Manhattan's Most Wanted,*" Evie went on as I glanced down and wrinkled my nose. "You made the cut. You are now one of eighty applicants being considered for the new season that starts next week. They called about fifteen minutes ago. I would have called sooner, but the phone started to ring so I'm just now getting to you. You have to go down to the television station by six—that was the latest appointment I could get you—for more questions."

I glanced at the clock. Five minutes shy of 5:00 P.M. I levitated a couple of inches and did a quick float to the bathroom, where I found Killer lounging on my favorite towel.

"You're in big trouble, mister."

Yeah, yeah, his gaze seemed to say, as if he knew I was already hooked on his sorry little black hide. *I'm shaking in my fur.*

"Are you there?" Evie asked as I eased down in front of the sink, turned on the water, and hiked my foot under the spray.

"I'm here, but you're not," I said to the oblivious cat. "Pack your bags, bozo, because you're out of here."

"Who are you talking to?"

"A stray I brought home."

"Is he cute?"

"Not that kind of stray. A cat."

"Oh, I love cats. I have two."

"Do you want another?"

"Sorry. My building only allows two pets. Listen, they're also going to do a five-minute interview tape, so be sure to wear something colorful."

"What about smelly?"

Evie laughed. "You're new to motherhood. Don't worry. It'll get easier. Just make sure you put fresh litter in the box every day and eventually the accidents will stop. There's always an adjustment period."

I hate you, I mouthed to the cat, who continued to smirk. I dried my foot on a hand towel and grabbed a handful of toilet paper.

"Aren't you excited?" Evie asked as I padded back to the bed and scooped up my morning surprise.

"Thrilled. I've always wanted a great big pile of poop."

"I'm not talking about that; I'm talking about *MMW*. Isn't it just the greatest? To think you might actually get to meet Mark Williams in person."

"Mark who?" I deposited the cleanup in the toilet and flushed.

"Williams. That cute weather guy. I just heard that he was picked by *People* magazine as one of their fifty hottest New Yorkers," Evie told me as I walked into the kitchen and grabbed an unopened bottle from the fridge. My gaze snagged on the milk and I contemplated payback for Killer.

Starvation.

Mutilation.

Painful death.

Unfortunately, I got the heebie-jeebies from all three, so I ended up pouring a saucer of milk for the cat and nuking a glass of O positive for myself.

"Since when does *People* pick fifty hot New Yorkers?" I leaned against the kitchen cabinet and sipped my breakfast while Killer lapped up the milk.

"They're doing it for every state. Sort of a tribute to local celebrities. The Big Apple issue comes out next week and will coincide with the first episode of the new *MMW.* I hope you make it."

"Uh, yeah, me, too." *Not.*

But while I had no intention of making the actual show, I wouldn't have minded another go with the rest of the women who'd made the cut. I'd done my best to circulate last night, but with Ty on my mind, I'd only introduced myself to maybe half. If I went back, I could meet the rest and even branch out to the *MMW* staff, from the single, twentysomething receptionist with the dark roots to the divorced camera guy with the foot fetish. Talk about some needy candidates.

Never fear, people. Lil is here.

"So are you coming to the office or are you going straight over to the station?"

"I'll swing by and check in first. How are things going?"

"Well, the reason I couldn't call you right away is because the second I hung up with the *MMW* producer, I had three phone calls from women who didn't make the cut. They want us to hook them up. I set up their appointments for tomorrow."

Great.

"And your mother called."

Not so great.

"She said she'd like you to bring at least one prospect with you on Sunday for the get-together."

I.e., the *hunt*.

Forget backyard barbecues and homemade ice cream. Being eccentric as well as anal, my father refused to let go of tradition. He felt it his parental duty to see that his children were able to stalk and subdue, in addition to plopping down a twenty at the local deli for the bottled blood type of the week. That, and he liked to show off his latest golf swing.

So we met each week at my parents' Connecticut estate to watch his Tiger Woods impersonation and ravage the more than hundred acres in the name of sustenance. Since this was the twenty-first century and born vamps liked to keep a low profile, we hunted each other—the *it* person—instead of plundering nearby malls and sinking our teeth into unsuspecting shoppers. The pot of gold? Extra vacation days from Moe's.

Since my brothers were all gainfully employed in the family business, they lived for the hunt and the extra days off. Max had flown off to Spain for an entire two weeks with his extra days. Rob had cashed in his to buy another Porsche. And Jack had used his to go scuba diving in the Amazon with a set of twin bimbos named Lolly and Dolly.

I, on the other hand, had my own fantabulous business far away from the printing and copying mecca. Therefore, I didn't enjoy the hunt in any way, shape, or form.

Still, I dragged myself to Conncticut every week. I was already the ungrateful, irresponsible daughter who refused to settle down and propagate the species with one of my mother's numerous fix ups. I was not going to be the ungrateful, irresponsible daughter who pissed away four hundred years of tradition *and* refused to settled down and propagate the species with one of my mother's numerous fix ups.

"Fill me in." Evie's voice pushed into my thoughts. "Since when did we start matchmaking for your mother?"

"Since last night."

"Is it another one of her friends?"

"No, nobody from the country club." Aka the Connecticut Huntress Club, an organization of born female vampires who met to interact and sip Bloody Marys (literally) and match up their unmatched children.

"Thank heavens. Those were the pickiest women I've ever had the misfortune to meet."

If she only knew. But I wasn't ready to declare my vampness to Evie just yet (if ever) for fear she'd freak and quit. She did a great job. Even more, she could spot a designer knockoff at fifty paces. And so I kept my fangs to myself and let her believe my mother and her friends were merely pompous aristocrats rather than pompous bloodsucking aristocrats.

"So who is it?" she wanted to know. "Who are we doing this time?"

"My brother Jack."

"But isn't he already getting married?"

"That's why she wants me to match him up. She's totally against the wedding."

"And you're going to do it?"

"I don't have a choice."

"Yes, you do. Just tell her no. Tell her that what she's asking of you is too much and you can't do it."

"You know, you're right."

"Of course, I am. Just bite the bullet and tell her. The fear of the unknown is much worse than the actual confrontation."

"I'm glad you said that. That's exactly what I needed to hear."

"No problem. That's what I'm here for—to help in any way I can. If you need someone to match up the biggest loser in the Bronx, I'm your girl. If you need someone to schmooze the landlord, consider it done."

"How about if I need someone to call and break the news to my mother?"

"Is Jack a leg man or does he prefer a nice ass?"

"I thought so. Wuss."

"What can I say? I have my own crazy mother to deal with."

"Any other messages?"

"Two bill collectors and my cousin. He said something about you promising him a date?"

"Not with me. We're going to match him up."

"*My* cousin? Good luck. You're going to need it."

"He can't be that bad."

"All I'm saying is that if you have a rabbit's foot, I'd definitely pull it out for this one."

"He seemed nice in a pierced, tattooed, reject sort of way."

"He also tried to French kiss me last Christmas under the mistletoe."

I shrugged. "He's desperate. You're an attractive woman. Things happen."

"He tried to French Fergie last Christmas under the mistletoe."

"Another cousin?"

"My great-great-uncle's elderly girlfriend."

"He's desperate. She was once an attractive woman. Things happen."

"When she didn't go for it, he tried to French her great Dane, Oodles."

"Sounds like I might need more than just the rabbit's foot."

"Exactly."

"That was a joke."

"If you say so."

"Anything else?" I rushed on, eager to kill the sudden visual, otherwise I would never look at Thumper in quite the same way. "Any calls from the opposite sex?"

"A guy named John called. Said you had his number."

"Anyone else?"

"No, Ty didn't call."

"I didn't say anything about Ty."

"You didn't have to. Look, I know you like him. It's obvious. Why don't you stop waiting and just call him?"

"It's not that easy. I'll see you in an hour," I told her and quickly hung up.

I eyed Killer, who'd crept out of the bathroom to stare up at me with bright green eyes. "Do it again," I warned him, "and we'll forget all about the rabbit and go for a cat."

I smiled evilly and he actually stepped back. I wasn't much when it came to hands-on annihilation, but I could bluff with the best of them.

Eleven
♥ ♥ ♥

I showered and changed and left Killer with my downstairs neighbor, Mrs. Janske, who owned two dozen cats and three birds. I promised her a case of air freshener (too many mothballs + too many pets = one stinky apartment) and she promised to call if he misbehaved or missed me (her words not mine). I headed off to work with minimal guilt.

The second I stepped out onto the front stoop, I knew Gwen the private investigator/schoolteacher/ depraved divorcée was on the prowl again.

Click, click.

The sound ticked away in my head as I headed around the corner and up the block.

Click, click, click.

I made a mental note not to do anything vampy— no shape-shifting or sinking my fangs into the cute guy who worked the newsstand. I was just going to act normal. That, and give her several decent pics to take back to her mother. Proof that I was just like every other New Yorker headed off to the daily grind.

I paused every few minutes to give her a good shot.

Me checking my watch.

Me buying the latest issue of *Vogue*.

Me vamping the newsstand guy because I forgot to go to the ATM to get money to pay for the *Vogue*—oh, shit.

Me prying the guy's hands off my ankles and getting the hell out of there before he tried to tackle me and declare his undying love.

Me on the next block checking my shoe for fingerprints and not looking the least bit winded.

Me retouching my lipstick.

Me flipping my hair.

Me flipping off a cab driver who hit a pothole and sprayed water on my shoes. (We're talking new Delman cotton wedges—I'd decided to go for the feminine, floral look. So *now*, especially with my embroidered Lulu Guiness clutch, a daisy quartz necklace, and a chiffon Moschino dress.)

Me fighting down a raging vamp temper as I watched the yellow blur disappear up the street. I came this close to hauling A after him and curing him of his discourteous driving once and for all.

I had a feeling that flaying a hardworking citizen

would be frowned upon by the city council, so I walked into Dead End Dating instead.

Evie had already left and Word was hard at work on the docking station in my office. Since I couldn't look at him and not think about poor Thumper, I quickly stocked up on business cards and answered all life and death e-mail. Nina One, aka Nina Lancaster—daughter of hotelier and ancient vampire Victor Lancaster, who owned, among others, the Waldorf Astoria, where she played hostess to feed her designer clothes addiction—wanted my opinion on her latest accessory acquisition. Meanwhile, the other half of the Ninas, Nina Two—of sanitary products fame—wanted my opinion on a birthday present for her commitment mate.

I quickly typed in *Love it!* Send. And *Forget the lingerie and wrap yourself in a spreadsheet.* Send. Word up: Nina One had fabulous taste and I coveted her every purchase. Nina Two was committed to Wilson the financial guru who got off watching the stock reports on CNN.

I ignored the three latest messages from my mother and headed out the back door. (Gwen was still parked out front with her camera.)

The smell of vitamins and carpet cleaner enveloped me as I stepped out into the small alley that ran behind the building that housed my business, a CPA, a mom-and-pop vitamin shop and a small interior decorating firm. I contemplated vaulting over the back fence and using my preternatural speed to run the several blocks to the television studio. So *not* happening with these shoes, I quickly decided. I wiggled my toes and zings of pain vibrated up my calves. *Ouch!*

I closed my eyes and focused. After a few seconds of visualizing myself as Vampy Von Bat, a loud flutter echoed in my ears. Suddenly I felt weightless (move over Jenny Craig). I put my tiny pink wings to good use and flapped toward the sky. I also sent up a silent prayer to the Big Vamp Upstairs that my new shoes arrived with the rest of me when I morphed back near the NBC studios. While I wasn't too worried, since I'd pretty much perfected my technique when running from the law a few months back, I wasn't taking any chances.

Please, please, please.

I left the alley behind, took a quick look to make sure that Gwen was still planted in a chair at a small café across the street, and flew several blocks over.

I landed in a nearby alley and breathed a sigh of relief when I saw my shoes materialize along with the rest of my outfit. Resolving myself to the sudden weight gain, I straightened my dress and rounded the building to go inside.

The lobby overflowed with women, some of whom I remembered meeting the night before, others I recognized but hadn't yet made contact with. The sight of the familiar gold and cinnamon decor brought a rush of memories, in particular, Ty's voice and the desperation that had laced each word.

"Hello? Earth to Ty?" I sent out the silent message and paused, hand on the glass door. Seconds ticked by and nothing. No shout for help, no crying in misery. Not even a whimper.

I fought down a rush of worry (I had a job to do and sitting around angsting wasn't going to help) and waltzed inside. The worry, much to my surprise, followed me. I know, right? I'm a born vampire. Translation: pompous, pretentious, self-centered, unfeeling creature of the night. But while I had one, two, and three down pat, I was having trouble with number four.

I couldn't stop thinking about Ty and how he might be hurting and how much I missed him and— *get a grip, wouldya?*

I tried a few breathing exercises to calm my nerves. When that didn't work, I decided to picture a scenario much worse than Ty's possible abduction, torture, and dismemberment.

I visualized the stack of bills sitting on my desk (eh). Then I pictured Evie's freaked-out face when I couldn't hand her a paycheck (maybe). Then I had a quick mental of Evie's father—a once upon a time financial wizard who now had ties to the mob—and how pissed he would be if he thought I was trying to take advantage of his precious little girl (and the winner is . . .).

I pasted on my most compelling smile and headed for the reception desk to check in.

I'd just gotten my info packet, complete with an assigned time at which I would give my taped interview in Studio A, when I heard the deep male voice directly behind me.

"Check out these puppies."

After Killer's little surprise, I wasn't the least bit interested in checking out anyone's Lassie or Spot, not when I was already debating serious bodily harm to one infuriating feline. "Isn't there a rule against animals in the studio?" I turned and came face-to-chest with John Schumacker.

He was incognito, his long red hair pulled up in a sleek ponytail. He wore a tasteful ivory suit (an inexpensive label, but still nice) and a pair of matching pumps. The jacket was fitted, outlining what could only have been a pair of double Ds.

"I took your advice," he told me.

"I said inserts, not beach balls." I stepped back to put some distance between us and gain a better perspective. They were still there, still huge.

He shrugged. "The salesclerk kept saying I needed fullness to balance out my height, so I figured I might as well go for broke." He cupped the twins and gave them a squeeze. "They look good, don't they?"

"They're going to look deflated if you keep grabbing them like that. You should be showing them off, not copping a feel."

"I can't help it. They're soft and malleable, just like the real thing."

Um, sure they were. "You haven't felt up many women before, have you?"

"Damn straight I have." When I narrowed my

eyes, he shrugged. "My wife," he admitted. "And Jennifer Sue Horowitz back in the tenth grade."

"Let me bring you up to speed. Saline is nice. Gel is even nicer. But neither come close to a flesh and blood woman." At least that's what we au naturale females liked to think. "So what are you doing here?" I asked him.

He held up his bag. "I'm still under cover. Miss High Heels over there made the cut and so did I."

"You're kidding, right?" He nodded. Any iota of satisfaction I'd felt at being chosen (as if anyone could resist a hot happening female *vampere*) melted faster than my eye makeup during last summer's blackout.

He shrugged. "I just answered most of the stuff on the questionnaire with a maybe—on account of there aren't too many females I know who can make up their minds—and bam, I'm right here with the rest of the chicks waiting my turn for an on-camera interview."

I couldn't exactly remember any of the questions myself. I'd been too busy sizing up the lovesick production assistant who'd handed them out. I'd mentally rifled through my database for that perfect someone to replace the two-timing jerk who'd left her for an underwear model named Shag—*after* he'd played dress-up with her favorite thong.

What was it with guys? Was nothing sacred?

"I guess you got lucky," I told John.

He tapped his temple. "It's all about know-how."

"Yeah, sure."

"Okay, so I got dealt an ace yesterday. Today's a different story. I'm not taking any chances. I'm fully prepared for the long haul. If she makes the cut, me and the boobies are moving up with her if I have to arm wrestle every damned woman ahead of me on the list."

"It's amazing what a fake rack can do to a guy's confidence level."

"You're telling me. I was a little freaked out at first, but then I put them on and bam, my clothes fit better and I actually looked pretty damned hot. At least that's what Ross said."

"And Ross would be?"

"Nobody. Just an agent at our office."

My instincts perked up. "She wouldn't happen to be married, would she?"

"Nah. She isn't much to look at. Nice, though. Fun to talk to. We do pizza and beer every Friday night."

Too cute. I arched an eyebrow at him. "A standing date?"

"Nothing like that." He shook his head. "We're just friends. She's not really my type."

I had a feeling she was exactly his type. He, like every other clueless male in the dating world, just didn't know it. Yet.

"Why don't you and the twins pass these out for me?" Before he could reply, I stuffed a handful of Dead End Dating cards into his hand and mouthed Go.

"I don't know. I'm not much of a salesperson."

"You've got boobs, John. You can do *anything*."

He seemed to think. "Okay, I'll give it a try. What do I say?"

"Just give a nice testimonial about how you're happily wed thanks to me and my staff and that you would highly recommend us to any and everyone."

"But I'm applying for a dating show."

"Just tell them that you're standing in for your cousin who couldn't make it today because of acute appendicitis or a bleeding ulcer or something horrible sounding, and that you, yourself, are happily engaged, and you owe it all to DED. They'll eat it up."

He looked doubtful. "I really should be taking pictures." He held up a leopard print key chain. "I'm not only committing everything to video, I'm taking backup stills just in case."

"So pass them out near your surveillance suspect." I gave him a little shove.

"I guess that'll work." He toddled toward a cluster of women and I made a mental note to find out Ross's last name.

I spent the next fifteen minutes exchanging cards and talking up my matchmaking service. I was so busy, in fact, that I didn't even hear my name being called until John elbowed me and pointed toward an irritated production assistant.

"Lil Marchette?" the man demanded when I walked up and gave him my most dazzling smile.

"The one and only."

"I've been calling you for five minutes." And he wasn't the least bit happy about it.

In fact, he was seriously considering crossing my name off the list and moving up an alternate to take my place. He—Marty Bezdeck—didn't need this aggravation. He'd moved out of his parents' house three months ago, into a flat he couldn't afford, to escape his five sisters. He'd had it with indecisive, perpetually late women who couldn't seem to make up their minds. In particular, his ex-fiancée Jeanine, who'd always arrived a half hour late for their dates and had refused to set a wedding date.

My chest hitched. I know, I know. I'm a great big cream puff, but the guy had actually gotten down on one knee and proposed in the middle of Madison Square Garden. Talk about devotion.

She isn't the only woman in the world. There's someone else out there for you. I stared deeply into his eyes and sent the mental message.

His blue eyes clouded for a brief second and then he gazed back adoringly at me.

Not that I'm that someone, I quickly added. *I'm nobody. Just another ditzy broad with really great highlights and incredible fashion sense. You'd be crazy to want me.*

Marty wasn't buying it. He asked me out twice while escorting me to the set where the interviews were being taped. He offered to get me coffee. And give me a ride home. He even offered to take Killer for a walk: He had his own cat *and* a pooper-scooper.

"You know, that sounds like a really good—" I

caught myself before I blurted out the rest of the encouragement.

This guy was on the rebound in a major way and I wasn't going to stomp on what was left of his heart. I was, however, going to find him someone to help him pick up the pieces. I slipped a DED card into his hand, told him to call me tomorrow afternoon, and turned my attention to the video camera that sat in front of me.

"Okay, here's how the interview goes," the camerawoman (Sheila, married, two kids, ridiculously happy—*awww*) told me. "I'm going to ask you some simple questions, you'll answer, and the camera will get it all on tape. Remember, this is your chance to shine, to show Mark what you're made of, and why he should pick you to be his dream woman."

"Mark?"

"Mark Williams. Mr. Weather." When I didn't seem clued in, she added, "Manhattan's Most Wanted bachelor."

"Mr. Weather," I blurted, nodding vigorously. "The honcho of hurricanes. The top dog of twisters. Of course. Everybody knows him." Everybody except yours truly. "Pfff," I made a face. "Of course I know Marcus."

"That's Mark."

"Mark, Markie, Marko, Marcus—whatever."

She gave me an odd look before shaking her head. "Okay, on three, you're going to stare at this blinking light and describe your ideal date. The one thing you think is the most ultraromantic thing to do with a man."

I nodded and thought of a dozen truly romantic activities—everything I'd ever envisioned in my hottest fantasies, from basking on a warm beach together to licking Dom Pérignon off one another in the moonlight. The thing was, the idea wasn't to nab myself a spot on the show. I was here to circulate. To promote.

When she counted down *three, two, one,* and said "Most romantic activity?" then pointed to me, I found myself blurting the most obnoxious thing that came to mind.

"A wrestling match."

"Come again?"

"Front row, side-by-side, surrounded by sweat and name-calling and guys with beer bellies scarfing hot dogs. *Tres romantique.*"

"Um, okay." The woman shook her head. "Next question: Who do you consider to be the world's most romantic man?"

"Stone Cold Steve Austin."

"And the most romantic woman?"

"Paris Hilton."

"Most romantic food?"

"Pinto beans."

"Most romantic color?"

"It's a tie between orange and black."

"Most romantic symbol?"

"Skull and crossbones."

"Most romantic song?"

" 'Can't Touch This.' "

"Most romantic saying?"

"Is it always that small?"

"That's a wrap," Sheila announced, killing the camera. She eyed me. "You do know this is a dating show, don't you?"

"Of course." I did the dazzling smile thing again. "Why else would I be here?"

Twelve

S wallow, you fucking idiot.

The command echoed through my head and I tried. Once. Twice. My throat burned, refusing to work. My mouth felt huge and swollen. I tried to swipe my tongue over my lips, but it wouldn't cooperate. My brain scrambled, my thoughts ran in different directions. Stop it. I had to stop it. To think about one thing and keep my guard in place. I couldn't let her in right now. I wouldn't—

Fuck!

Pain exploded, jagging its way through my body. I went up in flames, my nerves screaming. My pulse pounded and my mind raced even faster. Images rifled through my head, one after the other, years and years of memories that I wanted to forget, to block out, to keep buried deep.

Easy. Stay grounded. Right here. Right now. Nothing else.

I pushed my eyes open as wide as I could and tried to fix on the dark shape moving about. Footsteps thundered on the concrete floor, the noise bouncing off the brick walls.

Cold fingertips scraped over my bare skin. Hard leather slid across my flesh. Metal bit into my ankles and wrists. The icy slab of concrete at my back ground into my raw muscles.

My watery gaze hooked on the small window near the ceiling. The last remnants of daylight pushed into the dimly lit chamber. A blaze of colored lights lit the background and danced off the opposite wall. It was almost night. Again. I tried to calculate how many that made, but suddenly I didn't know. It seemed like ages since I'd sat upright.

At the same time, I could still feel the blood on my hands, sliding down my throat, twisting in my gut. That kill had ended my life and landed me here.

With him. And the pain.

Heat gripped my ankles, spiraling up through my body, holding tight to each nerve ending until I arched up off the table. The smell of smoke and burning flesh filled my nostrils. My temples throbbed. My heart pounded faster and faster, as if it would explode.

If only.

"Aw, it's not that bad, is it?" The voice was deep, controlled, familiar.

Misery and guilt and a dozen other emotions

churned in my gut. Desperation pumped through me. Panic pulsed, fiery hot and nerve-racking, up and down my spine.

"What you feel is nothing compared to what I feel," he told me. "What I've felt all these years."

The shadow moved to my other side, humming a catchy tune with each step, as if he were watering a garden instead of killing me inch by inch. Second by second.

He wouldn't.

Not anymore, now that he'd killed me once, way back when. He wanted me to hurt. To feel the pain. The regret.

That's what this was all about.

What my afterlife had always been about.

White-hot pain ripped through me and I arched again, coming up off the table. A strangled gasp worked its way up my ravaged throat. My thoughts scrambled again.

Memories stirred and images flitted in and out until the sensation died and I managed to snag my gaze on the window again. The lights danced and in the distance, beyond the thunder of my heartbeat, I heard the laughter. The music. The occasional ding of an arcade game.

Fire lashed across the bottom of my foot and I bit my lip. Blood spurted into my mouth, gliding down my throat, stirring my hunger.

"You feel it again, don't you?" The shadow moved closer, blocking out the window. "The agony?" Another prod and I hissed. "Yes, you feel it. It twists inside of you, like a cold, slithering demon, eating you from the inside out. It snacks away on your insides until you're just a shell of what you once were. Until you feel like giving up."

I ground my teeth against the lightning bolt of pain. Anger rushed through me, the primitive instinct to kill instead of be killed, and my lips pulled back, my fangs extended. I wanted to rip him to shreds. I would have, but he'd taken too many precautions.

"That's it, vampire. Show your true colors. You're a vicious bastard. It doesn't matter how many criminals you take down, or how much good you do the world. You'll never escape your true nature. You're an animal who rapes and pillages the weak. A murderer. You'll never change." Cold, rank breath whispered over my ear as he leaned down. "I won't let you . . ."

Now would be a really good time to wake up.

The thought pushed its way past the darkness that engulfed me and my eyes popped open. But there was more darkness. Pitch-black. Smothering.

"I won't let you . . ."

The voice echoed and I panicked. "You and what army?" I kicked and clawed and bolted upright.

Feathers rained down on me as reality struck and I realized I wasn't fighting for my life in some cold, dank dungeon.

Rather, I'd just battled it out with my favorite pillow and half a goose down comforter.

I'd obviously won.

My frantic gaze darted around the room, drinking in the familiar dark blinds, the cherrywood dresser, the scrawny cat that sat on my favorite rug and stared back at me as if I were Bugs, Daffy, and Sylvester all rolled into one.

My heart slowed a fraction.

O-kay. A dream. That's it. Just a bona fide nightmare. Nothing to get all freaked out about.

That's what I told myself, but deep in my gut, I knew it was more. My gut and my feet.

I hiked up one aching extremity and stared at the sole. An angry red line glared back at me, proof that the past few minutes had been much more than the result of my downing an entire glass of cold blood right before hopping in the sack. I checked my other foot. Same mark. Same pain.

What the hell was going on?

I eased my legs over the side of the bed, wincing as my tender feet hit the braided rug. My wrists ached and my back hurt and my ribs felt as if they'd been kicked a few dozen times.

I closed my eyes and did a mental rehash of the dream/possible alien abduction. (Give me a break, all right? I still had three hours of sleep left and my brain was a little fuzzy.)

Cold slab. Taunting voice. Torture. *Ty.*

Realization struck and my eyelids shot up. I bolted to my feet and pain knifed through me. Nothing compared to what Ty had felt.

What I'd felt.

He'd linked to me. Or I'd linked to him.

Either way, we'd been there together. Seeing. Feeling.

"Holy shit."

I took a step and barely caught a scream of pain. I contemplated floating to the kitchen where I'd left my purse, but then decided that was too much effort. I sank down to the bed, focused my attention on the expensive clutch, and willed it around the corner, straight toward me.

A few seconds later, I retrieved Ash's business card and snagged my cell off the nightstand. I punched in the number and waited for him to answer.

"I'm busy right now," came the deep voice. "Leave a message . . ." *Beep.*

"It's Lil. Lil Marchette. I need to talk to you ASAP." I left my number and punched the off button.

I sat there for the next few minutes, willing the phone to ring, but nothing happened.

Would you just chill? He'll call soon enough and you can tell him . . . What?

It's not like I'd gotten an address and directions while I'd been linked to Ty. No, the only thing I'd gotten was a disjointed conversation and a semidecent view of someone's basement, and a really weird smell—a mix of mustard and diesel and a sticky sweet scent that made my stomach churn. Talk about nothing.

But at least I'd figured out why Ty hadn't answered me when I'd called out to him. He'd (a) been too busy being tortured and (b) hadn't wanted me around.

I didn't know whether to be sympathetic or hurt.

I settled for both and blinked against the sudden tears that burned the backs of my eyes.

I was NOT going to cry. Crying accomplished nothing. Even more, it made me look like a big marshmallow rather than a badass über vampire.

Not happening.

I spent the next fifteen minutes *not* crying until I gave a final sniffle and wiped at my eyes. There. I felt a little better. Still lonely and helpless, but I could deal. I turned and swept the stray feathers off onto the floor for cleanup later. (In case you haven't figured it out, I'm not much for housework and would rather wear a powder blue polyester pantsuit than engage in any sort of domestic activity.)

Meow . . .

Killer's soft voice drew my attention and my gaze swiveled to where he sat beside the bed amid a pile of down. I frowned. "Aren't you supposed to be in the bathroom?"

You try snuggling up to a toilet. He blinked up at me. *I need some love.*

He *did* look a little sad.

Since he hadn't left me any more presents—none that a quick glance could detect—I decided that it couldn't hurt for me to pick him up and maybe let him lay at the foot of the bed. After all, he'd had a bath (Mrs. Janske) and a spritzing of Chanel (*moi*). There really was no reason to sentence him to the cold, gloomy tile of the bathroom. On top of that, I wasn't in any hurry to find myself accused of animal neglect.

No way was I even thinking of picking him up because I felt *that* lonely. And helpless. And scared.

I snatched him up and stuck him in bed next to me.

And then I did the only thing I could do since it was still daylight and I was a vampire (and they'd yet to invent an SPF strong enough to keep me from going *poof!*) I snuggled up with Killer and spent the next three hours watching the clock and worrying.

Thirteen

❤ ❤ ❤

"Let's go over it again." Ash sat in my office at Dead End Dating, his powerful body overflowing the leather chair, and eyed me.

I slumped over my desk. I was tired. Frustrated. Hungry. My feet hurt, and not because of the brand-spanking-new strappy paisley sandals I'd put on before leaving the house. While I knew the marks would heal in less than twenty-four hours—one of my vampy perks—I couldn't ignore the pain. Or the truth. Ty was in a *real* mess, and there wasn't a thing I could do to help him.

"Again."

"But we've been over it a half dozen times already."

"And each time we learn something new. Come on. Spill it."

"Okay." I went over the dream from start to finish while he nodded and took even more notes. "So what do you think? And if you tell me to repeat it again, I'm going to stake myself."

He didn't grin. He was too busy staring at his notepad. "I'm thinking he isn't too far away. It sounds like he's been confined for a really long time, which probably means that whoever snatched him took him straight to this basement and hasn't let up since." He eyed me. "You said something about smelling diesel?"

"And mustard. And something I'm not really sure of."

He seemed to think. "There are lots of industrial plants in northern Jersey. Or the smell could be from a large truck. There are trucks in and out of the city."

"And the mustard?"

He shook his head. "That could be the abductor's lunch for all we know, rather than a clue to Ty's whereabouts." He closed his pad and pushed to his feet.

"Now what?"

"I keep looking and you wait for him to slip up again and link with you."

"Isn't there something I can actually do? All this waiting makes me crazy."

He shook his head. "I'm checking out Ty's list of fugitive apprehensions and running the prints I pulled against every database in the country. That's all we can do until we get a solid lead." His gaze met mine. "Keep trying to reach him. He might be getting weak, which is why you were able to link up with him. If that's the case, then you'll be able to do it again."

I nodded, but at the same time, I was hoping that last night had been it. Ty would be found ASAP and I would be off the hook as the telepathically linked, fantabulously dressed girlfriend.

As much as I wanted to help, I didn't really do pain and suffering all that well. While I knew there were bad apples in every bunch, I'd actually seen the brutality for myself. And felt the pain of it. And the experience sort of scared the crapola out of me and put everything into perspective.

Take my stack of bills, for example. Inconsequential compared to life and death. My stack of business cards from the *MMW* applicants? Important, but it's not as if I'd burst into flames if I didn't follow up every single lead. The stack of messages from my mother reminding me about Sunday's mating prospect for Jack? Okay, so maybe that did qualify as afterlife and death (my own). But everything else? *So* off my list of *must do right now or suffer dire consequences*.

I summoned a smile. "Maybe today was the worst of it and he'll come walking through the door, completely unharmed. Or at least limping with no permanent damage."

"You don't really believe that, do you?"

I didn't. That was the problem. "I'll keep trying to contact him."

"Good, and stop thinking so hard about what happened."

"You're the one who made me repeat it a zillion times."

"To get the facts. Now it's done, so don't dwell on it. You might be inadvertently blocking a vital piece of information. Just try putting your mind on something else and, who knows, you might have a breakthrough and give us something solid."

"And if I don't?"

His eyes grew brighter until I actually had to blink. "We'll have to deal with the situation." He started to turn and I couldn't help the sudden curiosity that burned through me.

"Why are you so intent on finding him?"

He paused and shrugged. "I hunt criminals for a living, but there are so many that it's a full-time job. Ty's good at what he does and he eases my caseload. Usually bounty hunters get in the way, but he's the exception."

"Because he's a vampire."

"Exactly. When he brings in a bounty, he knows whether to bring them to me or hand them over to the police."

"But aren't you the police? You're a homicide detective," I pointed out. "At least that's what you told me."

"I am, but I don't work directly for the local police or the feds. I operate out of a smaller, more elite department. We function with a completely different agenda in mind."

"To serve and protect?"

"To retrieve and punish."

"Vigilante justice?"

"Quite the opposite. We're sanctioned by Big Daddy himself."

Hmmm . . .

In human terms, Big Daddy referred to the head of the FBI or CIA or even the president.

In vamp terms, it referred to a royal descendant of the daddy of all born vamps—at present Count Christoff Deville. I'd matched up one of his cousins—Francis—not too long ago. Since Francis was still sort of dweeby and, therefore, the black sheep of the Deville clan, I'd finally given up the hope that I'd be seeing any sort of token of gratitude—high five, new car, small country. Plus, I'd kind of matched him up with a human (big no-no), which would have killed my chances anyway. Not that I regretted pairing him up with Melissa. They were in love and living together. Big sigh.

As for Big Daddy . . . In were terms, B.D. meant the pack leader, be it wolf or bear or labradoodle.

I eyed Ash. Nix human. Forget vamp. Were? Nuh-uh. He *was* some sort of Other, I knew that much since I couldn't read him and he could make his eyes glow brighter than the sun at midday (or so I've been told). But since I'd led a sheltered, pretentious existence like every other born vamp, my knowledge of Other supernatural creatures was a teeny bit limited.

"We let the cops and the bounty hunters take out

the minor offenders," he went on, "while we concentrate on a select few. The most dangerous."

"The least human?"

He grinned. "You just might have the intellect to go with that mouth of yours."

I followed him out into the lobby where Evie still sat at her desk, looking office fab in a pair of leather and embroidered cork wedges, a cotton dress, denim vest, and Tina Tang gold vermeil bracelet. She salivated over Ash as he walked through the outer office and then disappeared through the front glass doors.

She sighed. "Can I have him?"

"He's not mine to give away."

"Married?"

"No."

"Girlfriend?"

"He said no."

She breathed a deep sigh. "That's what they all say. He's probably got a girlfriend. That, or he's gay. The good ones are *always* taken."

"Let's hope not," I told her, fingering through the stack of profiles she'd just entered into our database. I spared a glance at Word, who stood on a ladder in the far corner and drilled a hole in the ceiling for one of the docking speakers. "Any luck matching up your cousin's profile?"

"Sorry. Last night I was too busy watching a *CSI: Miami* rerun to catch *Animal Kingdom*."

I grinned. "Keep looking. I promised him three matches."

"*You* promised him," she pointed out. "Me work-

ing his profile is a major conflict of interest on account of we're related."

"Three times removed is not related."

"Okay, it's a conflict of interest on account of I
can't stand the sight of him."

I could see Evie's point. He *was* a little hard on the
eyes, and sad looking. Literally. Tonight he'd traded
his metal image for pure Goth, and painted black
teardrops down one cheek. His eyes were rimmed in
black to match his fingernails. "I'll admit he's a little
out there, but so is most everyone else. There are
tons of crazies in Manhattan alone. They just aren't
so obvious. I doubt he's worse than any of our other
clients."

"You haven't spent every Christmas of your life
hiding in the hall closet with Aunt Gretchen."

"Was she dodging him, too?"

"No, she's old and thinks the hall closet is the
bathroom."

"Oh."

"Yeah. So best of luck. I've got my hands full."
Her face brightened. "We had four phone calls from
MMW applicants who didn't make this last cut." She
held up a couple of checks. "And retainer fees from
two of them who stopped by while you were meeting
with Mr. Hunky Ass."

"That would be Hunky *Ash*."

She grinned. "Says you." She put the checks into
her cash drawer, slid the profiles into her ENTERED
file, and started to shut down her terminal. "There
are extra doughnuts and plenty of coffee. Oh," she

turned and grabbed two message slips, "and your mother called while you were in with Hunky. She said not to be late on Sunday, and don't forget the match."

As if I could.

She leveled a stare at me. "I know it seems like a no-win situation, but things could be worse." Have I mentioned that in addition to being a kick-ass fashionista, Evie is also an optimist like the ever-fantabulous *moi*? "Look on the bright side. At least you have good hair."

"That's true." I beamed for all of five seconds and did a little fluffing before my face fell.

"Brighter?" Evie asked.

"Blinding."

She seemed to think. "You do have a whopping three whole days to find a decent prospect. Cities have fallen in a lot less time."

So true.

Three was, well, *three*. As opposed to two or the dreaded one. That meant seventy-two hours. Oodles of time to find one itty-bitty born vampire and show my mother that I wasn't a total loser in the matchmaking department. An itty-bitty hot, smoking vampire. But not *too* smoking. I wouldn't want Jack to actually fall for her.

Not that he would. He was in love with Mandy. Hopelessly. Desperately. Forever and ever . . . Right?

I'd never actually asked him if he planned to make her into a vampire. But, of course, he would. If he didn't, then she would eventually start to sag. She would get insecure and start forking over the bucks for plastic surgery. He would stay his usual hot self and she would end up looking like the cat woman and . . . Well, he just *had* to. Another black mark on his already tarnished record, as far as my parents were concerned. Marrying humans? No. Making vampires? *Hell,* no. Made vamps were the scourge of the earth. The lowest form of vampiric life. Mere peasants (my dad's words not mine).

Hence my dilemma with Ty. No way would my folks ever go for him—if we managed to develop some sort of relationship, that is. *If* I managed to free him from whatever crazed psycho was using him for a voodoo doll—

The thought stopped me cold and my mind started to race. *Nah.* I hadn't heard any chanting. Or beating of drums. Or squawking chickens.

"Are you okay?" Evie's voice pushed into my thoughts.

"Um, yeah." I forced a smile.

"Because you look like someone just kicked your cat."

I thought of Killer. "I should be so lucky." I turned and headed back into my office to get to work.

Fourteen

Seventy-two hours turned out to be a lot less time than it sounded like.

For one thing, I had to deduct the ten hours spent sleeping each day, as well as the two hours for hair, makeup, shower, and scooping up cat poop. That left thirty-six minus the time spent working on my other clients, calming a freaked-out Mandy when the hotel cancelled her wedding date due to an overbooking, and worrying over Ty. In the end, I had all of ten hours to search for Jack's perfect match.

Which meant that by the time Sunday evening rolled around, I'd managed to come up with an impressive zero prospects.

I stood in my kitchen, nursing a glass of warm blood while I contemplated my choices.

One, I could show up without a prospect, piss off my mother, and suffer the consequences.

Two, I could not show up at all, piss off my mother, and suffer the consequences.

And three, I could just stake myself and get it over with.

I'd just reached for the letter opener sitting near my latest Visa bill when I heard Killer's meow.

I glanced down and big green eyes blinked back up at me.

"Before you end it," he seemed to say, *"could you move your ass over to the cabinet and get me something to eat? I'm starving, here."*

My fingers closed inches shy of the opener. It's not like I could let him starve. I was totally more responsible than that. I walked over to the pantry. A few minutes later, I spooned a can of Gourmet Kitty into a silver Pucci pet dish (I'd gone shopping) and set it on the floor next to a matching water bowl. Killer strutted over, sniffed, and started lapping up the treat.

I grabbed the letter opener. "I'm going for it," I said to the cat. He kept scarfing without sparing me so much as a glance. "No, no. Don't cry and beg. It's better this way. Really. I won't have to listen to my mom. Or worry about Ty." Or help him.

The last thought stopped me cold.

Well, that and the sinfully delicious thought that followed—me and Ty and hot, life-affirming sex to erase his totally horrific experience.

My conscience (yes, I have one) and my hormones

raged and I abandoned the letter opener. I was much too young (and too freakin' scared) to end it all. Besides, what would happen to Killer? And Evie? And desperate males and females the world over who would give anything—*anything*—to fall in love?

Geez, what was I thinking? I had people (and a snotty cat) who needed me. I couldn't take the easy way out simply because I was scared of my mother.

Not yet, anyway. Not without exhausting every resource.

Grabbing my cell, I punched in Nina One's phone number.

"Tell me again why I should do this," Nina said after I'd explained my desperate situation.

"Because I'm your best friend and I would do it for you."

"No, you wouldn't."

"Okay, so I wouldn't. But I wouldn't have to because you're not a matchmaker with an overbearing mother and a letter opener." Nina's mother had believed in the wine and wait method of child rearing. Namely, she'd drunk wine and waited for the nanny to deal with the children. She still drank wine and stayed as far removed from Nina and her brother as possible. Unlike my mother, she wasn't pining away for grandchildren. It was hard to pine when you were pickled.

"What kind of letter opener?"

"A sharp one."

"That's not what I meant. Where'd you get it?

Tiffany's?" Nina's addiction to designer couture and accessories was even worse than mine. Really.

"It's sterling silver with tiny diamonds in the handle. It's Cartier. My brothers got it for me when I opened Dead End Dating."

"It sounds divine."

"Get a grip. It's a letter opener."

"Sorry. We've been hosting a convention and I had to work five nights in a row, double shifts. I'm beat. And going into withdrawal."

"So go toss around some cash at the gift shop."

"I already have one of everything. A girl can only have so many I Love New York T-shirts."

"So what about tonight?"

"I would love to, but I have a date with this really cute French waiter—he does the graveyard shift with room service—and I promised I'd meet him in the penthouse tonight for a little midnight snack and quickie."

"You would choose sex over our lifelong, five-hundred-and-twenty-two-year friendship?"

"It's really good sex."

"Fine, if you won't do it for our friendship, what about for the white silk Donna Karan jacket that I borrowed this past New Year's Eve?"

"I thought I'd lost that."

"Apparently not, because I'm looking at it right now. So far, I've treated it as if it were my own, because we're such dear friends. But if we're not *that* close, then I don't really need to be careful. What do

I care if you hate me for spilling an entire glass of blood all over the front?"

"That's blackmail."

"I prefer to think of it as effective bargaining."

"What do I have to do?" she finally blurted.

"Just come with me to Connecticut and act interested in Jack."

"What about his girlfriend?"

"I'll distract her every now and then so you can cozy up to him in front of my mother."

"And the jacket?"

"You'll get it back in mint condition. Tomorrow." When she didn't answer, I added, my voice softer, "Please, Nina. This would really mean so much to me."

Several seconds ticked by. "Oh, all right. But you owe me."

"No problem. I'll give you—"

"And don't even think about offering me a free profile," she cut in.

"—free, um, coffee. And cream. *And* sugar."

"Forget it." She paused before delivering the verdict. "I want your Badgley Mischka sunglasses."

"The ones with the Swarovski crystals?"

"Those are the ones."

"But—"

"Or I'll call Pierre and tell him to meet me upstairs. It's quickie time."

"Deal," I muttered. *Bitch*.

"I heard that."

* * *

"Sorry I'm late," I told my mother when she opened the massive front door later that evening. "I couldn't decide between the Anne Kleins and the Jimmy Choos." I stared at my feet outlined against the expensive marble tile. "Jimmy won."

"Fine, fine." Jacqueline Marchette looked her usual stunning self in a black Emanuel Ungaro dress. The material that draped her body accented her tall, svelte figure. Her long, dark brown hair was slicked back into its usual chic ponytail. She had high cheekbones, rich brown eyes, and glossed lips. White gold mesh earrings dangled from her pale earlobes. She had one hand on the doorknob and a tumbler of vodka in the other. She reeked of French perfume, cherries jubilee, and major disapproval. "Just hurry and get inside." She spared Nina a look as she waved her glass. "Your father's already in the middle of his fourth putt and your brothers are here. *And* the human." The door thudded shut behind us. The ice in the vodka glass tinkled.

My mother wrinkled her sculpted nose as she led us toward the main living room where everyone was gathered. "I tell you, if I have to see that Molly fawn all over my baby one more time, I'm going to throw myself on the nearest sharp object."

"It's Mandy, Mom." The *click, click* of my shoes echoed in the massive hallway, keeping time with my frantic heartbeat.

I know, I know. She was my mother. She'd given birth to me. Fed me. Nurtured me. She wasn't going to end my existence if I happened to disappoint her.

At the same time, she was my *mother.* She'd given birth to me. Fed me. Nurtured me. She *wasn't* going to end my existence if I happened to disappoint her.

No, she would make me suffer.

"It's outrageous is what it is," my mother went on. "She keeps touching him." She took a long swallow from her glass as we reached the main room.

My oldest two brothers—Max and Rob—stood by a polished cherrywood sideboard. Max looked as handsome as ever in expensive casual—Guess jeans and a fitted, washed-out gray tee. Rob had gone for modest casual in a pair of Levi's and a navy henley, while my dad pulled off tacky casual in black, red, and white plaid pants and a red golf shirt. Max sipped a scotch on the rocks, Rob nursed a bottled beer, and my dad leaned over a small putting green, golf club in hand.

My mother nodded toward the couple who sat side by side on the tapestry sofa. "What did I tell you? She's holding his hand." She said it with the same outrage as *"She's plotting to destroy the entire born vamp nation"* or *"She's wearing a Dior knock-off."*

Let's see. Hopelessly in love. Wedding in three months. Joint checking accounts. "The nervy bitch," I murmured.

"Exactly." She forced a smile. "Everyone, Lil's here. And Nina."

Several pairs of eyes turned toward us and I gave a little wave before scanning the rest of the room in search of some sign that tonight was going to be even worse than I'd anticipated. An indentation in the couch. A pair of car keys that didn't go to the Marchette fleet of filthy expensive vehicles. A jacket or a pipe or—I swear I'm not making this up—a scorecard for total Orgasm Quotients.

Long story short: My mother wanted grandbaby vamps to carry on the Marchette line. Since no female was good enough for her three boys, the fate of this particular branch of the family tree rested solely on yours truly. Hence the constant fix ups.

At least until Mandy had entered the picture. My mom had been so freaked lately that she'd forgotten all about finding eligible, fertile son-in-law candidates. I'd been solo for the last six hunts.

I smiled. Make that seven.

"Remy's running late. He'll be joining us for dinner later," my mother informed me, wiping the smile off my face. "He's your date for tonight."

Fifteen

Did she just say Remy?

My heart jumped and if I hadn't been a perfect, pretentious born female vampire, I would have sworn I could feel the sweat popping out on my forehead.

Not *Remy*.

Don't get me wrong. I like the guy. As far as born male vamps went, he was one of the most tolerable. I grew up with him in the old country. We'd played connect the blood drops together and chased our human nannies and even terrorized the occasional small village. While I didn't see him that often now—I lived in Manhattan and he upheld the law as the chief of police in Fairfield—we still had a lot in common. Even more, I never had to worry about giving him the brush-off because I knew he didn't like me like *that*.

At least, I'd never thought so until my close brush with jail a few months back. He'd helped me out and I'd sort of promised him a favor, and, well, the debt remained unpaid. Now whenever he looked at me, I couldn't help but wonder if he was picturing me naked.

Particularly since I'd started to picture him naked.

"So where is she?" my mother asked as she came up beside me, effectively killing my anxiety over Remy's imminent arrival.

"Right there." I motioned to where Max poured a drink for my best friend. Meanwhile, everyone else tried to look awestruck while my pops demonstrated his latest twist and curl, and griped about his failed sniper attempt on Viola.

" . . . tried to take her out from several different vantage points. Who knew the woman could move that fast?" he told my brother Rob.

"She's a *were*, Dad. They have fast reflexes."

"I had five fully cooked pot roasts as a distraction and she still dodged every bullet."

"You really shot at someone?" Mandy asked. "Isn't that attempted murder?"

"Not during hunting season," Jack informed her.

"But that's Nina," my mother murmured. "She's hardly appropriate for Jack."

"Why not? Born vamp. Impressive Orgasm Quotient. Great shoes. Killer eyelashes." Nina had gone for the Christina Aguilera look, complete with multicolored lashes that shimmered every time she blinked. "I think I hit the jackpot."

"But all of you were in knickers together."

Thanks, Ma, for that great visual. "Look at it this way. She already knows what a shit he is, so there'll be no surprises a few centuries down the road."

She seemed to think. "True. I suppose it could work." She shrugged. "Anything's better than that Maxie."

"*Mandy.*"

"Whatever."

"Besides, Nina isn't going to actually hook up with Jack. This is just a little teaser to get him ready for the real prospects."

"You already have more lined up for the dinner party?"

"Do I have more?" I snorted. "I'm a professional, Mother, a detail-oriented perfectionist who is always fully prepared and leaves nothing to chance. Of course I have more." At least I was hoping like hell I would. "You're paying me good money and I fully intend to deliver."

"If she's really a prospect for Jack, why is she flirting with Max?" She eyed the blonde who leaned into my oldest brother and rested a perfectly manicured hand on his arm.

"That's not flirting. They're just talking. And laughing." And looking as if they'd like to strip each other bare and do the nasty right there on my mother's prized Berber rug. I snatched my mother's glass. "Let me get you a refill."

I made a beeline for the liquor and breezed by Nina. "Would you cool it?" I hissed.

"You told me to cozy up to him."

"Jack, not Max."

"I'm practicing."

"Well, stop it. Ooops, we're out of ice," I declared. I motioned to the human perched next to my youngest brother. "Mandy, can you help me get some from the kitchen?"

She popped up, excitement bubbling in her eyes at being called by her actual name. "Sure."

"Fab." I turned to Nina and whispered, "You've got five minutes to impress my mom. Make it good."

"As soon as I get home, I'm lining my cat's litter box with your Donna Karan jacket," I told Nina as we hid out in the pool house a half hour later while everyone else searched for the *it* person.

"Since when do you have a cat?" She gave me a curious glance.

I shrugged. "I'm trying an alternative diet."

"Ewwww."

Yeah, ewww. But it was the best I could come up with considering the fact that I was extremely upset. And pissed. I gave Nina the evil eye. "What the hell were you thinking?"

She shrugged. "You said to make it good."

"That meant a little smiling and flirting with *Jack*. It didn't mean a lap dance for Rob."

"I wasn't giving him a lap dance. My skirt got stuck on his zipper."

"Because you were shaking your moneymaker right on top of his Mr. Happy."

"Your father swung his club and I had to dodge. It was either Rob's lap or the floor."

"There was a rug to cushion the fall."

"Get over it. The night's still young. I'll give it another shot during dinner." She glanced at the diamond Cartier bracelet encircling her slim wrist. "How much longer do you think they'll be?" Her fangs peeked past her full lips. "I'm starved."

My father was *it*. In addition to being the head of the Marchette clan, he was also the grumpiest loser. "It could take awhile."

We spent the next hour dishing on the latest spring line and discussing our sex lives.

Okay, so we discussed Nina's sex life and my lack of one since Ty had dropped off the face of the earth.

"I hate to perpetuate the snob thing, but there's a reason the ancients turn their noses up at the whole vampire-making thing."

"Maybe they're just a bunch of old geezers who are set in their ways."

"And maybe they know something we don't." She gave me The Look. "All I'm saying is, I would forget all about this Ty person if I were you. There are plenty of other vamps out there—"

The shrill sound of a whistle drowned the rest of her warning.

I pushed to my feet. Thankfully, it was over. The hunt *and* the lecture.

"Awesome, Dad," I told my father when I reached

the patio to find him looking sullen. Rob wore a victorious smile and held up the whistle he'd ripped from my father's neck. (Quick update: The *it* person wore a whistle around his or her neck and the first vamp to get close enough to rip it free and blow took home the coveted vacation days.) "You held out longer than anyone *ever*."

"Way to go." Nina smiled and added her congratulations. "For an aging vamp, you've totally got it going on."

My father's gaze turned red and I seriously debated ducking beneath a nearby chaise longue.

"Why, thank you," my mother blurted, stepping between Nina and my dad's piercing glare. "Such a nice compliment, darling, don't you think?" she asked my father, placing a hand on his arm. "Even the younger vampires are impressed with your wisdom and cunning."

In addition to being an overbearing mother, Jacqueline Marchette had also perfected her ass-kissing skills. At least where my father was concerned.

She smoothed the collar of his golf shirt. *Pucker up*. "Have I told you how fast you were this evening?"

My father drank in her praise like a thirsty construction worker. His chest puffed out and he pushed his shoulders back. "I was fast, wasn't I?"

"The fastest." She smiled. "And so elusive. Why, I felt certain the children would *never* find you."

"I could have outlasted them all night, you know. But the point of all this is to hone their hunting skills.

If they never actually get the prize, they'll get frustrated and that would defeat the purpose."

"Such a wise vampire."

Such a load of baloney.

"Come," she told him, turning to lead him into the house. "You must be ravenous after such a spectacular demonstration of skill and endurance. Children," she called over her shoulder. "In."

Max high-fived Rob. Jack kissed Mandy. And I grabbed Nina's hand and started after my mother. The sooner the evening ended, the better. Maybe if we hurried, I could down a glass and Nina could do something flirty with Jack, and we could scram before Remy showed up—

"Uh, hi," I mumbled as I came up hard against the muscular frame that suddenly appeared in the doorway. I stepped backward and tried to control the sudden pounding of my heart.

Remy was tall and blond. He had green eyes and a smile that made my tummy tingle. Worse, unlike the other BVs, Remy had no scent, which ruled out my NOT liking him because I smelled like cotton candy and he smelled like something that totally did NOT go with the light, fluffy stuff. Like bananas Foster or chocolate cake or Oreo cookie brownies. I'd broken off many a relationship because a scent was too rich or too fruity or too something. My soul mate would be the perfect complement to me, his scent an enhancement of my own.

Remy spent his nights catching Fairfield's most wanted and so he took a special pill that had been developed by a top secret tactical weapons manufacturer. It suppressed his smell, which gave him an edge over all those criminal vamps and one megalicious matchmaker. They couldn't smell him coming and I had nothing to complain about to my mother.

Remy really was the perfect born vampire for me.

If I could get past the whole knickers thing, which, of course, I couldn't.

At least that's what I told myself.

Remy touched a strong hand to my shoulder and heat spiraled to my nipples. Bad nipples. "Slow down, Ace, or I'll have to arrest you for speeding."

Bring on the handcuffs, buddy.

I drop-kicked the ridiculous, outrageous, *never gonna happen* thought right out of my head and pasted on an apologetic smile. "Sorry. I'm just really hungry."

His gaze collided with mine and something sparked in the deep green depths. "That makes two of us."

I swallowed and yanked Nina up beside me. "Um, have you met Nina?"

"We grew up together, remember?"

"Good, then you'll have lots to talk about." I dodged him and headed for the sideboard. I poured myself a glass, my hands trembling so badly that I almost said to hell with it and chugged straight from the bottle.

Um, yeah. That's really going to happen.

I touched the crystal to my lips. Blood slid down my throat and sent a rush of ahhhh through me. My hunger eased and relief swept from my head to my toes. I wasn't really attracted to Remy. I was just hungry.

"I thought you wanted me to talk to Jack," Nina said when she sought me out after fifteen minutes with Remy.

I sipped my third glass. "Change of plans. You're doing just great." I held up my glass in salute to Remy, who stood across the room. "Just get back over there and keep him from coming over here."

"What about your brother?"

I eyed Mandy and Jack, who sat side by side while my mother glared at them from across an antique cherry coffee table. "I think it's time my mother heard the truth."

Sixteen
❤ ❤ ❤

"He really has some sort of bad infection?" My mother asked a few minutes after I hauled her into a corner and started to confess.

"The worst." I nodded. "Extremely red and very itchy and totally nasty." Was I the adverb queen or what? I made a face. "Total yuck."

"Lilliana," my mother nailed me with a stare, "that is the most absurd thing I have ever heard."

You and me both. I shrugged. "I didn't believe it myself, but Jack showed me."

The disbelief morphed to concern. "Really?"

"I saw it with my own two eyes." I made a face. "And I smelled it, too." I stuck out my tongue. "All I can say is, I know what I'm getting Jack for his next birthday. A great, big Ralph Lauren gift set."

"An *infection*?"

"With a capital I."

"But he's immune to any and all germs."

"Any and all *known* germs. This is something else. Something brand-new and ultimately powerful." I lowered my voice to emphasize dire importance. "A strain of bacteria that specifically targets vampires."

My mother gasped and I tried to look appropriately horrified.

"Once they annihilate all vamps, they'll go after weres and Others and, ultimately, humans."

"So this bacteria targets the most powerful first?"

I nodded. "And the best dressed."

My mother looked as if her brain were spinning ninety to nothing before she finally shook her head. "I just cannot believe it."

"Believe it." Please, please, *please* believe it.

"I can't imagine anything *that* powerful," my mother persisted. "Vampires are so superior."

"*And* highly sensitive. Which means that when a vamp is infected, the symptoms are magnified. Whereas the average human can just slather on some cream and get off with a little scratching and maybe a few weird stares from the people on the subway, a vampire has to undergo intravenous drug treatment and risk being shunned by all of the born vamp nation." I knew I was laying it on a little thick, but we're talking *my* mother. When it came to sniffing out a lie, the woman was Columbo, Sam Spade, and the entire *CSI: Miami* team all rolled into one.

"This is terrible."

"That's why Jack needs Mandy." I kept slathering it on. "She's a doctor."

"She's a forensic pathologist."

"Yeah, well, she's had a recent run-in with corpses who've kicked the bucket because of this nasty stuff. She's become an expert."

"Is that right?"

"She's done a ton of research and she's even responsible for developing the antibiotic."

"What would a forensic pathologist know about drug development?"

I eyed my mother. "Are you forgetting that her great-aunt something-or-other was burned at the stake for mixing up potions?"

"So she *is* working a spell on him. I knew it. I told your father that she was cooking up something, but he just refused to listen."

"She's contributing to science, Mom, not boiling horny toads and sprigs of witch hazel. This isn't witchcraft. I'm just saying that she *is* a descendant, which makes her better at this sort of thing than your average run-of-the-mill forensic pathologist." Hey, it sounded good. "Anyhow, she's perfected the injection on humans, but Jack is her first vampire."

My mom watched as Jack bent down to retrieve a napkin that Mandy had dropped—no, really. *My* brother.

"Poor Jack," my mother crooned. "No wonder he isn't acting like himself."

"So you see," I went on, "Jack needs Mandy. She

has to watch him closely, extremely closely, for all changes in his condition until he fully recovers."

"But he will, right? Make a full recovery?"

"Of course. But not before the wedding," I blurted. "Or the honeymoon. Also, with the antibiotic so new to his system—he just now started the treatments—he really shouldn't be getting overly excited or upset."

"Maybe we should forget the matchmaking prospects for now."

"My thoughts exactly."

"Which means you'll be giving me my money back, of course."

"Absolutely." I nodded. "Minus one-third, that is." Hey, I *had* shown up with Nina.

"Oh, well." My mother, like the proper born vampire she was, shrugged off her worry. "I'll just have to resign myself to the situation, I suppose."

Yes!

She looked hesitant for all of five seconds before her expression seemed to relax. "My, but Remy's looking very handsome tonight." She shifted her full attention to—uh, oh—me. "And virile, don't you think?"

And just like that, I was back to being the center of my mother's attention.

I fought down a wave of panic and did the only thing I could do in such a situation. I nodded and mumbled "Um, yeah." Then I traded the O positive for a shot of tequila and I started to drink.

Heavily.

* * *

"I think I'm turning into an alcoholic," I told Evie on Monday evening when I walked into the office early. My head pounded and I felt even worse than I had the day after the bridal fitting.

Of course, some of my bad mood could be attributed to the fact that Mandy had left a message telling me to meet her at Wedding Wonderland in less than two hours for another try-on session. That, and my lack of sleep. It had been forty-eight hours since I'd heard from Ty. My feet had healed, but the images still lingered, making me nervous and anxious and totally uncomfortable despite the fact that I was wearing my favorite pair of Circle of Seven jeans and the cutest Rock & Republic corset top.

I'd rehashed the scene, searching for more clues, but other than the mustard and diesel smell, I'd come up with a big fat *nada*. Ash was still running prints and I was still sleeping with Killer.

"Are we talking voluntary drinking?" she asked me, handing me two new client files. "Or drinking to escape neurotic relatives? Because I've been there and done that, and it doesn't count when your sanity's at stake."

"It was definitely an escape mechanism." I perched on the corner of her desk, flipped through the files—a pharmacist named Tania and a kindergarten teacher named Beckie—and gave her the low-down on Sunday evening (minus the hunting and blood drinking, of course). "But I also did Jell-O shots at Wedding Wonderland," I added once I'd finished, "and my mother wasn't even in the same state."

"How many Jell-O shots?"

"I lost count."

"How many shots at your folks' place?"

"Two. Three if you count the one that I threw at Nina when she brought Remy over to talk to me."

"Two shots hardly makes you an alcoholic. As for Wedding Wonderland . . . Come on, I'd drink, too, in that situation." She shivered. "We're talking off-the-rack dresses."

She had a point. "So no Betty Ford?"

Evie shook her head and handed me today's mail. "You'll have to find someplace else to hide out from your mother." Her eyes lit with excitement. "Someplace like, say, a cruise ship."

"Excuse me?"

She held up a message slip and waved it in the air. "You made the final cut," she blurted. "You're dinner cruising on the Hudson tomorrow night." When I didn't seem anymore clued in, she squealed, "You're going on a group date with Mr. Weather!"

After calming an overly excited Evie (can you say too much caffeine?) and promising to bring back an autograph from Mr. Whoever—I walked into my office, pulled out John Schumacker's card, and punched in his number.

"Schumacker, here. What can I do for you?"

"Tell me you got cut."

"I'm dusting off the old life jacket right now."

My ego deflated—the only thing I'd had going for me since I'd rolled out of bed and stepped in Killer's latest surprise. "Are you sleeping with someone at the television station or what?"

"Don't I wish," he told me. "You?"

I thought of Ty. "Don't *I* wish." I stiffened against a wave of crappiness and tried to look on the bright side. Another date, another chance to mix and mingle and promote my business. That, and I could give John a nice little shove toward his own happily-ever-after with Rosie.

I'd called and fished for information at his insurance agency and discovered that her last name was Wheaton. She was single, had never been married, and had no kids. She liked sports, in particular basketball and baseball. She could bowl a perfect strike and she made a mean gelatin salad for the company picnic. She'd also been named insurance adjuster of the year three times running and—and this was huge—she liked John. I'd talked to three people—all males subject to my vampy wiles—and they'd confirmed that she'd mentioned him around the office.

I perked up. "What about your case?" I asked him. "Did she make it?"

"You bet your ass she did." I could practically hear him rubbing his hands together. "She's about to slip up. I can just feel it."

"Sounds like this is really turning out to be your stepping-stone up the insurance fraud adjuster's ladder." Talk about a mouthful. "Why don't you go out and celebrate?"

"No time. I need to check my camera and my video cam. And one of my boobs is leaking. I'm going to swing by La Perla and pick up a new one."

"Just a quickie celebration. Maybe you and Rosie and a couple of beers?"

"Nah. I'll wait until I actually crack the case open. Then I'll do it up right."

"A steak dinner and candlelight?"

"A keg and a disc jockey. I'm going to have a party. You're invited."

"Great." Not.

I said goodbye to John and turned my attention to my computer. I spent the next half hour searching my ever-growing database for a few possibilities for my newest clients—both of which were courtesy of *Manhattan's Most Wanted*—and dodging phone calls.

First call? My mother, who wanted to know if I'd heard of Dr. Pierre Mancuso, a born vampire and leader in viral research.

Second? Nina One, who wanted her jacket back.

Third? My mother, who wanted to remind me about the dinner party and inform me that she'd also invited Remy.

Fourth? My mother, who wanted to remind me about the dinner party *again*, and inform me that she'd also invited Remy's mother.

Because, of course, one born vampire mother obsessed with grandchildren wasn't enough. We needed two.

The Fifth call? A frantic Mandy.

" . . . forgot all about Claude. He's the groomsman

from Paris," came her frantic voice. "He e-mailed Jack his tuxedo measurements last night and I was supposed to bring them with me today to give to Shirley because she has to order them right away or we run the risk of not getting the exact ones we want, but I'm already here and I forgot and Jack isn't picking up the phone and I really, *really* need you to stop by our place on the way over here and pick up—"

"Consider it done," I said, snatching up the phone.

"Oh, good. You're there. I was going to try your cell next, but I was hoping you would be at the office instead, but just in case—"

"Mandy," I cut in, closing out my computer file.

"What?"

"Breathe." I clicked on shutdown and listened as she inhaled and exhaled. "Good girl," I crooned. "I'll stop by your place." I closed the files and grabbed my purse. "Just relax. Everything is going to be okay."

"Says you. Shirley managed to get her hands on an additional three dozen dresses."

"Oh, goody." Oh, shit.

Seventeen
♥ ♥ ♥

"Ooooooooooooo . . ."

My brother's voice carried from inside the apartment.

"Ahhhhhhhhhhh . . ."

"Uhhhhhhhhhhh . . ."

Someone was either getting laid, or watching a *Sesame Street* episode on vowels.

A loud moan punctuated the thought. Definitely number one. I should probably come back later.

The thing was, I knew Mandy was at Wedding Wonderland. Which meant Jack was inside with someone else. Which meant . . .

I stiffened and banged on the door. Wood grumbled and groaned beneath the force of my fist (I *am* Super Vamp). A few grunts and I knocked again. Harder. My knuckles made indentations in the wood. I drew back and was about to rip the thing off its hinges when I heard Jack's voice.

"It's open. Eeeeeeeeeee . . ."

Oh. Well. Okay.

The knob turned and I walked into the large apartment. Much larger, in fact, than my own, but Jack made at least ten times my salary at Moe's, not to mention he still drew a nice allowance from my folks for helping with the family biz.

I headed down the small foyer and stalled in the doorway that led to the living room. Shock beat at my temples as my gaze fixed on the two people in the center of the room.

He couldn't be . . . No way was he actually . . . *No!*

Jack was sprawled on a portable massage table, a sheet draped over the lower half of his body. He lay facedown, his back gleaming with massage oil. Hans, my mother's personal masseur, leaned over him, his massive hands kneading and working while Jack ooohed and ahhhed.

My gaze narrowed. "Just what the hell is going on here?"

Jack's head bobbed up from the table. "I'm getting a deep tissue."

"I can see that." Jealousy reared its ugly head and I stared pointedly at Hans. "What is *he* doing here?"

"Mom sent him over. She called this afternoon and said I've been working too hard." Hans rolled and pushed and Jack's head wobbled. "That I should take the night off and she would have Dad cover for me at Moe's. She sent Hans over to help me relax."

Okay, here's the scoop. I covet Hans. He has the biggest, most fabulous hands *ever*. But like her favorite Dior blouse, my mother never lends him out. I've begged. I've pleaded. I've even considered subbing at Moe's.

No Hans with the hands.

"How come you get to borrow him?" came my sullen question. Just as the words were out, the answer struck. Terrible infection. Poor Jack.

"Beats me, but she said I should keep him for as long as I want." Strong, massive fingers grabbed a shoulder blade and pressed. Jack's mouth dropped open and drool pooled in the corner. "What . . . are . . . you . . . doing . . . here?" he finally asked, each word accompanied by a loll of his head.

My own muscles screamed, *"Me, too!"* and I fought down the urge to shove my brother off and hop up on the table myself. "Mandy forgot the measurements for Claude's tux. She tried to call, but she said your cell is off. So is the answering machine."

"This is a Do Not Disturb moment." He motioned to the mahogany desk set up on the opposite side of the room. "The measurements are in the middle drawer." His head dropped and he started to moan.

I knew the feeling. I'd had one massage via Hans when my mom had been away at a Huntress convention in Spain. The airlines had been limiting baggage, and so she'd been forced to leave him at home. I'd begged for two days before the Swedish hunk had finally agreed.

Okay, so I'd cried and he'd been so freaked out that he'd begged me to stop. (He *so* didn't want to risk my mother's wrath.) One thing had led to another and, well, tada! Those meat hooks had been all over me.

I shivered at the memory. We're talking pure ecstasy. There's no other way to describe it. The oil seeping into my skin. The rough fingers pushing this way and pulling that and—whew, is it hot in here, or is it just me?

I picked up my steps and snatched open the drawer. If past experience served me, I had about three minutes to get the hell out of there before Jack—

"Ohhhhhhhh . . ."

Uh-oh. Too late.

My preternatural instincts kicked in and I moved so fast I made myself dizzy. The door slammed shut behind me and, hurray, I was safe!

Sort of. I could still hear him.

I'd love to say it was the vampy thing and I'm just special, but he was now screaming. The entire building was privy to his "Yesssssssssssssssssssssss!"

The old woman down the hall stuck her head out, saw me, and gave me a disapproving frown.

"Oh, no, it's not what you think—" I started.

Slam!

Down on the first floor, a college-aged girl peered

out and grimaced. A fiftysomething woman with a cheating husband gave me the evil eye.

"It's not—" *Slam! Slam!*

I'd just reached the door to the building when I heard the creak of hinges behind me. I whirled. "I didn't do anything, all right!"

"Lil? It is you! I thought I heard your voice out here."

I drank in the woman smiling at me and my own expression eased into a grin. Rachel Sanchez was twenty-four with long brown hair and an olive complexion. She was short and petite, with big, bright brown eyes and a cute nose. Once upon a time, she'd been hooked on Jack (who hadn't?). She was now a Dead End Dating client. One of my most difficult, as a matter of fact.

You try matching up a *were*-Chihuahua.

Luckily, in addition to being a *were*, she was also patient. She beamed. "Thanks so much for the dog biscuits."

"Thank you for going out with the sanitation worker. I know he wasn't really your type."

She shrugged. "Nothing ventured, nothing gained."

Atta girl.

"So you wanna come in and have a drink?"

"I'm on my way to an appointment," I started and her face fell, "but I suppose one quick drink wouldn't hurt."

"You're just in time," she told me. "It's apple night."

"Apple what?"

"See, me and the girls from work get together every Monday. Sort of like a celebration that we all made it through the first day of a new week. We used to do nachos and chocolate cake, but then Denise, one of the girls, gained twenty pounds. So now we try to make something that's healthy. Tonight it's appletinis and apple pie."

"How is that healthy?"

"Appletinis are liquid, so they don't count, and the apple pie is made with a low-fat crust and artificial sweetener."

Hey, it made sense.

I followed her into an apartment with the same layout as my brother's, through the living room, and into a small kitchen.

"The other girls aren't here yet. Just Susie. Suze," she motioned to a twentyish girl with short brown hair, a pug nose, and brown eyes, "This is Lil. Lil, Suze."

My gaze met with the girl's and . . . Nothing. I couldn't read a thing, which meant she wasn't human. I did, however, have the sudden urge to scoop her up and cuddle, which told me she was definitely a *were*.

A Chihuahua like Rachel?

Maybe. Maybe not.

She wore a yellow T-shirt and white Capri pants. Her nails were painted a bright peach. I watched as she slid on pink mitts and retrieved a freshly baked apple pie from the oven.

She set the hot dessert on a trivet, pulled off the mitts, and walked over to where she'd cored the apples. She sniffed a Granny Smith before slicing it into quarters and lifting one to her mouth. She started nibbling, her two front teeth chomping away at the fruit.

I can't explain, but just like that an image of Word popped into my head. Crazy, right? What could they possibly have in common?

"You like to bake?"

She beamed. "I love it." She nibbled some more.

"What about pizza?"

"I'm afraid I've never actually made one."

"I meant do you like to eat pizza?"

She grimaced. "Too greasy. Since Rach and I have been doing the healthy-eating thing, I've given up all junk food."

Which eliminated every single favorite listed on Word's profile.

"What about beer?"

"Too many calories."

"Music?"

Her eyes lit. "I absolutely love boy bands. Backstreet Boys. *NSYNC. Even the old ones like Bell, Biv, DeVoe and Marky Mark and the Funky Bunch."

It would never work.

Even so, there was just something about her that drove me and kept the questions pouring out of my mouth.

"Favorite color?"

"It's a toss-up between yellow and mango orange."

"What are your thoughts on piercings?"

"Barbaric."

"Men wearing eyeliner?"

"Gay."

"Men wearing glasses?"

"Geek."

She nibbled some more and I should have taken the cue to stop, forget this girl, and drink my appletini.

I eyed Suze, my mind racing. "You're a *were*, right?"

She looked nervous for a split second, her gaze zigzagging to Rachel, who held a martini shaker in one hand and a glass in the other. "It's okay. She's not a real vampire."

A rush of happy went through me.

Because I was onto something, I reminded myself. *This* close to matching up a difficult client, which never failed to fill me with euphoria, and the giddy notion that true love was out there, waiting for any and everyone brave enough to reach out (awww).

No way was my heart suddenly pumping so fast because I actually *liked* Rachel's statement. I was a vicious, bloodthirsty vampire and I would show them—just as soon as I satisfied the niggling in my gut.

"You *are* a *were*." It was more statement than question, but Suze nodded anyway.

"Chihuahua?"

She smiled. "Right size. Wrong species."

"Cat?"

"Hardly."

"Possum?"

"Nah."

"Skunk?"

"No, but I have been called a skank before."

Haven't we all? My curiosity kicked into overdrive. Okay, this was it. I was going for broke. "Rabbit?"

She shook her head. "Squirrel."

"Close enough."

Eighteen

❤ ❤ ❤

"They're all so beautiful," Mandy declared after trying on thirty-two more dresses for the second time in three hours. "I just can't decide."

I stood near the edge of the velvet sofa, downed my third Jell-O shot, and croaked, "More."

Shirley retrieved the now-empty tray (Mandy had done four and her mother a whopping five) and smiled. "I'll be right back."

I was just about to settle back and return calls on my cell while Mandy wiggled into the next dress when she grabbed my arm and hauled me off the couch. Her eyes were lit with desperation. "You have to help me decide." She shook her head and eyed the rack full of white fluff. "There are just so many. And they're all so . . ."

Busy? Outdated? Ugly?

" . . . so *white*," she finally finished. "I'm getting a headache."

"It's the tequila. No more shots for you." I pried her fingers loose from my arm and stepped back, wobbling a bit in my Charles David lace-up sandals. Not that I was snockered. Not yet. I blinked until the blurriness faded and eyed the dresses. "Okay," I said. "*Okay.*"

"Okay what?"

"Okay, I'm going to do this. Fix this. Make it all better." I blinked again and stood up straight and my mind cleared enough for me to think. "Have you ever had a wedding fantasy?" I turned to Mandy. "You know. Dreamt of the Big Day? With all the trimmings?"

"Well, yes."

"Did you picture a certain dress?"

"Several of them."

It figured. "Did they all look just alike, or were they similar in cut and style?"

She seemed to think. "They were kind of similar." An idea seemed to strike and I knew she was following me. "Not exactly, but they had lots of things in common."

"Good." I motioned toward the sofa. "Sit." When she plopped down and wiggled for comfort, I added, "Now I want you to close your eyes and picture the different dresses. I'll ask you questions and we'll toss out everything that doesn't fit with the mental. That might not get us all the way down to one, but it should narrow things a bit."

She nodded. "Okay." She closed her eyes and I gave her a few seconds to get her juices flowing.

Okay, so I gave myself a few seconds to get a grip. Either way, we're talking win-win.

"Straight or full?" I finally asked.

"Mostly straight. But not too straight. I need to be able to keep up with Jack when we walk down the aisle." She cracked an eye open. "Vampires walk down the aisle, don't they?"

Never. "Of course."

She smiled and closed the eye. "Is it working?"

"We're definitely making progress." I retrieved eight of the thirty-two dresses, set the rejects off to the side, and kept the possibilities hanging in front of us. "What about material? Satin or silk?"

"Yes. I mean, I'm open to either. Or both."

"That rules out the taffeta." I rifled through the stack and pulled out seven dresses to add to the Not in this Galaxy rack.

"What about lace?"

"Yes, but not too much."

That cut five more from the Back to the 1980s collection.

"Poofy bows?"

"I'm not really big on bows. Or beads. I don't like a lot of clutter."

That eliminated nine more. I eyed the remaining trio. "Sleeves or strapless?"

"I definitely want strapless."

Adios three amigos.

Relief swept through me and I smiled. "All done."

"Really? Which one did I—" Her eyes opened and she stared at the empty rack. "But there's nothing there."

"I say we consider it a sign from God." Whoops, did I say that? My bad. "I'll make an appointment at Vera Wang. I'm sure they'll have something wonderful."

"But I can't go there."

"Of course you can. I have connections. I can get us an after-hours appointment. We'll sip champagne, eyeball dresses, and have a fab time."

She shook her head. "Let's do it again."

"You're kidding, right?"

"I have to pick something *here*." Her desperate gaze struck mine. "Shirley's family. She went to a lot of trouble to get as many dresses as possible so that I would have plenty to choose from. And she's been staying open late. And she's making all these Jell-O shots and she's even throwing in the unity candle for free. I can't just walk out and hurt her feelings."

"I can."

"Really?"

"Uh, yeah. I'll tell her."

Mandy's eyes lit with hope. "You can do that?"

"I'm a badass vampire. We rape and pillage the way some people jog and play tennis. Crushing someone's hopes and dreams? Snuffing out their livelihood?" I smiled. "I am so there."

That's what I said, but somewhere between the raping and snuffing, I sort of lost my enthusiasm.

When Shirley returned with another round of

shots and a hopeful expression on her face, I lost my
nerve, as well.

"Have you made a decision?"

Mandy and her mother stared at me. I cleared my
throat. *You can do this. Release your inner vampness. Just open your mouth, maybe even flash a little
fang, and let it rip.* "She wants to try everything on
at least one more time," I heard myself say. "Then
she'll sleep on it and pick her favorite first thing tomorrow."

"I will?"

"She will?"

Mandy and Mrs. Dupree spoke in unison. Meanwhile I flashed them a look that said *Hello? Lying,
here. Follow me.*

"I will," Mandy blurted.

"Most definitely," Mrs. Dupree agreed.

Ah, the look. Works every time.

"Excellent," Shirley replied. "Then we can move
on to the veil and shoes and accessories."

"Lucky us."

"Actually, you really are. I have a bunch of new
vendors who are sending me stuff left and right. I just
got in this conch shell necklace that looks as pretty as
a picture with the dress that has the little navy sailor
bows."

I smiled. "Fab."

Shirley beamed and held up the tray. "Shot?"

"Please." Mandy grabbed eagerly for the lime. I
took a green apple and Mrs. Dupree settled back
with a watermelon and a raspberry.

The next few hours passed in a blur of dresses and tequila and self-pity (my own). The more I stared at all the lace and pearls and swaths of fabric, the more I kept picturing myself instead of Mandy. And the more I missed Ty.

Made vamp. Born vamp. So *not* happening.

I knew a future with Ty wasn't in my realm of possibility (or my mother's), but I couldn't kill the images no matter how much I tried. Nor could I squash the worry that niggled away at me and made me all the more anxious to call Ash. Again.

"I know what you're thinking," Mandy declared as she tried on one Southern belle monstrosity in particular. Shirley had gone to retrieve the matching straw hat (yep, ya heard me, *straw*) and veil, and we were alone for the first time since I'd wimped out.

"You do?"

She nodded. "You don't have to say a word. The look on your face says it all."

My look says I'm pining away for a made vampire?

"I can see it in your eyes."

Oh, no.

"You think I look awful." She faced the mirror and threw up her hands in disgust. "Maybe we should just forget the whole thing. I'll never find a decent dress. The hotel booted us out and all the other decent hotels are booked. The only place that's free on our date is my Uncle Nino's hamburger joint. He wants to serve chili-cheese fries." She sniffled. "And I'm beginning to think that your mother hates me."

"What makes you say that?" Other than cracker-jack intellect, of course.

She shrugged and the floppy sleeves of the white dress sagged on her shoulders. "She never talks to me. At first, I thought it was because she didn't really know me. But I've been to oodles of hunts and I've tried talking to her, and she just doesn't bite."

"That's actually a good thing."

"Maybe." She shrugged. "But she also glares at me a lot, as if she can't stand me. What do you think?"

This was it. My chance to come clean and stop carrying the burden of my mother all by my lonesome. I would simply tell Mandy how much my mother detested her and go from there. The girl had a right to know. I mean, really. I would want to know if the love of my life's mother *hated* my guts.

I think.

"She doesn't hate you," I told her.

"What makes you say that?"

Yeah, what? "She just doesn't warm up to people very quickly." Okay, so technically she was a luke-warm vampire who would never warm up, but that was beside the point. "Just give her a little time."

"She doesn't think I'm good enough for him."

"No, actually, she doesn't."

Her gaze collided with mine. "I knew it!"

"She thinks you're too good. Don't take this the wrong way, Mandy, but Jack's a real shit. Believe me, I've seen it. We've all seen it. She just doesn't want you to wake up one day and realize you made a mistake." Okay, so this was my fear for Mandy, not my mother's, but who was I to argue details? "She just wants you to be sure."

"I know how Jack used to be. I mean, I've never seen it, but I've heard. A player. Sleeping with different women every weekend."

I nodded. "And during the week."

"But he's changed. He's a wonderful man. Committed. Loving. And everyone deserves a second chance, don't you think?" Without waiting for my reply, she added, "Even a player like Jack."

"You're sure?"

She seemed to think. "You know what? I am." Her shoulders stiffened. "I've actually never been more sure of anything, or anyone, in my entire life." She leveled a stare at me. "I know I'm doing the right thing by marrying him. Deep in my heart, I *know*."

I smiled. "Then that's all that matters."

She seemed suddenly aware of the tears streaming down her face. She sniffled and wiped at her cheeks. "You know, you're right. Who cares if I'm wearing a hideous dress and eating chili on THE most important day of my life? I'm marrying the vampire I love. The vampire who loves me. We don't need a fancy location or an elaborate ceremony. We don't even need favors for the guests. The almonds tied in those cute little satin baggies. We just need each other."

Yeah, right.

I wiped at a traitorous tear that slid down my own cheek. "You're not going to wear a hideous dress or tie the knot in a greasy diner." I sniffled. "And no

way are you wearing white and going within twenty
feet of a platter of chili-cheese fries." I stiffened.
"Not if I can help it. You're going to have the wedding of your dreams."

"Really?" Her eyes glimmered with newfound
hope and I nodded.

What can I say? I'm a sucker (no pun intended) for
the big H.

"You're so wonderful, Lil. I'm so glad we're going
to be sisters." She seemed to gather her determination as she slapped more tears from her face. "So
what are we going to do?"

I forced aside my own crazy notions of love and
marriage and Ty, and pasted on my most convincing
smile. "Don't worry about a thing. Just finish trying
on the rest of these and leave the details to me."

Nineteen

♥ ♥ ♥

After we finished up at Wedding Wonderland, I took a cab straight home. I drank a glass of freshly nuked blood, fed Killer a can of cat food, and then spent the next few hours on the computer researching alternatives to the wedding dress situation. When I felt certain I had a workable plan, I tackled the ceremony location.

"I need a favor," I told Nina One when she answered her cellphone.

"I need my jacket. And my sunglasses."

"You can have them both if you do me this one itty-bitty favor."

"I'm not seducing Remy. He's nice and all, but I'm not ready to squeeze out a couple of born vamps right now and his mother is worse than yours."

No, really? "This isn't about Remy. I need a ballroom." I explained the Mandy situation and ended with a dramatic, "If you do this for me, I'll do *anything*."

"Bajra cashmere scarf?"

"I was thinking more along the lines of my first-born. My second, too, if you validate parking."

"Sorry, but I prefer more immediate gratification. Like, say, sometime in this century."

"Thanks a lot." I closed my eyes and pictured my all-time favorite accessory *ever*. At least until Hermés came out with their fall collection in three months, two days, and sixteen hours. "Okay," I blurted before I could change my mind. "It's yours."

"Really?"

"I said so, didn't I?"

"I'll check our schedule and see who I can bump." She paused and I could hear her fingers flying over the keyboard. "It'll be tricky. We already have a banquet for the bar association scheduled for that evening." More typing and my anxiety level kicked up a notch.

"Maybe I'll call Lola and see if she can work something at the Plaza," I said. The minute the words were out, the fingertips tapping the keyboard on the other end of the line stopped cold and the earth stalled on its axis.

Lola Bettancourt Camden was the daughter of real estate tycoon and born vamp extraordinaire Hamilton Camden. Her father and Nina's frequently competed for the same high-end properties. The running score as of yesterday's buyout of the Chase bank building put Hamilton in the lead while Victor Lancaster ran a close second.

Following in their fathers' Gucci footsteps, Nina and Lola frequently went head-to-head for rare and extremely hard to come by designer couture. My Bajra was a one-of-a-kind. A gift from my mother, along with my own closetful of lime-green Polos and beige Dockers, when she and Dad had handed over the NYU locations of Midnight Moe's to yours truly for my last birthday present.

I'd given back the copy centers (the uniforms had my name embroidered on them, which meant they were mine until they started to decay or I had a run-in with a sharp object), but I'd snapped up the scarf faster than Killer went through a dish of Tantalizing Tuna.

"You wouldn't call Lola," she finally said, her voice accusing. "You hate Lola."

"She's a bitch, but that doesn't mean I wouldn't strike a little deal with her in the name of family."

"Let's see . . ." The fingers started moving again, faster this time, and I smiled. "I *could* tell the bar president that we've had a recent lawsuit filed against us by a disgruntled guest and that one of their members is handling the case, which would make a dinner at our establishment a direct conflict of interest."

"Brilliant."

"I'll move the bar dinner to the Omni," another one of daddy Lancaster hotels, "and put the Marchette-Dupree wedding in its place right here." I heard more typing followed by a "There. All done."

"You're the best."

"You WILL follow through this time, right? Because it's been a full twenty-four hours and I still haven't seen my jacket or the shades."

"I'll drop them by tomorrow."

"Cross your heart and hope to pierce a virgin in the eye?"

Ugh. Had we been that bloodthirsty as kids?

Goober alert! Fangs. Coffins. Night skulking.

Okay, so we had been that bloodthirsty as kids.

"I do," I grumbled.

"Say it."

I rolled my eyes. "Cross my heart and hope to pierce a virgin in the eye."

"And say, 'Thank you, Nina.' "

"Thank you, Nina."

"For tonight and for last night."

"For tonight and for last night."

"Don't mention it. I move things all the time. Reservations *hates* me. Except for George and Chuck. They think I'm the shit. But Anna and Megan? Haters, the both of them." Her voice took on an edge of excitement. "I don't usually like to stop by at your folks' place because they're so . . . Well, you know how they are."

Unfortunately, I did.

"But last night was kind of fun. I haven't seen your brother in ages. I remembered him as this stuck-up, full-of-himself gigolo, but he's really changed. He's actually kind of nice."

Max? Rob? Or Jack? All three fit the initial description. Jack, however, was the only one who hit pay dirt on the change part. And the nice. Or at least seminice since Mandy.

"I'm afraid he's already taken."

"Oh, no. By who?"

"Hello? That was the entire point of me dragging you all the way across state lines. Jack's getting married to Dr. Mandy. My mom is freaked. Remember?"

"Not Jack, silly. I'm talking about Rob."

"*Rob* has changed?"

"It's so obvious. He's older and, well, more mature."

"Were we at the same party? The one where Rob arm wrestled Max for dibs on the comfortable recliner?"

"He won," she declared. "I was so impressed."

I was *so* not hearing this. "Let me get this straight. You're interested in Rob?"

"I think there's a little something there. A connection. Do you think he's attracted to me?"

Let me think about this. Nina walks upright. Drinks blood. Has a vagina. "He adores you."

"Really? Did he say that?"

"Not in so many words, but I know my brother. Trust me, he would *do* you in a heartbeat."

"Excellent. Maybe I'll tag along for the next hunt."

"We're not hunting this Sunday. I mean, we probably will (on account of we haven't NOT hunted in over three hundred years and my dad was big on maintaining tradition), but not until after my mom's dinner party."

"I accept."

"You're not invited. Unless," I added, my mind racing, "I get to keep the sunglasses."

"But I earned those," she whined.

"True, but I'm going to earn them back by giving up my seat at the dinner table so that you can sit next to Rob."

"All right."

"You're kidding, right?"

"No. Keep them. Listen, I have to hang up. There's a long line at check-in. We have a convention in town—romance writers, or something like that. I'll see you tomorrow for my jacket." *Click*.

I hung up and stared at the phone in disbelief.

No way, no *way* did she just give up a pair of Badgley Mischka's for a piddly orgasm, or even ten of them. Like me and a few other megalicious female vamps, Nina had an impressive two-digit Orgasm Quotient. Designer couture came first while doing the humpty-hump ran a close second. Never were they reversed.

Unless . . .

A smile crept across my face.

"Nina *likes* Rob," I told Killer, who sat on my lap, his head resting on one knee. "Isn't that great? Maybe they'll hook up and I'll be an aunt."

I pictured myself herding a few dozen little Robs and Ninas through the department store, Barney's (wearing my favorite Rebecca Taylor chiffon dress), and the smiled faded. We're talking chiffon. As in susceptible to fingerprints and frantic little hands tugging and pulling and *rrrrip*!

Oh, no they didn't!

They didn't. I drew in a deep breath to calm my pounding heart. I was getting way ahead of myself. I tuned out the image and shifted to one where Nina and Rob stared adoringly into each other's eyes (after writing me a big fat check for services rendered) and said I do. *Much* better.

I sighed and Killer meowed.

I rode the wave of contentment for several more seconds before I upended back into a sea of crappiness.

It was the middle of the night, I was a hot, happening *vampere,* and I was desperately alone (except for Killer, but I didn't count him because then I would have felt that much worse because I now had a big pile of kitty litter sitting in my bathroom just waiting for me to take the plunge). My two best friends had found someone (Nina One had Rob (sort of) and Nina Two had her commitment mate, Wilson). Jack had Mandy. Max had half the socialites in Manhattan, including one of the Hiltons (but you didn't hear that from me). Come Friday night, Word would have Suze. My mother had my father. And I had fantabulous hair.

Yep, my afterlife sucked, all right.

Meow.

Killer's soft call pushed into my thoughts and I glanced down to see him staring up at me with un-blinking green eyes.

Enough with the pity party, already. You don't know real despair until you're half-starved and stuck in an alley playing bitch to a pit bull named Big Boy.

True enough.

I pushed away the doom and gloom and tried to concentrate on scoping out an appropriate restaurant for Word to take Suze. I Googled and scrolled through the list of possibilities. Should they go upscale or low-key?

The question echoed in my head and reminded me of my own personal dilemma. Chief of police or renegade bounty hunter?

I thought about Remy and how perfect he was—refined, with a hefty fertility rating, which made me think about Ty and how imperfect he was, rugged with no fertility rating at all, and how it didn't really matter.

I liked them both.

Actually, I liked Ty more.

I scribbled down the names of two different bar and grills and powered off the computer. I found Ash's phone number and punched it into my cell. He answered on the fourth ring.

"Do you have any leads?"

"Not since you called me about six hours ago."

"Is that all it's been?"

"Yep."

"Are you sure? Because it seems like a lot longer."

"I'm timing you."

"Oh." I set Killer on the floor and pushed to my

feet. "I don't do waiting very well." I paced the floor. "I just really need to know that he's okay."

"The only thing I can tell you is that we did pull a second set of prints from his doorknob. I matched them up to a felon from Brooklyn. He just got out of prison after doing eight years for armed robbery."

What? "They only give eight years for armed robbery?"

"Give or take time off for good behavior. He walked about three weeks ago and word on the street has it that he was gunning for Ty. Ran his mouth all over town about how he was going to gut Ty and eat his tongue."

"Ewww."

"And then he just disappeared."

"With Ty and his tongue?"

"Professional opinion?"

"Yes."

"I doubt it. Whoever—*whatever*—took Ty was a lot more of a badass than your average human thief. Even so, his prints shouldn't have been there, so we're following up."

It wasn't what I wanted to hear and so I reversed back to the inefficiency of our justice system. "Eight years? For an armed burglar/tongue eater? That's *it*?"

"That's the justice system."

"But he should still be locked up, confined to criminal tongues instead of those belonging to kind, decent, law-abiding citizens."

"Sure, he should. And so should half the criminals

in New York, but the system is overcrowded. There's just not enough room."

"Which is just cause to turn violent, twisted offenders out into the street?" My fingers tightened on the cell phone and my vision was a glazed vivid crimson. "What the hell are we paying taxes for? So guys like that can walk up and down Fifth Avenue and pull a Hannibal Lecter? So they can kidnap and torture and—"

"Easy, there, Norma Rae," he cut in. "I'm on your side. I'm just giving you an update."

I reined in my temper and drew a deep breath to calm my pounding heart. "Fine. I'm sorry. But I'm writing my congressman."

"Have at it. In the meantime, I'll see what I can do about locating the felon. I'll let you know if I turn up anything."

It wasn't the answer I'd wanted, but it was better than nothing.

A tiny lead.

A thread of hope.

I latched onto it and held it close as I crawled into bed next to Killer and closed my eyes. Ash would find the felon who would lead him to Ty before he had his tongue eaten, or worse.

At least that's what I told myself.

But the more I tried to reach Ty, the more the silence continued, and the more I started to think that maybe, just maybe, it was already too late.

Twenty

I spent the entire day tossing and turning and feeling like the only Diet Coke in a fridge full of O positive and AB negative.

Translation: useless.

Which explained why I, the Countess Lilliana Arrabella Guinevere du Marchette, forfeited her twelve hundred-thread-count sheets for a vacuum cleaner.

No, really.

I was that desperate to *do* something, sleep eluded me, and so it seemed like a good idea. Much better than lying in bed and staring at the ceiling.

Waiting.

Worrying.

I did the rugs and dusted. I even swept the bathroom. When I finished, I paused near the sink and eyed the toilet brush.

Okay, so I wasn't *that* worried.

Besides, I'd killed what was left of the daylight. The sun was just about to set and I had a busy evening ahead.

I hopped in the shower and then went through my nightly ritual of hair and makeup and more hair. I pulled on a cream-colored, ultrashort, Foley embroidered silk dress and flat gold sandals, and then topped off *The Stepford Wives* meet Twiggy look with a leather Coach clutch, crystal earrings, and my sunglasses. I grabbed Nina's Donna Karan jacket and the scarf and headed out the door.

I might have felt like crap, but I looked as vampilicious as ever.

Obviously I wasn't the only one who thought so, because the camera started flashing the minute I stepped out in front of my building.

I so wasn't in the mood for this.

Before I knew what was happening, my preternatural feet had carried me across the street. I faced a startled Gwen, who looked as if she'd just seen a ghost.

Way to go, Lil. Low profile, remember?

"You," she gulped, "that is, you were just . . ." She pointed across the street before her frantic gaze swiveled back to me. "And now you're . . ." She pointed and swallowed again. "Just like that."

I remembered flipping through channels earlier before resorting to the vacuum. "I'm an illusionist. Like that Criss Angel. You know, the magician guy."

"But I thought you were a matchmaker?"

I smiled. "Actually, I am. I'm just an illusionist in my spare time. And since we're on the subject of dating—"

"We are?" she blurted.

We are. I sent the silent message. Not that she would get it. Unless her hatred of men had turned her into a card-carrying lesbian, or at least a bisexual.

She stared blankly back at me. A good sign or a bad one, depending on how one looked at it. I decided to go for the positive. She wasn't reading me, which meant that she still liked men—even if she did think Lorena Bobbitt should be the first woman president.

"Meeting people these days is so difficult, it's no wonder so many hook up with total losers," I offered.

"They're all losers."

"The majority, maybe. But there are those rare few worth their weight in gold: men who'll serve you breakfast in bed and rub your feet, men who won't fart in bed or hog the remote control."

"Really?" She looked as if I'd told her the world was flat and born vamps really did volunteer for community service.

"You bet. You've just been fishing in the wrong pond. You need a guide. Someone to bait your hook and cast your line." I handed her a card. "That's where I come in. An attractive woman like you shouldn't be having coffee all alone." I eyed the untouched cup sitting on the table.

"Oh, I wasn't having—I mean, yeah. I was sucking up the coffee." She nodded vigorously, freaked that she'd been about to blow her cover. "Um, I can't leave the stuff alone." Right. One glance into her frantic gaze and I knew she hated coffee as much as her ex. Their first date had been at the Espresso Bean and she still couldn't set foot inside the place without threatening someone with bodily harm.

I smiled. "You should find someone who shares your passion for, er, coffee."

"I should, shouldn't I?"

"You're attractive. In the prime of your life. You deserve more than a cheating ex."

"I do, don't I?"

"There's more to life than being someone else's gopher." The words tumbled out before I could stop them, but she didn't seem to catch the slip that I was onto her, or that I saw much more than the average, fabulously dressed hottie. "You could be having fun, instead of running all over New York playing Magnum PI for your mother."

"I could, couldn't I?"

"Call me and I'll hook you up," I told her. "Guaranteed."

Excitement lit her eyes as she stared at the card. Her expression faltered as she seemed to think. "Is it really expensive?" She shook her head. "Because I'm on a tight budget right now." Mr. Ex had taken her to the cleaners and stuck it to her royally, the poor thing.

"Actually, I'm running a special right now for coffee lovers who have their own cameras." I was so lame. But I'd had a sleepless day and my brilliance was running on fumes. "A free profile, plus two prospective matches, provided, of course, that you bring your camera to your first appointment and take a few pictures for Dead End Dating. I've been meaning to add some visuals to my Web site." What can I say? I wasn't on empty yet.

"Deal." She smiled and I smiled.

I turned and headed up the street, and this time, no one followed.

I dropped off the jacket and scarf to Nina at the Waldorf. In return, she gave me several pamphlets for the hotel and a confirmation for booking the wedding date.

Next stop? Jack and Mandy's place.

Ten minutes and a scary cab ride later (were there any other kind in the city?), I climbed the steps of Jack's brownstone. I rang and he buzzed me up. I was just about to knock on the apartment door when it whooshed open and I found myself staring at a round, chubby, pink-cheeked face.

"Harriet?"

"Good evening, Miss Lil," the old woman told me. She wore the usual starched black dress and pressed white apron. She sported a tiny black cap atop her short, silver hair. "Lovely to see you."

Harriet was my mother's personal maid. She was a zillionth-generation descendant of the actual au pair who had cared for my mother when she was a child. My mother treasured Harriet almost as much as her collection of rare Chanel perfume bottles. My mother couldn't live without her.

Until, apparently, now.

"What are you doing here?" I asked the old woman.

"Helping out Mr. Jack." She smiled again and motioned me in. "Have a seat. Can I get you a spritzer? Club soda? Glass of blood?"

"I . . . uh, no." My gaze shifted to Jack, who lay sprawled on the sofa, the remote control in his hand. On the coffee table in front of him sat a stack of his favorite magazines (*GQ* and *Maxim* and even a few copies of the rare *Aristocratic Vamp*), two bottles of the most expensive, imported blood on the market, an extra pillow, and a brand-new iPod with docking station. "Mom sent all this stuff, didn't she?" He nodded. "And Harriet, too?"

"I'm supposed to take it easy," Jack told me. "And Harriet's here to make sure that that happens." He grinned. "I still can't believe it."

"What?"

"That Mom finally came around. She's accepted Mandy and now she's trying to make it up to me for acting like such a lunatic."

"That," I nodded, "or she thinks you've caught a rare bacteria and need 24/7 medical assistance."

He frowned, despite the fact that Harriet had

handed him a glass of his favorite blood type and even tucked a napkin under his chin. "What are you talking about?"

I wasn't going to say anything. Take it to the grave, I told myself.

Then again, I wasn't actually going to the grave and eternity was a really long time to perpetuate a lie. Even more, it was much too long to watch Jack laze around and be pampered. Been there, done that (Jack *was* the youngest boy of the bunch and the most spoiled).

"I might have mentioned something about your condition," I told him.

"I don't have a condition."

"No, but let's suppose you did. I might have mentioned it to her to emphasize the fact that you actually need Mandy. For more than just sex."

"I do need Mandy for more than just sex."

A few months back, such a statement from Jack would have totally wigged me out. Since Mandy had come on the scene, Jack had turned into a decent guy and I'd stopped waiting for someone to jump out and yell *"You're being punked!"*

"I know that and you know that, but Mom doesn't get it. What she does get is that you're her baby boy and your livelihood is being threatened."

"She gets that?"

"She didn't at first, what with you being a Super Vamp and all, but then I explained that this bacteria is something new and rare and only affects Super Vamps. Now she gets it."

"In other words, you lied to her."

"For a good cause." I told him about her hiring me to match him up, and he nearly spurted a mouthful of the red stuff back out at me.

"You're kidding, right?" he asked as Harriet rushed over to dab his chin. "She hired you?" He pierced me with a stare.

I nodded. "She even paid a rush fee."

"What a cold-hearted bitch."

"She was desperate," I blurted. Wait a second. What did I just say? Was I actually defending the obsessive, overbearing Jacqueline Marchette? "She felt like she had no choice." Uh-oh. I was. "You're her son. She thought she was doing what was best for you."

"Breaking up my relationship with Mandy is not what's best for me. It never will be. I love her. I've never loved anyone the way I love her. Hell, I never even knew such a thing existed." He pushed to his feet. "This is going to stop."

"I already stopped it. Mom's through gunning for Mandy. The wedding is on. Just appreciate the cease-fire and relax."

"If she tried once, she'll try again."

"Maybe not."

"And maybe you're delusional." He shook his head. "I have to do something. Right now. Before things get worse." His gaze collided with mine.

"Tell me you're not going to do what I think you're going to do."

He nodded. "I'm going to give her the old heave-ho." He reached for his cell phone and waved it at me. "It won't be easy and it won't be pretty, but I'll just have to deal with the fallout. She has to know that she can't just stick her nose in whenever she feels like it. She has no say in what I do or don't do. Not now. Not ever. And I'm going to tell her so." He glanced at the cell phone before shifting his expression to the massage table set up in the dining room. "You bet your ass I'm going to tell her."

"Just as soon as your session with Hans?"

He nodded vigorously. "Just as soon as my session with Hans."

"Wimp."

Twenty-one

❤ ❤ ❤

"I can't believe we're here," John commented as we stood at the entrance to the main dining room of *The Lady of the Sea,* a small charter ship that offered dinner and dancing and a spectacular view of the Hudson at midnight.

Several television cameras had been set up around the large room, each manned by a man or a woman wearing a headset and a microphone. The frantic producer stood a few feet away, a clipboard in hand as he eyed the crowd and checked off arrivals. The finalists (fifty, to be exact) mingled here and there, drinks in hand, awaiting the arrival of Manhattan's most wanted bachelor. Near the bar, a big-band trio played an instrumental version of "Disco Inferno."

"But we are." My nostrils flared and I drank in the aroma of too much perfume, lots of hair products, and an overabundance of nerves. "For whatever reason," one that still eluded me, "we made the cut just like everyone else."

"Not *we* as in you and me. *We* as in me and my girls." He cupped his chest. "La Perla had to special order this time and I almost didn't get them today. I'm not lopsided, am I?"

I eyed him from head to toe. He was wearing a navy blue silk dress with cap sleeves and an Empire waist and silver sandals. My gaze ventured back north and stopped on the area in question.

"They're perfectly even, and even bigger than the last time. Did you gain a cup size?"

John grinned. "I figure these babies are what got me this far, so the bigger the better." He arched his back. "They're a little heavier than I first thought."

"Think of them as a safety measure. They'll make nifty flotation devices if we hit an iceberg."

"We're on the Hudson. There are no icebergs."

"Then you're good to go if we hit a Dumpster or a dead body."

I checked my stash of business cards, eyeballed a few prospects that I was particularly interested in— attractive, successful women desperate enough to try a dating service should they get booted off tonight— and waltzed into the dining room, John following in my footsteps.

We mixed and mingled for the next half hour. Then the producer herded everyone into a group near the doorway. The musical ensemble launched into an instrumental of "There she is, Miss America . . ."

The doors opened. A round of applause erupted, followed by a collective murmur of excitement.

I took a few steps back, determined not to be caught in the stampede (we're talking fifty women, biological clocks ticking, and one elegible man), and sized up the man who appeared in the doorway.

Mr. Weather was so handsome and rich and full of himself (I'm a vamp, I can tell these things) that I actually wondered if he'd been stranded on a lavish French estate as a child and raised by a pack of born vampires.

Think Tarzan, but with a black Gucci suit rather than a loincloth.

He was tall and tanned, with blond hair and green eyes, and a smile dazzling enough to charm a city full of viewers.

John nudged me. "He's kind of cute."

"Don't tell me the ta-tas are going to your brain?"

He shrugged. "Since when is it a crime for a man to appreciate another man's appearance? It's not like I'm going to touch the guy. Hell, I'm not getting within five feet of him. No sirree. Unless," he added, "I have to. I've got a job to do, after all. And, well, duty calls."

Um, sure.

I made a mental note to phone Rosie ASAP and get her on board with my Match-Up-John-Schumacker project before he stopped worshipping from afar and started asking for hair how-tos and clothing tips.

I watched as Mr. Weather floated into the room, his trademark smile firmly in place, his eyes gleaming with a predatory light, along with just the right amount of humility, as he drank in the harem of attractive women.

A production assistant followed hot on his heels, arms overflowing with long-stemmed red roses. Manhattan's most wanted smiled, plucked a rose from the bunch, and handed it to the first woman he met. He repeated the process with each encounter and the minutes started to creep by.

After ten minutes and three contestants, I gave up watching the ritual and retrieved a glass of wine from the bar. I know, I know. Hello AA. But I needed something to keep me from going off the deep end while I waited my turn at a rose. I tried talking to a few of the other women, but all attention seemed fixed on the man making his way through the dining room.

While John homed in on his fraud suspect (at least that's the excuse he'd given to make a beeline for the bachelor of the hour), I finished off my first glass and retrieved another, and traded standing for a seat at a small table in the far corner. I was in the middle of my third glass, snapping my fingers to an off-key version of KC and the Sunshine Band's "Get Down Tonight," when I felt a hand on my shoulder.

"Hi, there." The voice was deep. Smooth. And oh, so irritating. I've been around five hundred years, ladies. That means I've heard every pick-up line, seen every suave move. Suffice it to say, I wasn't one to be schmoozed very easily, which is why I'd given up one-night stands in favor of finding my soul mate.

I turned, our gazes locked, and the facts ticked off in my head.

Mark Williams. Loaded. Liked looking in the mirror. Loaded. Liked looking at his hair. Loaded. Liked admiring his pecs. Loaded. Liked eating in five-star restaurants and admiring his butt. Loaded. Liked having his teeth bleached. *Loaded*.

He smiled, obviously expecting me to fall all over him to make the next cut. But I hadn't wanted to make this cut, so I narrowed my gaze and stared at his mouth. "Crowns or veneers?"

"Excuse me?"

"You've obviously had a lot of dental work. Did you cap what was there or go for a new set?"

He looked stunned for the space of three heartbeats before his expression eased into another smile. "You're the funny one."

"Excuse me?"

"I liked your tape."

"You did?"

He shook his head and chuckled. "Pinto beans," he snorted. "That was a good one."

I *know*. Mr. Weather snorting, but there it was. Loud. Sincere. And in total contradiction to my raised-by-vamps theory.

"You have a wonderful sense of humor."

"I do?"

He nodded, and when he smiled, his expression

seemed softer and more genuine. "I'd love to talk to you some more, but I've got to spread myself around."

"No, no. I completely understand."

"Maybe we can hook up later? You know, catch a few minutes to really get to know each other. Just the two of us."

"Definitely." My hand closed around the rose he handed me and I actually felt a tiny thrill of excitement.

He liked me.

Not that I *wanted* him to like me.

That was the point. I was clearly sending out my *do not like me* vibe, yet here he was, slobbering all over me and begging me to meet him later. (*All right,* already. I know that's not *exactly* what was happening, but I'm the one giving the recap and I say he was definitely slobbering.)

I *so* had it going on.

Too bad he wasn't a certain made vampire who hunted tongue-eating criminals for a living.

The thought stirred visions of Ty, and I quickly went from feeling hyped up to feeling totally icky. Particularly when we all sat down to dinner and I was forced to push around a plateful of grilled salmon and wild rice.

I picked and forked and even pretended to eat a few bites that I quickly spit into my napkin using my ultrafast reflexes and the occasional, "Look! Mr. Weather just lost his pants!"

I watched John's Adam's apple bob and my own

hunger stirred. I definitely should have had more than one glass of AB positive before I'd left the house.

Gathering my own control, I tamped down on the urge and sucked down yet another glass of wine. I'd made it through dinner and was drinking in the aroma of chocolate cake with raspberry sauce when John elbowed me.

"Lookee, lookee! She's dancing."

My attention shifted to the microscopic dance floor and the tall blonde swaying provocatively in the center. She wore high-heeled suede boots, an ultrashort black dress, and a seductive expression that stated very clearly what she was feeling at the moment, and—lemmetellya—it wasn't pain.

Beside me, John was going nuts. He kept lifting his clutch and mumbling into the clasp.

"Indigestion," I blurted when the other women at our table stared pointedly at him. "She takes pills, but nothing seems to work. Her doctor suggested she try meditation to help with the pain. The purse is her focal point. That's it," I rubbed his back. "Focus. Chant. There you go."

Since John was competing with dessert for everyone's attention, our tablemates quickly scarfed down the explanation and turned their attention back to scarfing down the chocolate cake.

Stop acting like an idiot. I sent the mental thought, but he wasn't looking at me and so I had to resort to another Super Vamp technique. I popped him upside the head.

"What?"

"You're making a fool of yourself. Stop holding up the purse and mumbling."

"I need a good shot, complete with commentary." He grinned. "This is it. I'll get my promotion, for sure."

"Not before you get committed." I motioned toward the dance floor. "Why don't you stand up? Move around a little. Maybe you can get a better vantage point?"

"Good idea." He bounced up from the seat. "Promotion, here I come."

I watched him pick his way around the perimeter of the room. He hung back. He dipped behind an overgrown ficus. He planted himself behind a waiter holding a water pitcher. But no matter where he moved, he couldn't seem to get a clear shot and so he kept moving, circling, until he stood on the opposite side of the room.

I saw the frustration play over his features as he tried to zoom in on his subject through the other dancers. It wasn't working. He couldn't get the shot.

Like hell.

Determination fired his eyes and he stiffened. He stuffed the purse under his arm, did a quick shift and fix on his boobs, and then took a wobbly step forward.

He inched his way out onto the dance floor, swaying and shimmying toward the center, the clutch firmly under his arm, the end aimed effectively at his target.

The song ended and a faster song took its place. Everyone on the dance floor picked up the tempo, including John. He started to shake. To wiggle. To bounce.

Now I don't want to sound like a skeptic or anything because, obviously, if vamps exist (as well as a whole group of weres and Others), then anything's possible. But I've never really believed in people who had premonitions or psychics or fortune tellers, or anyone else who claimed to predict the future.

Rather, I liked to think that the future depended, ultimately, on the choices one made, that there was no predestined path and that things could turn on a dime just like that. And, if so, then getting a glimpse of it ahead of time would be virtually impossible.

Right? Right.

At least that's what I'd always thought.

Until I saw John do a twist and twirl. A sense of disaster swept over me. A frantic "Oh, shit" echoed through my head.

I braced myself and sure enough, he twirled again.

His body went left. His boobs went right.

And the whole evening went to hell via express delivery.

Twenty-two

❤ ❤ ❤

Things happened really fast from that moment on, but to me it felt like a horror movie unfolding slowly, painfully. John, freaked that his breasts were now slipping and sliding across the dance floor in opposite directions, took a nosedive to catch one. His long red hair slapped at the air and then jumped ship, exposing a dark brown buzz cut.

A loud scream ripped through the ballroom. The music stopped. The producer went nuts. A dozen pairs of eyes swiveled between the dance floor and yours truly and—

I quickly shut my mouth and the screaming stopped. What can I say? We're talking a *buzz* cut.

The fraud suspect jumped back. Her heel smashed down on insert number two and solution squirted all over the wood floor.

The woman next to her slipped, grappling for the brunette next to her as she landed on her ass. The brunette went down, clutching at the blonde next to her, who reached for the redhead next to her, and so on, until the only person still upright was Mr. Weather. Uh-oh.

I caught a quick glimpse of the bachelor's shocked face as a woman tumbled into him and he tried to catch her.

Before I could think, I shot to my feet. I crossed the room and hit the dance floor in two seconds flat (they don't call it preternatural speed for nothing). My hands filled with all that cool, smooth Gucci. I caught Mr. Weather just as he was about to tumble backward and disappear into a sea of French manicures and strappy stilettos.

"What the hell?" he mumbled as I steadied him on his feet and smoothed the rumpled lapel of his jacket. He blinked and shook his head, as if trying to understand that the blur he'd just seen had been yours truly.

"I had a couple of energy drinks before I came," I blurted. "It's a wonder what taurine can do."

"Uh, yeah." He shook his head again and blinked a few more times. "You're really strong."

"I take vitamins, too. You can't have too much B14."

"That's not a vitamin. It's a bingo number. I think you mean B12."

"B12, B14—I take the entire B family. And the rest of the alphabet, too." I made a show of flexing my arms and sent the silent message. *I'm the most buff specimen of female perfection that you've ever seen and you're appropriately wowed. You're also anxious to get the hell out of here, find the nearest bathroom, and make sure none of these bitches messed up your hair during the collision.*

"I really need to take a leak. Thanks again."

"It was nothing. Just forget it."

Yeah, right.

While I could make Mr. Weather forget if I wanted to, I couldn't work my vamp magic on a room full of women. My gaze swept the surrounding faces. Most were too busy mourning ruined dresses or mussed hair to even notice me (yeah, baby). But there were a few who stared as if I'd just turned into a giant bobble head.

Or a vampire.

I ran my tongue over my teeth. Nope. No fangs. I smoothed my hands over my dress. No soft, pink bat fuzz.

My only slipup had been shooting across the room like a cannon in full view of everyone and, more important, the four video cameras currently recording everything on tape, all in the name of Gucci.

Mr. Weather walked toward the men's room. The staff stylist followed him, flat iron in one hand and a bottle of Spritz It in the other.

I was just about to try to do some damage control with a nearby cameraman when two security guards, followed by several of the boat's officers, stampeded past me. They headed straight for John, who was scrambling to his feet.

The guards nabbed him just as he made it upright and hauled him off the dance floor. Meanwhile, a half dozen production assistants started peeling women off one another.

"But I didn't do anything . . ." I heard John plead as security dragged him from the room. "Wait," he struggled and wiggled and tried to dig in his feet, but he'd lost his shoes in the chaos and he couldn't seem to get a grip on the carpet. "Don't." He tugged and pulled and cast a frantic glance my way. "I can't leave my hair!"

The 26th Precinct of the New York City Police Department wasn't nearly as bad as I thought it was going to be. Of course, I wasn't one of the poor saps being paraded by in handcuffs. No, I had it parked on a metal chair near the busy information desk.

"Nice hair," the woman sitting next to me said.

My hands tightened on the red wig that lay in my lap. "Thanks." I slid a glance at the woman and smiled.

Debbie Ray Lawrence. Twenty-five. Born and raised in Trenton. She'd been in the city for two years. Part-time college student. Full-time escort. No current relationship. Her last boyfriend had been a shitbag named Sonny. He'd wiped out her three-hundred-dollar savings and eaten the last Rice Krispies bar before leaving her for a stripper named Lou. He'd claimed that Debbie didn't have enough

experience for him, which had led to her current oc-
cupation. No man would ever leave her again for being a schmuck in bed. But while she now knew what
she was doing, she wasn't so sure she liked it. She'd
still never had an orgasm and, to be honest, she
didn't really understand what the fuss was all about.

There was a ton more stuff—her fav color, food,
congressional candidate—but I was tired and Debbie
was extremely long-winded. I smiled and cut the connection.

"Amateur or professional?" she asked me.

"Definitely professional."

"Yeah, I figured as much. You've got the look perfected."

"I do?" I hadn't been aware that matchmakers had
an actual *look*. I glanced down. Fab shoes. Great
dress. I did have it going on in a major way.

"So how much do you charge?"

"For two or three?"

"I was thinking one."

I shook my head. "I never just do one. It's either
two or more, otherwise it's really not worth my time
and effort. I mean, what are the odds of hitting pay
dirt with just one?"

"That's true, but two seems like an awful lot."

"Are you kidding? I've done tons more. I did a full
dozen just last month."

"In one night?"

"Oh, no. That would be too tiring. I spaced them
out over a few weeks."

"Oh, okay. That makes much more sense. I've done that before."

"You're a matchmaker, too?"

"No, I have a pimp who sets up my dates. I just make sure the guy gets off. What about you? Do you have a pimp?"

I shook my head. "I'm not a hooker. I just hook up people."

"So you're a pimp?"

My thoughts went to Viola and the reproductive fest I'd been responsible for several months back. In the name of procreation, not pleasure. We're talking survival of the species. "Sort of."

She nodded. "Interested in taking on any new girls?"

"Only if you're interested in giving up your current profession and finding the love of your life."

"Love sucks most of the time. I'd rather have cold hard cash."

"You and me both. So what are you doing here?"

"A friend of mine lost her purse and didn't realize it. She tried to ditch a cab fare and the driver called the cops. He pressed charges and now she's here. I'm her *go to* person: If she needs help, she goes to me. If I need help, I go to her. What about you?"

"A friend of mine lost his mind, and I'm here to make sure no one commits him."

We chatted for a few minutes and I gave her a handful of Dead End Dating cards to pass out to her girlfriends (just in case they got tired of men paying them for sex and wanted to go back to giving it away for free) before Ash finally walked into the station. He was my only connection with the NYPD and so I'd called and asked for his help.

He had two men with him. Both shared his dark good looks and pitch-black eyes. The man on his right, however, wore his hair long and loose, while the man on his left had his hair buzzed to the scalp. All three had the same flame tattoos decorating their right arms. They were hot and hunky and . . . demons.

The thought registered as I noticed the way they drew the attention of every female in the busy room. Only vamps could mesmerize like that. Or weird cult leaders.

Since Ash was neither (he hadn't once slipped me a pamphlet or asked me to drink a glass of Kool-Aid), he had to be a demon.

Specifically, an incubus.

I felt a lightbulb go on over my head. Duh. That was it. I should have known.

Rumor had it that my great, great, great, great grandmother's lady's maid had been seduced by one. One minute she'd been sleeping like a baby and the next she'd been rutting and bucking and begging some stud muffin for his seed (my mother's words, not mine). Anyhow, the stud muffin had given it to her and then, poof! he'd disappeared. Half the castle had claimed an incubus. The other half had claimed a no-good stable boy by the name of Sean. But no one really knew for sure.

I'd never met a demon myself, let alone three, until now.

So far no one was bucking or rutting or begging, unless you count the con artist in the corner who was trying to talk one of the cops out of her badge, which meant there was a slight possibility (shocked gasp) that I could be wrong.

I made a mental note to Google demons the moment I got back to my computer and pushed to my feet just as Ash and his buds approached.

"Thanks for coming," I told him.

"No problem. Me and the boys were headed to the Bronx on a case." He motioned to the guy with long hair and said, "Mo, this is Lil. Lil, my brother, Mo." He motioned to the buzz cut. "This is my other brother, Zee."

"Hey," said Mo.

"What's up?" asked Zee.

I smiled and felt my stomach quiver beneath their scrutiny. I had a sudden vision of the three of us, naked and panting and . . . *oh, boy.*

My smile died and the three Prince brothers grinned.

Forget Google. They most definitely *were* demons— that, or I was really sexually frustrated and susceptible to anything in pants. While this had been the case before Ty (we're talking one hundred years without a serious relationship), it wasn't the case now. I'd had really great sex (albeit for only one night) and satisfied my urges for at least a good six months.

Which meant I was staring at three demons of sexual delight.

"I called the desk sergeant about your friend on the way over here," Ash told me.

"Friend?" I forced aside the lewd and lascivious images and struggled for a coherent thought. "Oh, yeah, my friend. John. Did you find out anything? They didn't arrest him, did they? I mean, I know he murdered his dress when he dove onto the floor, but that isn't against the law, is it?"

"They didn't arrest him, but the show's producers aren't very happy. They want to press charges for female impersonation."

"But that isn't against the law."

"Exactly, which is why nothing's going to come of it. But management did file a restraining order. Schumacker won't be allowed to set foot inside any of the network buildings ever again and he won't be allowed within fifty feet of Mr. Weather, or any of the female contestants."

"What about his fraud case?"

"It turned out to be legitimate, but during the ruckus, she slipped and now she's in the emergency room about to undergo a laminectomy on her lower back."

"Oh, no."

"That's why John's still in the interrogation room, even though everyone's told him he's free to go. He says his life is over and he would rather stay here than go home and eat SpaghettiOs until he kicks the bucket." He leveled a stare at me. "You have to get him out of here. He's driving everybody nuts."

I thought of poor John sitting back there, feeling like his life was over. I could sympathize. Ty had been kidnapped by a psycho, my preternatural fall from grace had been caught on videotape and I still hadn't figured out an answer for the wedding dress situation. I was definitely feeling pretty icky myself. The urge to go home and plunge face-first into the kitty litter was pretty strong.

But while I didn't have a shoulder to cry on (not unless you count the three sets standing in front of me, but I *so* wasn't going there), John did. He wasn't alone in the world, even though he might feel like it at the moment.

I pulled out my phone.

"You calling for backup?" Ash asked. I nodded and he added, "A couple of gonzo guerrillas to drag him out?"

I smiled. "I've got a better idea."

I'd never actually met Rosie, the adjuster from John's agency, but I knew her the moment she walked in.

The clues? She was dressed in rumpled jeans, an oversized sleep T, and house slippers, as if someone (guilty) had gotten her out of bed in the middle of the night. Her eyes were filled with worry.

Oh, and she had *Ask Me About Life Insurance* emblazoned across the front of her shirt.

"Rosie?" I met her near the information desk. "I'm Lil. I'm the one who called you."

"Where is he? Is he all right? Can I see him?"

If I'd had any hope that Rosie would be as interested in John as he was in her, one look into her blue eyes was enough to convince me that my instincts had been dead wrong.

Rosie didn't like John.

She loved him. Hopelessly. Desperately.

Awww.

"He's in the interrogation room, but he's fine," I assured her.

"No one's beating his face into the table or shoving pencils up his nose to get him to spill his guts?"

"Not yet, but if he doesn't vacate the premises soon, they're likely to start." I explained the situation and how low he was feeling.

"That's terrible," she told me. "Just terrible."

"I know. That's why I called you." Time to start laying the groundwork. "I thought if anyone could make him feel better, it would be you. He talks about you all the time."

"He does? What does he say?"

"That you're a really good friend." Her face fell and I rushed on, "And that he *really* likes you."

"He said that?"

"Well, not in so many words, but I know that's what he was thinking."

"How do you know?"

Because I'm a lean, mean, mind reading machine.

"Just a lucky guess, but I know I'm right. He really does like you; he just doesn't realize how much. Yet."

"We've worked together for six years. Six years of lunches and softball. Six years of Friday night beer and pizza. He knows my life story and I know his. If he doesn't know how much he likes me by now, he never will."

"Men are slow. Extremely slow." She seemed to think and her face perked up. "They're also creatures of habit. He's used to you being his buddy. The key is to spice things up and show him you're more than just the beer and pizza girl."

"You mean I should order spaghetti instead of pepperoni?"

"I mean you should jump his bones the next time you see him. In addition to being slow, men are clueless. Unless it's written right in front of them, even tattooed on their foreheads, they won't get it. You have to go in there and tell him what you really want from him. Outright. In plain English."

"Really?"

"That or you could strip naked and show him, but since there are cops watching I'd save that part for when you get him home. Right now, though, you should definitely tell him how you feel. Confess. And flirt. Can you flirt?"

"I can wink and whistle. And I can even turn my eyelids inside out."

"Winking is good. I'd nix the whistling and the eyelids. You want him to want to have sex with you, not have you exorcised."

"Good point." She shook her head. "But how do you even know that this will work?"

Because I'm an ultra vamp and I know these things. "Women's intuition."

"He must be feeling like an idiot. This case was the opportunity of his lifetime."

"No," I stared deep into her eyes. "You're the opportunity of his lifetime."

What can I say? I'm a sucker for the big L.

She smiled. "You might be right." She stiffened and seemed to gather her courage. "He definitely needs a wake-up call."

I smiled and handed her the hair. "Go in there and get your man."

Twenty-three

♥ ♥ ♥

When Rosie left to coax John out of the interrogation room, I walked over to Ash to get a quick update on Ty.

"Any news?" I asked him while Mo and Zee strutted over to a nearby vending machine. No sooner had Mo fed his quarters into the slot, than an entire row of hookers rushed forward to give their support in helping lift the drink from the dispenser.

"We located the burglar," Ash told me.

"With Ty's tongue?"

He shook his head. "Just his own. Says he went to Ty's place to confront him, but no one was there. The guy also said he found the loft just the way we did— a mess. He didn't call the cops for obvious reasons."

"Did he see anything suspicious?"

"He's got so much coke up his nose that he can

barely see his feet." He shook his head. "I'm afraid we're back to square one." He eyed me. "He whispering any sweet nothings your way?"

"Don't I wish." I did, I realized. With all my undead heart. I missed Ty. I missed talking to him and lusting after him. I missed him lusting after me.

A longing that must have shown in my eyes because Ash touched my arm with a firm, comforting press of his fingertips. Yep, he was an incubus, all right. He had to be. Heat sizzled through me and stirred my hormones.

The slutty bitches reared their ugly heads, gave a half-hearted *yowza* then settled back into *nah, I've got a headache* mode. It was nearly morning, my muscles were weak, and I hadn't slept in three days. Forget hot, incredible, mind-blowing sex with an ultra hunky incubus. All I wanted at the moment was my bed, my Victoria's Secret jersey knit pj's, and Killer.

Not because I liked the cat, mind you.

It's just he was going through an adjustment period, what with his new surroundings, and I didn't want him to feel unwelcome. Then he might freak out on me and start marking his territory on my couch or my Serta Pillow Top. The one thing I needed even less than an old, snotty cat was an old, snotty, psychotic cat *and* smelly furniture.

"Thanks, but no thanks," I told Ash. "I'm just not in the mood.

"Really?" He looked stunned, as if "nah" wasn't in the realm of possibility.

Then again, if he *was* an incubus, it totally was
NOT in the realm and I'd definitely thrown him for a
loop. Guilt wiggled its way through me and I heard
myself say, "It's not that you're not uber sexy and I
don't want to, it's just that I'm washing my hair today."

"Yeah." He nodded. Disbelief and shock played
tag team on his face.

"And my cat's hair."

"Right."

I smiled. "But definitely next time."

He seemed floored for a split second before a grin
curved his lips. "Ty did say you were different."

"I thought he said I had a big mouth."

"After he said you were different." His grin
widened and he winked. "He was right."

"Would that be different in a good way or a bad
way?"

"Good for you. Bad for me." His gaze sizzled with
sudden heat. "Unless you change your mind."

"Sorry, buddy. It's not going to happen. One man
is enough in my life."

"Ty?"

"Killer."

He winked and motioned to his brothers that it
was time to go.

"But while I'm not interested, I know someone
who is." I pointed out Debbie, who sat waiting for
news about her friend. "Maybe you and your posse
could show her what she's been missing all these
years."

His gaze collided with Debbie's and her cheeks turned pink. I knew she was having the same hot thoughts about the Prince brothers that I'd had.

"I've got work right now," he told me, "but I'll see what I can do later."

I nodded, watched him turn and then I found myself standing all by my lonesome.

I checked on John and Rosie, found out she'd coaxed him from the interrogation room into the bathroom, and smiled. I said goodbye to Debbie and handed out a few more cards to several officers on my way to the door. Then I caught a cab and headed home.

Killer, as usual, was thrilled to see me when I walked in the door. I'd barely stepped inside before I had to brace myself for his excitement.

He spared me a sleepy glance—*Keep it down, would ya? I'm trying to nap here*—and then snuggled back down on one of my discarded blouses (the rat fink).

A gun and a small coffin. That's all I needed and my world would be right again.

I forced aside my destructive thoughts—I didn't do destruction all that well *either*—and headed for the bedroom. I changed into my favorite pj's, warmed myself some AB negative, checked the blinds, and climbed into bed. I drank my breakfast and then eased down onto my back. I stared at the ceiling and listened to Killer snore.

I threw a shoe and boinked Killer on the head and then I stared at the ceiling and listened to my neighbor snore until her alarm went off and CNN started to blare. I thought about boinking her with my other shoe, but I didn't think my aim was that good (we're talking a Jimmy Choo not a boomerang), so I flipped onto my stomach and stuffed my head under the pillow. I held the down pillow tight and tried to drown out the noise at the same time I tried not to think.

To freak.

Had I really done my Superman impression in front of *everyone* just to save Mr. Weather and his primo Gucci suit? Had I really committed myself to finding the perfect wedding dress from among Shirley's blast from the past collection? Had I really lied to my mother? Had I really turned down the chance to have the most incredible sex of my entire life with one of the devil's own? Had I really fallen head over heels for a made vampire?

No, no, no, and oh, no!

At least that's what I told myself. (While I didn't do death and destruction all that well, I kicked ass at denial.)

Even so, my mind kept replaying the past few weeks, the previous night, until even I (the proverbial queen) couldn't ignore the truth. I sucked at being a born vampire, and not in the good way.

If I made the finals and any of the footage aired, I was so going to find myself a prime target for the SOBs (Snipers of Otherworldly Beings). While my fellow humans would assume it was some trick of the cameras and dismiss it as some really clever reality TV, the SOBs could spot a vamp at fifty paces. They would make me right away, not to mention I would draw the attention of the entire born vamp nation, the majority of which prided themselves on keeping a low profile. I would be a disgrace.

Oh, wait. That was me already.

But only within the warm, comforting embrace of my own family.

This would take things to a much higher level. I had a hard enough time dealing with my own mother's disapproving frown. Multiply that by a gazillion, and you would have the general consensus at the next major vamp event. I would be ostracized. My business would take a major hit. Everything in my closet would be repossessed except for the Moe's uniforms. I would be evicted. I would end up living on the street wearing Dockers and lime-green Polo shirts, sucking on rats for sustenance, and muttering to myself about the good old days.

A tear slid down my cheek and I slapped it away.

Okay, I told myself. Okayyyy. So what if I'd taken a few wrong turns and now found myself stuck on a dead-end road? All I had to do was backtrack. Rewind, so to speak. I would just tell Shirley she didn't have a decent dress that could be worn in this particular decade. I would come clean with my mother (after the wedding, of course), and I would take Ash up on his offer the very next time I saw him. And I would go cold turkey on Ty once I saved his afterlife and made sure that he was safe.

As for *Manhattan's Most Wanted . . .*

A mute point, I told myself.

It wasn't like I would come even close to making the final cut. I'd said all of three sentences to Mr. Weather. He didn't know me, and I didn't know him, and there were a ton of other girls who'd been shaking their asses in front of him on the dance floor. Sure, I'd been the best dressed. With the most fantabulous hair. And a really rockin' shade of magenta sunset lip gloss. But men didn't notice things like that. If they did, then I wouldn't be in business.

Clueless, remember? No, men noticed boobs and asses, and there'd been far too many of them right in his face for him to pick me.

Me making the final ten was right up there with the Hudson turning to wine or Oprah picking a novel for her next book club selection that didn't make me want to slit my wrists.

I.e., it's *never* going to happen.

"You made the final ten!" Evie beamed the moment I walked into Dead End Dating on Wednesday evening.

The news stalled me in the front lobby and I nearly dropped the latte I'd picked up at Starbucks.

Obviously, Evie noticed my sudden distress because she rushed forward, plucked the latte from between my fingers, and went back to her computer.

"You're kidding, right?" I asked her.

"I wouldn't kid about something so incredible. They just called. I was jotting down a note from your mother: she wants you at her place early Sunday evening to help set up for the party. Anyhow, a limo will be picking up you and the other nine girls Friday night to take you to Devan's on Central Park for dinner. You'll each have an entire fifteen minutes with Mr. Weather that will be taped and broadcast on Saturday night. Isn't that terrific?"

"Yeah."

"And you're supposed to wear something colorful for the camera, something to make you stand out."

"No problem. I'll be the one in the killer heels with a bull's-eye painted over my heart."

"Don't be so negative. Just because you're open to love and commitment doesn't mean that some guy is going to come along and shoot you down." Evie had obviously taken my realism as a metaphor. "You have to be positive. Besides, Mr. Weather doesn't seem like the heartbreaker type. He's so cute."

I wasn't sure where being cute contradicted being a shit, but I was too upset to object.

She reached for a stack of messages while I gave myself a quick mental pep talk.

You still have your health.

You still have a great bod.

You still have three credit cards (out of sixteen) that aren't anywhere close to the limit.

So what if you're going to be on local television on Saturday night? It's a cable channel, for Damien's sake. How many people could actually watch? And—and this was the mucho important thing—it's a *dating* show. News flash: Born vamps don't date.

Not in the traditional sense. They hooked up, had sex, declared their undying commitment, had more sex, squeezed out some baby vamps, and—you guessed it—had even more sex. They didn't have candlelit dinners or dance in the moonlight, or anything else that could be considered remotely romantic. Meaning there was a 99.9 percent chance that no one in the born vamp community would even see the show.

The SOBs were another story, but since it was a local broadcast, the only attention I was likely to attract was Vinnie and his brother, Crusher, a couple of SOBs out of Jersey. They handled all takedowns for this area and, or so my mother said, could be bribed with a little green and free office supplies. (Being an SOB wasn't just about staking vampires and popping a couple of silver caps into an unsuspecting *were*. Vinnie had a business to run: expenses, balance sheets, taxes.)

Which meant I wasn't totally S.O.L. at the moment.

"There's one more cut after this—from ten to five, then it's down to the final two. If you make that," she beamed again, "you get to be on the *Today* show."

On second thought.

I tamped down a sudden case of nerves, arched an eyebrow, and went for the whole ultra cool vamp image. "Is that all?"

"Shirley called and said she needs a dress decision today."

"Oh, no." Bye, bye ultra vamp. Hello freaked out maid of honor. "Today?"

Evie nodded. "Otherwise there won't be enough time to order it. Unless you pick something off the rack."

Her words registered and snapped me out of my panic. My mind started to race.

"If you decide to go for rack," Evie went on," the seamstress still needs six weeks to make the appropriate alterations—"

"That's it," I cut in. "We can have the dress altered. All this angsting and the answer has been right there all along. So obvious. So easy." I smiled for the first time since climbing out of bed. "You're a genius, Evie. A total genius."

"All in a day's work." She sipped her latte and went back to her computer.

I walked into my office, phoned Mandy, and told her Evie's sudden brainstorm.

"Do you really think you can find someone to fix whatever dress we pick out?"

"Sure we can. Granted, we can't go to any of the other bridal shops around town because they would all want to take credit for the dress, if they'd even touch it in the first place. And we can't let Shirley's seamstress do it because then she would know that we hate the dress."

"Won't she know that anyway when we show up at the wedding with a different dress?"

"A fantabulous dress," I told my soon-to-be sister-in-law. "Which she will get full credit for. She'll be so busy signing up brides that she won't have time to wonder what happened."

"Maybe."

"Would you stop being so negative? It's all going to work out."

"Your mother stopped by today and brought Jack dinner."

"My mother stopped at your place?" Jacqueline must really be worried. "That doesn't sound so bad." I tried to play off the gravity of the situation. "A bottle from Giovanni's or the new imported stuff from Angelo's?"

"A Rockette named Lola. I told you, she hates me. She wants to break us up."

"Lola isn't a break-up attempt. She's food. Surely Jack didn't—"

"No. He loves me. But what's going to happen in ten years when I start to get old and Lola doesn't?"

"Was she a vampire?"

"No, you're missing the point. There will always be another Lola and Jack will always be young."

"And so will you if you're really serious about committing to him."

"I know. I mean, we've discussed it. He's going to turn me. We just thought we would wait until after we got married. I mean, there's no rush at this second. I'm just letting my nerves get to me. With the dress on top of that, I can barely function."

"You'll soon be able to cross that off your list of freak-outs because this is so going to work."

"You're sure we can find a seamstress?"

"It's a needle and thread, not rocket science. There has to be *somebody*."

Twenty-four

♥ ♥ ♥

"**S**orry. I only do minor alterations. You couldn't pay me enough to touch a wedding dress." *Click*.

I crossed yet another name off the list Evie had printed out of local seamstresses and dry cleaners.

While it wasn't hard to find someone to perform basic stuff—hems, waist tucks, tapering—no one, I repeat NO ONE, wanted to touch a wedding dress.

"They have specialists for that," Jowanna Truman told me. She was seamstress number twenty-three on my list of—ahem—twenty-five.

"Do you know anyone who could help me out?" *You do*, I sent out the mental thought on the off chance that Jowanna, mother of five and devoted wife to Tim, might be attracted to the same sex and, therefore, putty in my manicured hands. *You know someone who would be happy to help me. Ecstatic, even. And you're going to give me their name right now.*

"I've got a girlfriend who does wedding dresses, but she already works for two downtown designers. She's got her hands full."

Hey, you can't blame a vamp for trying.

I contemplated making my standard offer—love and happily ever after courtesy of a Dead End Dating profile and three prospective matches, but Jowanna's husband owned the dry cleaners adjacent to Seams Sew Good, her alterations shop, and so they met for lunch—and for a quickie—everyday. (I'd gleaned this info from Tim, who *had* been putty in my hands. Too bad he didn't know any seamstresses other than his wife.) Together, they were a pretty solid couple, which meant they didn't need a matchmaker. Maybe a babysitter for the kids on account of they were driving Tim up the wall and he'd like for once—just ONCE—to be able to watch the Knicks without a bunch of yip-yap going on.

But I digress.

Point is, no go.

I hung up the phone and eyeballed the last two possibilities. Both were in Chinatown—i.e., New York's Asian mecca—and while I had nothing against some really tasty chai or a silk kimono, I'd already called one seamstress in the same locale and hadn't understood a word she'd said.

I know, I know. Ultrapowerful vamp. Impervious to bullets, bruises, and bunions.

But we're talking an *accent*.

I set the list aside, checked my e-mail, and flipped through folders for our latest Dead End Dating clients. Four were women who'd been at the dinner cruise (and hadn't made it to the final ten). Three actually wanted dates while one, I was pretty sure, just wanted the inside scoop on my Speedy Gonzales impersonation. She'd filled out a profile and asked for a personal meeting with *moi*.

"She said she needs the best of the best and won't work with any dating expert besides you." That's what Evie had told me.

I'd spent all of five seconds gloating—hey, I *was* pretty good—before reality had kicked in. Reporter. Hot vampire with really hot shoes. It was a bad headline just waiting to happen.

I eyed the fifth folder in my stack. Gwen Rowley. Part-time PI and full-time man hater. I turned to my computer and did a few searches for men with an interest in amateur photography. I hit pay dirt twice. I ran another search for men with obnoxious mothers. Half the names in my database scrolled across the screen. Okay, narrow the search to men with obnoxious mothers in city government. There. One match.

Three possibilities. Can I follow through or what?

I buzzed Evie to pull the three charts so I could take a closer look before I turned to the dinner-cruise women. I was just about to do another search when it hit me.

What was I doing cold-calling seamstresses? I should be tapping my own database, searching for someone, anyone, that I'd matched up. If they felt eternally indebted to me for their happiness, I could surely talk them into doing a few nips and tucks on one of Shirley's dresses.

I typed in sewing and waited for the bevy of choices to scroll across my screen.

A single name popped up and I groaned.

Esther Crutch. Esther was a made vampire I'd be-friended when I'd first opened my business. I'd been trying to hook her up ever since, but she wasn't ex-actly the easiest match. Problem one? Esther had been turned into a vampire back in the 1800's when beauty equaled ten to twenty extra pounds and zero makeup. While she'd invested in enough MAC to im-press even me, there wasn't a thing she could do about the extra baggage she was carrying around on her hips. Problem two? She wanted to spend eternity with a made male vampire who appreciated full-figured women and enjoyed *Bonanza* reruns. The thing was, no male MV appreciated a full-figured anything. They all wanted to kick it with Jennifer Lopez or Jessica Biel. And since they had gobs of charisma and sex appeal (see Webster's for *vamp*), they could. Also, since they were so busy kickin' it, they had no free time for TV.

I brought up Esther's profile and scanned her likes and dislikes. Sure enough, she'd listed sewing under *Hobbies*. Along with crochet, macramé, and ceram-ics (yawn).

Picking up the phone, I punched in her number.

"Hey, Es. It's Lil."

"Lil? I'm so glad you called! Thanks so much for the face cream you sent over. I loved it."

"Did it work?"

"No, but it smells really good. Like cucumbers. And it tastes good, too."

"You ate some?"

"No, but one of my cats did."

Okay, I know I should have been freaked that some poor feline had slurped up a two-hundred-dollar jar of cream, but the stuff was completely organic and harmless. Which meant I freaked on the real disaster. "*You* have a *cat*?"

"Why, yes. Actually, I've got four. I used to hate animals. In fact, I swore I would never get even one. But then I found this stray and she followed me home."

Yikes. Where have I heard this story before?

"One thing led to another and there I was, cuddling on the couch with Mindy. Now I have four total. What about you?"

I thought of Killer. "Nope. No cats." I told you I did denial really well. "Not a single, smelly, needy, snotty one."

"That's a shame. You're really missing out. Animals are wonderful company. Provided, of course, you train them to stay off the furniture with one of those spray bottles. I just squirt Miffy on the nose when she does something she's not supposed to and bam, instant cooperation. Oh, and make sure you change the litter every day. And don't put the box too close to the phone. Why, I tripped just yesterday trying to pick up a sales call and landed face-first—"

"Not a possibility," I cut in. "Not for me. No cats, remember?" I faked a shiver. "Just the thought gives me the creepies. Listen," I rushed on, determined to get us off the topic, "I'm calling because you mentioned in your profile that you liked to sew."

"That's right. Don't tell me you've found someone who likes to sew? Because I'm right in the middle of this gorgeous quilt and it would be so much fun to have someone help me out—"

"No, no quilters." I don't even want to think what a made vampire who likes to quilt would look like. "I'm not calling about a match. I'm calling to ask a favor. See, I've got this wedding dress that needs alterations. It's for my brother's fiancée and it just isn't right the way it is. I thought if we could find someone who knew how to use a needle and thread, they might be able to change it up for us."

"Gee. Yeah." She sounded as doom and gloom as I suddenly felt. "I did make my own clothes and everything," Esther had grown up predepartment store, "but they didn't look anything like what's out there today. As for an actual wedding dress . . . I've always wanted to try one, but I never had the chance." Her voice ended on a note of melancholy that made me feel like the worst matchmaker in Manhattan.

I couldn't even match up poor, lonely Esther.

I was a loser. I was worse than a loser. I was a needy loser trying to scrounge a favor out of a poor, lonely, desperate vampire.

Enough with the pity party, already. There's no sense in the both of you being desperate. Just get on with it. You can make it up to her later.

I sucked it up and gathered my determination. "You could think of this as training for the real thing, which, I'm sure, is just right around the corner."

"Really?"

Yes. The lie was there on the tip of my tongue, but for some reason it stalled. "I don't have any prospects," I heard myself say. Hey, I didn't do guilt any better than murder or mayhem or polyester. "But as soon as I'm finished with my brother's wedding and a few other pressing issues that are on my plate right now, I'll find you someone. I swear. I'm going to hit every made vamp hangout in Manhattan. And Queens. And Brooklyn. And I'll even head out to," I swallowed, "Long Island."

"No way. You would do that for me?"

"If you'll do this for me. Please, Esther. I really need your help."

"I suppose I could give it a try. I still have my sewing machine around here somewhere. But just don't expect too much, okay?"

"Believe me, nothing could be worse than what we've got."

Literally.

While Mandy had called Shirley and picked the least hideous of the bunch, it still had a dozen yards of itchy tulle. And mega beads. And bows. And ick. I felt certain anything Esther came up with would be an improvement.

At least, I was hoping.

I held tight to the notion and chatted for a few minutes about a new stomach wrap I'd seen at my tanning spa just last week. Esther promised to try it (she tried everything on the off chance that her vamp DNA would give out and she would somehow, someway morph into Nicole Ritchie).

"Thanks, Lil. I'll talk to you later."

"Yeah." I summoned my courage and stopped her just before she hung up the phone. "Wait." I licked my lips as the question formed. "Suppose I did have a cat, which I don't. But just *suppose* I had this friend who had a cat and he kept clawing at her favorite leather sofa. What sort of bottle would my friend buy to discourage the bad behavior?"

"Are we talking scratches or gouges?"

"Slicing and dicing."

"Get an extra large garden variety, fill it with water, and nail the little bugger every time he even looks at the furniture."

I smiled. "I can do that."

"There's a new sheriff in town," I told Killer later that night as I held up the bottle I'd picked up on the way home. "And her name is Lil Marchette."

Twenty-five
♥ ♥ ♥

"I don't see how this is going to help me have a great date," Word said as I attacked his hair with a comb and a bottle of detangler Thursday evening.

We were in my office, Word seated in front of me in a chair. He eyed his reflection in the small mirror I'd set up on my desk. Evie had left the moment I'd walked in with my bag of tricks.

"I know you want to help him but trust me. He's a lost cause."

Since I didn't know the meaning of the word, I'd walked into my office to face Thursday night's challenge: Turning Word from scary into succulent—or at least palatable.

"Trust me," I told him, setting down my comb and reaching for the bottle of spray. "Women love a man with good hair."

"I don't want her to love me."

"Trust me. Women are more likely to like a man with good hair." I sprayed a full minute before grabbing my comb. "Did you wash it like I asked?" I struggled to pull the comb through but it wouldn't budge.

"I washed it three days ago. I didn't see a reason to wash it *again*."

"No, no. Of course not. Then you might actually smell like soap instead of an old gym sock." I thumped him. "What's wrong with you? You have a date tomorrow night. Aren't you the least bit excited?"

"Of course I am. I've had a walking boner for days. Ouch." He rubbed his head where I'd thumped him again. "What did you do that for?"

"Can't you think about anything besides sex? Don't you want a woman to admire you? To appreciate you? To look into your eyes and fall head over heels?"

"I'd rather have sex."

I blew out an exasperated breath and drank in another to help slow my pounding heart. *Easy,* I told my inner vamp. *Do not attack. He's just a kid.*

"That or a blow job."

My fangs slithered forward and I hissed, and then I pinched his arm like a mother.

He yelped and nearly toppled the chair. "What'd you do that for?" he managed after several gulps and a few girly whimpers.

"Because you're an idiot. I've found the perfect

woman for you and you're going to screw it up because you can't think beyond your dick." *Human* males.

Then again, I'd just described every male from made vamp to born, were to demon.

I drew another deep breath. I wasn't going to pinch. Or thump. Or kick. Or rip his balls off. No, I was going to reason with him. To appeal to him on his own level.

"Trust me," I tried again, spritzing more detangler onto his spiked locks. "Women get extremely turned on by men with good hair. And good hygiene. And nice clothes—or at least clean ones. And they'll practically orgasm on the spot if you open the door for them or look them in the eyes rather than the chest." Okay, so I knew I was fudging the expectations a little, but I needed a surefire way to get Word's attention.

His eyes brightened. Bingo. "You mean, she might actually come, too?"

It was clear Word hadn't considered anything beyond his own good time. Another trait human men had in common with the other various species.

"As foreign as the concept is, yes, it's possible. And highly likely if you play your cards right. And I can tell you one thing, if you think it feels good when you get off, it's nothing compared to how you're going to feel if she gets off, too."

"No way."

"Total way."

He touched his hair and eyed his reflection before

seeming to come to a conclusion. "This had better work or I'm disconnecting the entire docking station *and* the speakers."

I smiled. "Like a charm." I gave up my present course of action and opted for a new idea. I set the comb and detangler aside.

"What are you doing?"

"It's what we're doing." I grabbed my purse and motioned him to follow me.

He pushed up from the chair. "What are *we* doing?"

"Finding a shower."

His eyes lit and he gave me a hopeful look. "Are you going to get in with me?"

"Not without a decontamination suit. Now move."

I took him to my place, herded him into a hot, steaming shower, handed him shampoo and a bar of soap, and left Killer sleeping—er—guarding the door until I returned.

I headed several blocks over via furry pink bat (I didn't trust Killer's guard dog instincts and the thought of a naked and wet Word mucking around my apartment for any length of time made me sort of queasy) to Pierre Claude's, a small men's shop owned by one of my fave designers.

Pierre was a genius with cut and color, and also a born vamp. He wasn't committed and I secretly suspected he was gay, which was another reason I liked him. Not because I prefer gay men in order to avoid investing in a real relationship (did I mention that I'd started watching Dr. Phil since I wasn't sleeping very well?). No, I liked him because gays were as unheard of among born vamps as, say, matchmakers.

"So what are you looking for today?" Pierre asked me, flashing me a dazzling smile. He wore a tailored white shirt, black slacks, and trendy black cowboy boots. He had a tape measure hanging around his neck. "Top? Bottom?" His eyes lit. "Undies?"

"You don't do undies."

He nodded. "I do as of yesterday." He pulled a pair of red silk nothings from his pocket. "What do you think?"

"If you can't wear it, you could always floss with it."

He grimaced and stared at the underwear. "Oh, well. It's still in the cooking phase. You want chic? Ultra chic?"

"Something simple."

"Jeans?"

"That would be good. Maybe a silk shirt or something clingy to show off muscle definition."

He growled and wiggled his eyebrows before reaching for a few suggestions. "These might work."

I eyed the black button-up. "Too Tim McGrawish."

He pulled out a red one and I shook my head. "Too Tom Jonesish."

He pulled out a blue spotted shirt and I grimaced. "Too Blues Cluesish."

"Why don't I leave you alone and go get a glass of champagne?"

"I'd love a glass."

"Not for you, darling. For me." He shook his head and muttered "Female vampires," as he walked away. "This is why I'd sooner castrate myself."

Um, thanks a lot for *that* image.

I spent the next few minutes flipping through his latest collection until I'd found a few possibilities. I handed over my credit card and headed back home. I arrived to find Word wrapped in nothing but a table, plopped on my sofa, Killer curled up in his lap.

"You were supposed to keep him contained," I told the cat.

For a few scratches behind the ear and an extra can of cat food, I'll jump ship for anybody.

"You wouldn't happen to have on underwear, would you?"

"Nope."

I swallowed against the sick feeling in my stomach and tossed the clothes at him.

"What's this?"

"There's an outfit for you to wear tonight to sort of acclimate your body to decent fabric, and another for tomorrow night." When he continued to stare, I added, "It's your new look."

"But I like my old look."

"You're the only one." I pointed toward the bathroom. "Go."

When Word started to grumble, I rolled my eyes heavenward and gave my loudest, most ear-splitting

"Yesssssssssssss!" followed by lots of panting and moaning and a long, shuddering sigh.

His ears turned red and I was pretty sure he'd decided to change. Just to emphasize my point, I grabbed the super deluxe water bottle.

Killer took one look, jumped to the floor, and scrambled for cover.

"You wouldn't," Word told me.

"Oh, wouldn't I?"

He made a beeline for the bathroom to change while I disinfected the couch.

"What do you think?" he asked a few minutes later when he returned.

I swept a glance from his head to his toes and tried not to grimace (at the toes, not the in between). "You look hot."

"Really?" Hope fueled the one tiny word and I actually went sort of soft. Sure, he was obsessed with sex. But he was young. Inexperienced. Deep down he really and truly did want to find that special someone and his insecurity was proof.

"Really." I stepped forward and ran my fingers through his freshly washed hair. "You look good with the whole wet head look. I say we leave it as is." My gaze dropped to his face. The peach fuzz that had covered his chin was now gone, his skin freshly shaven and slapped with aftershave. He smelled good, and I couldn't help but smile. "I'm really proud of you." I slid my arms around him and gave him a sisterly hug.

Which lasted all of five seconds before I heard his voice.

"Enough to have sex with me?"

"Don't ruin the moment." I finished my hug, stepped away, and left him to gather his dirty clothes from my bathroom while I answered my cellphone.

A quick glance at the caller ID and my heart kicked into overdrive.

"What is it?" I blurted the moment I hit TALK.

"We have a lead," Ash told me.

"You're kidding. Really?"

"One of Moe's contacts ID'd Ty. He claims he saw him with a man a few weeks ago right around the time he would have disappeared. He's giving us a sketch and we're going to see if we can trace the man's identity. Moe's contact said he heard Ty call the guy something that sounded like Morgan. Or Borgan. Something like that. Does that ring a bell?"

My mind rushed back through the scene, but I couldn't come up with anything solid. "Maybe. I'm not sure."

"Well, think about it and call me if you make any kind of a connection or remember anything else. And FYI, you can fire up your computer. You'll be getting a new client soon."

I perked up despite my anxiety. "You're lonely and ready to settle down?"

"No, but Moe and Debbie had such great sex last night that she doesn't want to settle for any more losers. She's giving up the profession and going back to college full-time. And she's going to let you match her up."

"Great," I said, but I didn't actually feel it in my gut. In my mind, I was still rehashing the episode with Ty and the shadow. "I give a finder's fee."

"Sex?"

I snapped out of worried mode and frowned. "What is it with males and sex?"

"Sex makes the world go 'round, sweetheart."

"So sayeth a man. A free profile and one potential match. And I'll throw in a dozen doughnuts. Take it or leave it."

"Debbie can have the free profile. She'll need it. She's on a budget."

"How about the doughnuts?"

"A man can't have too many Krispy Kremes."

I couldn't resist. "A man or a demon?"

He chuckled. "You still don't know?"

"I'm betting demon."

"Think," he said. "And give me a call."

"I have been and I've even Googled entities from hell. You've got all the characteristics—good looks, flaming eyes, sex appeal. That, or you're taking some new pheromone that makes you irresistible to the opposite sex."

"I meant think about Ty and the man who was with him."

"Oh." I pushed aside all the thoughts muddying my brain and pictured Ty's face.

"See what you can come up with."

"I will." And I did for the rest of the night and all

through most of the next day—until I started cleaning, that is.

I know, I know. Was I sliding into a pile of domestic muck so deep I might never climb out? Maybe, but I couldn't seem to help myself. I needed a distraction. That on top of the fact that I'd had Word in my bathroom and on my couch, and was a woman on a mission.

By the time the next night rolled around, my apartment was spotless and I was dead tired. No, really. To the point that I seriously considered calling the producers of *Manhattan's Most Wanted* and telling them I'd been stricken with a dangerous bug and was now quarantined at a local hospital.

At the same time, I couldn't *not* show without stirring real suspicion because of what had happened during the dinner cruise. I already had one reporter interested in me. I wasn't going to shake things up even more. I mean, really. What normal, sane woman in her right mind would forfeit a chance to get to know Manhattan's hottest weather guy? Nada. That's why I had to go. Otherwise someone would suspect I wasn't a normal, sane woman. Enter Vinnie and his brother, and I'd be paying through the nose with highlighters and reams of copy paper.

Which left me with one choice—show up, be obnoxious, and get Mr. Weather to cut me himself. I would then react in typical reality TV fashion—cry and act appropriately offended because, of course, after three pseudo dates I'd fallen madly in love with him. That, or I could cuss and spit in typical VH1 fashion. But that might lead to an *I Love Lil* series and I so wouldn't be able to explain that to my folks. No, better to go for the waterworks and go sobbing into the night.

Bye, bye reality show.

Not that I would be able to breathe a sigh of relief or bask in the impressive number of clients I'd picked up thanks to the show. I still had to find Ty, make it through my mother's dinner party, and fix Mandy's wedding dress.

I forced aside the sudden icky feeling that crept over me. One problem at a time.

Twenty-six

"Get. Out. Of. *Here*." Esther's mouth dropped open as she stared at the ornate white dress Mandy and I had come by to drop off at her place on Friday evening. "I've never seen anything like it."

"I know it seems overwhelming, but I have the utmost faith in you." I patted her on the back. "You can do it."

She stared at the dress, struck speechless for a long moment.

I totally knew the feeling.

"It's just so . . ." she finally started, but her voice faded away as she swallowed a huge lump in her throat.

"I know, I know. It's loud. And busy. And scary. But so was the entire DKNY collection last season, but then they hired Janie Strausberg and look at it now. Tasteful. A bit eclectic, but I'm down with that. And hip. She took a bad situation and turned it into a positive. And that's what you're going to do."

She dabbed at her eyes and guilt rifled through me. "There, there. Please don't cry. Because then I'll want to cry and I so don't need to be crying since I'm going to be in front of a handful of television cameras in less than two hours." Which was why I'd cried on the way over with plenty of time to retouch.

Mandy and I both had.

"It's just so . . . *beautiful*."

"I know we're asking a lot, but . . . What did you just say?"

She sniffled and wiped at her damp eyes. "I said it's the most amazing dress I've ever seen." She stared in awe. "I've always wanted a dress just like this."

"Like *this*?"

She nodded several times. "Down to the tiny bows lining the hem. And dotting the skirt. And that great big one in back."

"*These* bows?"

"And the beaded bodice."

"*This* bodice?"

"And the six-foot train with the extra doodads."

"*That* train?"

"Why, it's straight out of my favorite fantasy. There isn't a thing about it that I would change." Her gaze collided with mine. "This can't be the dress you were talking about."

"Of course not," I blurted.

Mandy nudged me and shot me a *tell her* look.

I stiffened. Enter ballsy, do anything, dare anyone, don't-take-shit vampire extraordinaire. I opened my mouth, and prepared to give it to Esther straight. *It's the worst dress in the Free World and if we weren't so desperate, we would take it out, shoot it, and put it out of its misery.* "Maybe."

Yeah, yeah, my aim was definitely skewed, but we're talking Esther's *dream* dress. I couldn't very well tell her the thing had starred in the last *Nightmare on Elm Street* and that she really, *really* needed to get a life because she was obviously clueless when it came to fashion.

My gaze swept the small but tidy apartment, the old movie posters—everything from *Giant* to *The Lone Ranger*—lining the wall. Yep, she was a few accessories shy of a complete outfit when it came to decorating, as well.

My attention shifted to the pile of knitting that sat near the couch, the stack of crossword puzzles piled on the coffee table. And she *so* needed to spice up her extracurricular activities. Honestly, the made vampire was lonely and depraved enough. Who was I to pour salt on the wound by telling her her dreams sucked, as well?

"So where's the real dress?" she asked. She motioned to the ancient sewing machine that sat in the corner. It looked like an old-fashioned wrought iron desk, with pedals rather than a footboard. "I'm armed and ready."

Mandy nudged me and I cleared my throat. Just

do it. "Look, Esther, it's like this. Everyone has different tastes. Some people like cheesecake. Some prefer chocolate. Some people like Brad Pitt. Some women go ga-ga over Toby Keith. It's all about personal preference."

"What are you trying to say?"

"That maybe," I swallowed, "possibly," another swallow, "this might be the dress." There. All done. And I didn't spontaneously combust or turn into a big cat turd.

"But that's crazy. What could you possibly want to change about something that's already perfect?"

Mandy and I exchanged glances. "Everything," we said in unison.

"You're kidding, right?" She glanced past us. "This isn't some game show, is it? Am I being punked?"

"Don't I wish." Hey, we're talking Ashton Kutcher. He didn't rate a full ten on my Orgasm-O-Meter, but he came in a solid seven at least. I cleared my throat and focused on the white blob. "You don't think it's a tad on the busy side?" I asked Esther.

She shook her head. "Certainly not."

"What about poofy? You have to agree that it's a little poofy."

"No."

"What about full?"

"Not in the least."

"What about distracting?"

"It's a wedding dress. It's supposed to draw everyone's attention."

I shrugged. "Good point," I said and Mandy elbowed me. "Listen, Esther. Mandy here isn't the big, distracting dress type. She likes things more simple."

Esther nodded. "You mean plain."

"Exactly. While you or I wouldn't think twice about jumping into this baby, Mandy really doesn't have the joi de vivre to pull it off."

"Thanks a lot."

I patted Mandy's shoulder and gave her a pleading look that said, "Follow me, okay?" "Mandy isn't an extravagant person. She's more wholesome. Conservative. Blah." Mandy stiffened and I kept patting. "You don't want her to feel uncomfortable, do you?"

"No, no. Absolutely not. It's her wedding day. She should feel like a queen."

"Exactly. And that isn't going to happen if she has to wear this dress. She wants something that fits her personality better. That's where you come in. You can nip here, tuck a little there, and it'll be perfect for her."

"What changes did you have in mind?"

I pulled out the two-page list Mandy and I had jotted down on the cab ride over.

Esther took one look and shook her head. "This is a lot more than a few nips and tucks." She shook her head. "Maybe I'm not the right person for this."

"Nonsense. You've got the experience. The know-how. And a whopping six weeks to get it all done."

"That's impossible." She gave another shake of her head. "I can't do this."

"Maybe she's right," Mandy piped up. She wore a worried expression and a hopeless light glittered in her eyes. "This is a stupid idea."

Ditto. "No, it isn't. It's a glam idea, and it's going to work." It had to because it was all I'd been able to come up with. "That, or you can wear the dress as is."

"Or I can not wear it at all and call the whole thing off."

"Over this lovely thing?"

Mandy shook her head. "Please. Would you stop saying that?"

"That it's lovely?"

She nodded. "It isn't. It's awful."

Esther looked as if someone had kicked the big fat tabby parked on her couch. "You really think so?"

"No," I cut in. "I mean, yes, in her eyes, but to each his own, remember? You think it's lovely and, therefore, it is. But you're not wearing it. Mandy is, and she isn't as excited about the whole thing." I stared Esther in the eyes. "She isn't half the woman you are," I told the made vamp. "She can't pull off this look."

She seemed to think. "Not everyone can do petticoats," she finally admitted.

"Exactly, which is why we'd like you to rip them off and taper the skirt down some."

"But," she started and caught her lip. She cast a glance at Mandy, who looked as if someone had actually kicked her instead of the cat. Sympathy flared in her eyes. "I suppose I could cut out at least one of the petticoat layers."

"Really?" Mandy looked hopeful and Esther nodded.

"Maybe even two." She eyed the dress again and her hand dove beneath the layers of fabric. "But I won't lie. I'm not so sure we can taper the skirt without compromising the integrity of the dress, and I won't do that." She gave her head a firm shake. "I couldn't live with myself if I butchered this precious creation."

I waited for the birds to chirp and a cloud of fairy dust to rain down on us.

Instead, my cellphone rang. "Just do what you can," I told her before I punched the talk button and repeated Suze's address for the fifth time. "Now stop stalling and GO ON THE DATE."

"All right, already," Word mumbled before the line went dead. I punched off, slid the phone into my purse, and told Esther how grateful we were for her help. "Just do what you can," I added.

She agreed, halfheartedly, and Mandy and I caught a cab for the morgue. Mandy was on duty tonight and I was dropping her off on my way.

"You're looking very colorful tonight," Mandy said as we barreled down Fifty-seventh. "And glittery."

I'd gone all out with a hot-pink Chanel dress, silver Louis Vuitton handbag, strappy Manolo Blahnik stilettos, and enough jewelry to weigh down the average mob hit. Makeup wise, I'd gone for a cross between Fairytopia Barbie and Lil' Kim. Glitter eye shadow. Lots of eyeliner. Sparkling Ruby MAC lips, Pink Obsession glitter blush, and Dazzling Dust nail polish.

"I'm trying to make a statement," I told Mandy.

"And that would be *Don't bother me. I'm in the middle of an acid trip*?"

"*Don't pick me. I'm a camera hog.*"

She shrugged. "That was my second guess. So what do you think will happen with the dress?" Mandy asked.

"Are you asking Lil the realist or Lil the optimist?"

"There is no Lil the realist."

"That would be door number two, then. Let's see . . . Esther will realize that the dress is a hideous monstrosity, and since she's a die-hard romantic who fantasizes about her own wedding, she'll go above and beyond the call of duty to make yours as extra special as it can be. She'll kill herself day and night until the dress is a vision of loveliness. You'll walk down the aisle, say, "I do" with a smile on your face, and you and my brother will live happily ever after."

"She's not going to pull off the bows, is she?"

"Not a chance."

She seemed to think. "This is hopeless, isn't it? Your brother and I . . ." She caught a sob. "We're not going to make it."

"That's crazy. The two of you are already making it. You're living together. You're putting up with him and he's putting up with you. You don't mind that he leaves his dirty socks on the floor and he doesn't mind that you drape your wet bras all over the bathroom shower." When she gave me a questioning look, I shrugged. "I'm a vamp, remember? Anyhow, you're dealing with the bottles of leftover blood that he keeps leaving on the counter and he's dealing with the granola wrappers all over the nightstand. He's putting up with your work schedule. And you're putting up with our mother."

"And Luc."

I nailed her with a gaze. "She sent over Luc, too?" She nodded, and a rush of envy shot through me.

Luc was my mother's favorite manicurist. He could do a French mani in ten seconds flat, and he gave the yummiest paraffin-wax hand treatments. And his pedis? My. My. *My.* Talk about delish.

"Tell Jack I absolutely hate him," I added. My gaze zeroed in on the fingers that Mandy had curled around her purse. "You, too?"

She looked sheepish. "He's right there at our beck and call. It seems like such a waste just to let him sit around and watch cable all day. I mean, really, Jack can only get his toenails filed so many times a day, you know?"

Yep, unfortunately, I did.

"I could always postpone the wedding," she added after a long moment. "I don't want to, but sometimes I think it's the only thing left to do. Nothing seems to want to work out."

I thought of the two voice mails I'd had when I'd

checked my cell messages before arriving at Esther's apartment. There'd been one from Evie about a few recent clients, one from Word wanting to verify Suze's address, and zero from my mother. I couldn't remember the last time she'd gone a full twenty-four hours without calling me.

She was obviously too busy doling out servants to Jack and plotting ways to break up his relationship with Mandy to bother with her daughter.

Hip, hip, hurray!

For now. But if Jack and Mandy called it quits, then I would be right back where I started.

"Nonsense." Determination gripped me. "The hotel is a sure thing and I'm confident that Esther will come through for us." Just like I was confident I could get myself X'd off the reality show (fingers crossed) and find Ty (fingers *and* toes crossed) before it was too late. "We just have to think positive."

"That, or we could suck down a few chocolate martinis before you drop me off."

I glanced at my watch and thought of my crazy—and slightly uncertain—evening ahead. (Yeah, I had a plan, but that didn't mean it was going to work.) "I *do* have an hour before the *MMW* limo picks me up."

She nodded. "That settles it then. Positive is out. Getting sloshed is in."

I was *so* going to need an AA meeting when my afterlife finally settled down.

Twenty-seven
♥ ♥ ♥

I'd just stepped out of the cab in front of Dead End Dating when a black limousine rolled up to the curb and a uniformed driver got out. He opened the door for me and I climbed in with the other nine finalists.

Ten minutes later, the car pulled up to Central Park where the official date would launch with individual carriage rides for each of the finalists with—you guessed it—the infamous Mr. Weather. Meanwhile, the rest of us would suck down cocktails and talk to the cameras at a sidewalk café that had been set up, complete with tables and a uniformed waitstaff. Lights twinkled in the trees overhead. Beyond, the moon hung high in the sky and the stars glittered hot and bright and . . .

Deep sigh.

It truly was the most romantic setup I'd ever seen, right down to the white carriage wrapped in a garland of red roses.

The producer herded everyone over to the sidewalk café while a kindergarten teacher by the name of Pamela Sue Mitchell, who was up first, headed for the white carriage and Mr. Weather.

He looked as perfect as ever in a pair of black Armani slacks and a royal blue shirt. His hair had been coiffed with gel and his fingernails buffed and polished. He held a single rose as he waited for the first contestant, a smile on his handsome face.

I put on my best game face and stepped forward.

I moved at the speed of light, zooming in between Pam and Mr. Weather before anyone realized what had happened.

"Me first, me first," I cried. I snatched the rose from his hand and leaned in front of him just as the camera zoomed in on us.

I beamed for a close-up while he blew out a mouthful of my hair.

"What are you doing?" he asked as he pushed me out of the way.

"I'm always first," I told him. "Just relax and go with it. The cameras are rolling." Before he could get out another word, I climbed into the carriage and settled into the seat, my rose in hand.

Mr. Weather exchanged a few words with the producers before they finally came up for air. He pasted on his smile and climbed in beside me while a production assistant herded a shocked Pamela back toward the makeshift sidewalk café.

"I like your enthusiasm," he said, but he didn't sound half as happy as he looked.

My own smile widened. "You haven't seen anything yet."

Just as he settled into the seat next to me, I shrieked, "Wait, wait. I have to get a picture of this."

"There are a dozen cameras recording everything."

"It's not the same thing. There's no guarantee that this will make it on the air and I *have* to show my friends. They are never going to believe this." I pulled out the disposable camera I'd picked up on the way over.

"Nick"—Mr. Weather started to motion to one of the producers—"could you help us out here?"

"Oh, don't bother him." I shoved the camera into his hand. "You can handle it. Just aim and click." I struck my best pose.

"But I thought you wanted to show your friends?"

"I do. They are so not going to believe how good my hair did tonight. We're talking yummy perfection." When he just sat there, I waved a hand at him. "Go on. Snap a pic. In fact, snap a couple. I've got family, too."

The camera *click, click, clicked* and I shifted into several different poses. There. Here. Now. Perfect.

"You're a sweetie." I snatched the camera from his hands and stuffed it back into my purse.

"Don't you want to get a picture of us?"

I shook my head. "No."

"Are you sure?"

"I guess I could." I eyed him. "But do you really want a bunch of pictures circulating with your hair looking like that?"

He touched a hand to his head in alarm. "What's wrong with it?"

"Well, for starters, you've got a ton of strands out of place."

He shook his head. "I don't have even one hair out of place." Another shake. "That's crazy."

I shrugged and pulled out the camera. "Hey, it's your career."

He flashed me an exasperated look and his gaze collided with mine. Bingo.

His gaze sparked as I stared deep into his eyes and sent the silent message.

I'm just confirming what you've thought since leaving your Park Avenue apartment. Tonight just isn't your hair night. While most of it is cooperating beautifully, there are those few wayward strands that keep working themselves loose. You tried telling the studio stylist that they weren't cooperating, but she wouldn't listen. And now look what's happened. Everyone is noticing. Staring. Smirking.

"Forget it," he blurted. "No pictures. Please."

I patted his hand and gave him an understanding look. "Don't worry. I'm sure no one else will notice. Oops, then again, some of this is going to be on television so it's possible someone might notice."

Like, say, several million viewers.

"I need a mirror!" He shot to his feet and a production assistant rushed forward, mirror in hand. Mr. Weather spent the next few minutes smoothing and slicking at several invisible hairs near his temple while I posed for camera shots with the carriage driver.

Fifteen minutes later, we settled into the carriage and the ride started. The horses clopped their way around Central Park for several minutes while a small golf cart filled with the producer and two cameramen kept time next to us. Another camera guy rode up front with the driver, the lens trained on us as Mr. Weather explained the difference between a funnel cloud and an actual tornado.

Yawn.

Literally.

I opened my mouth and let loose the biggest, loudest *aggghhhhhh* I could manage, followed by a "Sorry for zoning out. It's not you. Really."

We kept riding, he kept talking, and I kept yawning for another five minutes until we were deep into the park. I leaned free of the door, summoned my inner vamp, and directed a furious red glare at our horses.

They stumbled and danced as the driver fought for control. The camera guy fell from his perch, hitting the ground and rolling out of the way just as the horses reared up.

They bolted, and just like that, we were speeding through Central Park. The wind rushed at us and I shouted, "Yippee," while Mr. Weather tried to duck for cover and save his carefully styled hair.

I smiled and pretended indifference to the damage being done to my own (a vamp had to do what a vamp had to do) and shoved my hands into the air, leaning and twisting like I was riding the Big Boy at Coney Island.

Just as the thought struck, I had the crazy sensation that it meant something, but then the carriage twisted and I forgot everything except putting on a great show for the golf cart speeding in our wake.

Ten minutes and lots of whimpering later (Mr. Weather, not the horses), the animals calmed down (courtesy of yours truly and more Super Vamp mind skills) and the carriage finally came to a stop.

I swallowed my heart, which had jumped into my throat (I'm a vamp, not a stuntwoman) and summoned a look of pure excitement. "Wow." I turned to Mr. Weather.

He wore a stunned expression, his hair standing straight up, his skin a pale, pasty white despite his spray-on tan.

I jabbed him. "That was *so* cool. Let's do it again."

"I have to get out of here," he mumbled. He shook his head, as if trying to get a grip. "Get me out of here!" he yelled, and the entire crew rushed toward us.

"But you've got nine more carriage rides left," I reminded him as he scrambled to his feet. "Unless you're feeling me as much as I'm feeling you." His gaze collided with mine. "If that's the case, why don't you go ahead and send everyone else home. We'll take another ride, just the two of us, and see just how fast this baby can go."

He gave me a horrified look and fumbled to open the door.

"Wait," I called after him as he landed on his feet and stumbled forward. *Stop,* I willed. *Turn.* He did and I snapped several quick pics before he got his bearings. "I can't wait to post these on my MySpace page."

His mouth dropped open and he looked ready to cry. He whirled and rushed toward the hair and makeup tent that had been set up near the café.

I gave the evil eye to a couple of pigeons flying overhead. They promptly dropped a couple of presents. Mr. Weather screamed, tried to dodge, and slid across the pavement.

I smiled, pocketed my disposable camera, climbed out of the carriage, and headed for the other contestants, who had been watching from the sidelines.

I spent the next two hours sipping club soda and watching, with satisfaction, as Mr. Weather walked around Central Park with each contestant. It wasn't half as romantic as a carriage ride, but it was much easier on the hair. The evening ended with Mr. Weather saying goodbye to each participant. I stood in line and waited my turn, confident that I'd already made a lasting impression, one that he wouldn't soon forget if the mustard-yellow stain on his shirt was any indication.

"I had such fun," I told him when he reached me. "I wish, hope, yearn, pray that we can do it again. I just know we'll make fab babies together and every year we'll celebrate our wedding anniversary with a sentimental stampede through Central Park."

"Uh, yeah. Sure." He gave me a quick peck on the cheek before hurrying to the next woman. "Whatever."

I smiled, an expression that only widened when the producer approached me with the news.

"I'm afraid Mr. Weather isn't interested in getting to know you further. We hope you've had a positive experience on our show and we thank you for your interest in *Manhattan's Most Wanted*."

I summoned a flood of tears and spat, "The bastard!" as an assistant whisked me toward a waiting cab. Five other contestants followed, all equally broken up.

We split into groups of twos and climbed into the back of each cab, all equally torn up over our near brush with married bliss.

"I know we could have been beautiful together," I sobbed to Pamela, the kindergarten teacher who'd followed me into my cab.

"You guys did make a cute couple," she said, rubbing at her own eyes. "If it wasn't me, I thought for sure it would have been you."

Well, uh, yeah. I am a hot, happening, babelicious vamp.

"We would have had six sets of fraternal twins," I

said. "Six boys and an equal number of girls, and two nannies."

"I wanted four sets myself, but only one nanny. I'd planned to care for the kids myself using the Richard Alcott method of child rearing. What about you?"

"Definitely." Who the hell was Richard Alcott? "And at Christmas we would all drive upstate and pick a fresh tree at one of those farms and then gather around the fireplace in our eight-thousand-square-foot Connecticut mansion and drink hot cocoa."

"And sing Christmas carols."

I wouldn't go that far. "Oh, well." I sniffled and shivered. "I guess I'll just have to settle for a breast enlargement. Or maybe a tummy tuck. Something to cheer me up."

She flashed me a smile. "I'm getting my porcelain veneers replaced."

We chatted a few more minutes about various plastic surgeons. Actually, she chatted and I nodded because, obviously, being a Super Vamp, I stood a bigger chance of meeting Godzilla than a plastic surgeon.

The cab dropped Pam off at her Upper East Side apartment, and then whizzed back out into traffic and headed for my place. A few more minutes, several jarring turns, and I was home.

I climbed out, tipped the driver—a lonely, single twentysomething with nice abs and an addiction to *Dr. Quinn: Medicine Woman* reruns—with a Dead End Dating card, and a mental "You will call." The driver gave me one of those dazed and confused smiles, a huge thank-you, and then he pulled away. I was halfway up the front steps when I smelled the strange aroma.

My nostrils flared and the scent of mustard and diesel slid into my nose and made my heart pound. I glanced around, my gaze slicing through the darkness, but there was nothing there. Just sidewalk. A few plants here and there. More buildings.

My ears perked and dozens of sounds filtered through. The purr of Mrs. Janske's cats. The voice of a local announcer doing the nightly news. A couple arguing about mothers (were they the bane of everyone's existence?). The sound of potatoes sizzling on the stove. The whistle of a teapot. The *pop, pop, pop* of a popcorn machine—

Wait a second. My mind played a quick game of *Which of these sounds do not belong?*

The *pop, pop, pop* continued. Along with the voices. The sizzling potatoes. The groan of metal and the rattle of wood. The creak of a doorway. The sound of footsteps echoing on the concrete. The lash of a whip—

A fiery *whack* jagged up my back and I stumbled on the steps. My anger stirred, my fangs extended, and I whirled to face my attacker.

There was no one behind me. I turned. Left. Right. Around. My gaze cut through the darkness. I didn't see anyone.

But I could hear them. The footsteps. The crack of leather—

"*Shit*!" I cried as white-hot pain ripped through my arm and I fell toward the front door of my building.

I blinked against the pinpoints of light that danced in front of my eyes and felt for the door handle. I didn't know who or what, but something was after me and I had to get away.

I turned the knob. Metal groaned and twisted. The lock snapped open and I stumbled inside. I almost went for Mrs. Janske's door when I heard the voice, so pained and pleading, so Ty.

"*No.*" His frantic plea echoed through my head.

The whip cracked and the pain exploded and I fell to my knees for a long, heart-stopping moment.

"*There's more where that came from.*"

The strange voice beat at my temples, trying to push past the heat that gripped my senses, but it was no use. I couldn't think. Or see. Or hear. I could only feel. The white-hot sensation. The cold floor biting into my knees.

When I finally managed to get my footing, I stumbled toward the elevator. A few seconds later, I reached the safety of my apartment. I barely made it a few feet before another pain hit and I fell face-first to the floor.

I fought against the fire that danced up and down my spine. I panted. I wasn't sure why except that I felt like I had to do something and I knew—thanks to my mother who, on every one of my birthdays, felt compelled to share her horrific experience enduring hours and hours of hellacious labor—that breathing really fast, in and out, could sometimes help. It didn't do jack.

The only thing it did do was jar me out of whatever mental connection I'd had with Ty.

I lay there for several minutes, calling out to him, trying to reestablish the link, but he obviously wasn't answering.

Because he didn't want to?

Or because he couldn't?

The questions haunted me as the pain, slowly but surely, subsided. The gripping sensation turned to a steady throb and I became aware of my wet fingers and the soft fur brushing against my palm.

I cracked open one eye to see Killer licking my hands. He paused. His big green eyes collided with mine.

Get up, already. I'm hungry.

No "Gee, I'm sorry you've fallen and you can't get up" or "Wow, you must really be hurt to still be lying there like that."

"I hate you," I told him as I staggered to my feet.

Yeah, yeah. We've already established that. Now get your ass in the kitchen and open up one of those little cans before I get ugly.

I headed for the kitchen, found some cat food, and left Killer lapping up his snack while I headed into the bathroom. I peeled off my hot pink dress and eyed the angry red welt that ran diagonally across my back. Another oozed on the back of my arm. The left cheek of my ass. The back of my thigh.

What the hell was happening?

But I already knew. Ty had shut me out for so long but his will had finally dwindled. He'd endured too much. The pain. The confinement. His strength was sapped, his control fried. He was dying now, his defenses crumbling once and for all. Which meant he could no longer keep me out if I wanted to get in. We were one and the same now.

"There's more where that came from."

The voice echoed and my wounds throbbed and I knew then that the night was just starting.

Twenty-eight

❤ ❤ ❤

"Open your eyes."

I tried. Not because he told me to, but because I wanted to. I wanted to be conscious, eyes open, mind alert. My senses alive. Anything was better than lingering somewhere between afterlife and permanent death, lost in the pain, mindless with it.

But the hunger was even worse.

My gut twisted and clawed and my throat burned. My insides churned, pushing and pulling, driving me crazy. I felt my fangs against my swollen tongue, grazing the tender flesh, drawing a thin line of blood. But my own blood wasn't enough: too slow and sluggish and cold.

I needed fresh blood. Then I could think. Fight.

As if my thoughts had conjured it, I felt a drop of sweet, delicious heat against my lips. My mouth opened and my tongue moved of its own accord, lapping and sucking.

More! the hunger demanded, and it came, flowing sweetly into my mouth.

I drank greedily until there was no more.

But I needed more. Another taste. Another chance.

I forced my eyes open and stared through a blur at the shadow that loomed over me.

"I knew that would wake you up." The shadow grinned, the expression a startling break in the black mask of his face. "Time to rise and shine."

The words registered, but they couldn't get past the hunger that growled and clamored for more sustenance.

I licked my lips and blinked. "More."

"Oh, you'll have more, all right, but not by my hand. I've been the gracious benefactor long enough. It's time you started fending for yourself." He turned and walked to the corner and suddenly there were two shadows. Logan, that was his name, larger and more sinister, and a silhouette maybe half his size.

"Come along now," he said to the small, belligerent shape.

No. The dread welled, but then excitement came rolling in, crashing over me and washing everything else away.

I was hungry, and finally he was going to give me something to eat. It had been so long, so long that I'd stopped counting the days since I'd last eaten. I cast a quick glance at the window. Darkness again. More lights. Music blared in my ears, mingling with the thunder of my heart and the frantic pop, pop, pop of a machine.

"Now, now, don't fight. It'll be much easier if you don't fight." Logan laughed. "Then again, that's the point, now, isn't it? The harder you fight, the more exciting, eh?" He jerked the shadow the final few feet into the dance of colored lights that spilled from the window.

"Please, mister." The young boy tugged and pulled at Logan's hand. "You better let me go. My mom will be looking for me."

"She can look, my friend, but she won't find you. There'll be nothing left to find when my friend, here, is done."

I heard the creak of metal, felt the chains on my wrists tighten and release. And then days, weeks of confinement staggered to a halt. I was free.

I struggled to sit up, my gut clenching, my throat burning.

My gaze swiveled to the young boy tethered to the table. The steady thump of his heart echoed in my ears. I heard the blood pulsing through his body and my mouth watered. I gripped the stone table, my fingers clamping around the edge to keep from reaching out. One swipe and it would all be over. I could feed and gain my strength. I could escape.

"How gallant," Logan said as he moved toward the doorway. "Fight all you want, but you won't last long. The hunger is too fierce. It rules you. Take a taste, Ty Bonner. You know you want to."

But I wouldn't be able to stop with just a taste. I was too hungry, my control too tentative. I felt my fingers loosen. My vision narrowed. My gaze centered on the pale ivory throat, the pulse beat.

"That's it. Give in. Give in to a night you shall never forget, and then you can regret it for the rest of eternity. Just like I do." The door creaked and slammed shut. The lock clicked.

My own heartbeat grew louder, drowning out the music and the boy's cries, and the damnable pop, pop, pop. I reached out.

"Ty?" The soft, familiar voice pushed into my head and stopped my hand in midair. "Can you hear me?"

My fingers closed, my nails digging into my palms. My own blood drip-dropped onto the floor and my body shook with unfulfilled need.

"Please, Ty. Answer me."

But I couldn't. I didn't want her here, in my head, seeing the temptation, feeling the pain.

I closed my eyes, but I couldn't bring myself to close my mind. I didn't have the strength.

Even more, I needed hers and so I held tight to each word that echoed through my head.

"I'm worried about you. I need to know if you're okay. Not that I like you or anything," she went on, her voice soft, hesitant even. "Okay, so maybe I like you a little. And I could possibly like you more than a little if you would just help me out here and give me some sort of clue so that I can help Ash find you. He's looking for you. We both are, but obviously he's better at it than I am because he does it profession-

ally. On the other hand, if he were looking for a date, he would obviously be clueless and I would have to help him . . ."

She kept going the way she always did and I let her. I welcomed it because it gave me something to focus on, to drown out the need and resist the urge that churned away inside of me.

"It's okay," I told the boy and for the first time, I actually believed it.

It was okay.

For a little while, anyway.

Ty was okay.

I knew it as I lay there in the darkness. He was right there with me. Calm. Controlled. For now. But it wouldn't last long. The Logan guy would come back and then Ty would be in deep shit and the boy . . .

In my mind, I saw him crouched there, his green shirt glowing like a neon sign in the darkness. Tears ran down his cheeks, washing away the mustard stain near his mouth—

Holy shit.

I bolted upright as reality rained down on me and the pieces fell together one after the other.

Mustard.

Diesel.

The blare of music.

The colored lights.

The constant dings and the rattle of wood.

A fire lit under me and I scrambled from bed. Suddenly frantic, I tugged on a pair of jeans and pulled on the first shirt that touched my hands. I stuffed my feet into generic flip-flops (was I stressed or what?) and reached for my cellphone to call Ash.

He didn't pick up.

I left a frantic message informing him where to meet me, and then sent a text message just in case. Stuffing the phone into my pocket, I grabbed my purse and headed for the nearest window. I shoved the glass up, closed my eyes, and focused my thoughts. In a matter of seconds, the sound of bat wings echoed through my apartment and startled Killer out of a sound sleep as I morphed into my fuzzy pink friend.

And then I hauled ass to Coney Island, all the while trying to shake the possibility that I might not make it in time.

While I still had at least three hours until daylight and no doubt that Ty was being held somewhere on the island, I didn't know exactly where. Which meant every second counted.

Otherwise . . .

I forced the thought aside and concentrated on hanging on to Ty's thoughts as they rolled through my head and the images played in front of his clouded vision.

I could do this, I told myself, flapping away toward my destination, my mind's eye fixed on the dungeonlike room and the boy. I could reach Ty and Junior, and save them both.

And if I couldn't?

I had a feeling we would all be fucked.

Twenty-nine

❤ ❤ ❤

I followed the West Side Highway toward the Brooklyn Battery Tunnel. The city was a blaze of lights below me as I zoomed closer to Brooklyn, and on toward the beach and the boardwalk.

It was just after midnight on a Friday night and the attractions were starting to close up. In my mind I replayed the sounds I'd heard—the metal groaning and the wood rocking and shaking—and zeroed in on Astroland rather than the Wonder Wheel, which blinked in the distance.

The amusement park lights twinkled and flashed. The Top Spin flipped and whirled, giving a last *yippee!* to the stragglers intent on sticking around until the very end. The Astrotower stood like a sentry keeping watch over the area. My gaze fixed on the Cyclone. The massive roller coaster loomed above the other rides, a blaze of neon against the pitch-black sky.

I landed behind one of the concession areas, smack-dab in a puddle of something pink and sticky. I morphed and the flapping quickly faded into the frantic sound of my own heart. I glanced down at my rhinestone flip-flops, now ooey and gooey, and re-sisted the urge to scrape them off. I didn't have time to worry about my shoes.

I know, right? Was I totally freaked or what?

But we're talking life and death and Ty.

I rounded the building and started walking. My ears prickled, drinking in the sounds, fitting them together with what I'd heard in my head earlier that night.

What I could still hear if I closed my eyes and con-centrated.

His wall had completely crumbled now, and so I was there with him, flat on my back on the hard con-crete. Every once in a while, my eyelids fluttered open and I saw the swirl of lights on the cement wall. The young boy's whimpers echoed in my ears, mak-ing my gut twist, reminding me that salvation was close.

Too close.

Hold on. I sent Ty the silent message, begged him to be strong, and picked up my steps.

I moved through the amusement park, moving closer to the roller coaster and sifting through the barrage of stimuli. I listened, picking up every sound, turning it over, letting it guide me.

The tinkle of the music.

The frantic *whoooshhhhh* of the coaster.

Ka-chunk, ka-chunk.

Cha-pow.

Ba-da-bing.

I felt like I was starring in a bad kung fu movie as I turned this way, took a few more steps that way. I half-expected a masked ninja to jump out at me (or a ravenous vampire), and so I kept a careful watch on my back. Unfortunately, that put my feet at risk, and I stepped down on a fully loaded ketchup packet. I was thanking the Big Vamp Upstairs that I didn't spray the leg of my Chloe jeans when I heard the familiar sound.

Pop, pop, pop!

I forgot all about the ketchup. My head snapped up. My ears prickled. My gaze swiveled to the food stand just to my left. They offered everything from popcorn to sodas, hot dogs to pretzels. A large tub of mustard sat on the counter next to a bucket full of ketchup packets.

Dread rolled through me, followed by a rush of anxiety. My heart pounded and my blood rushed as I scanned the surrounding buildings. Another ride. Another concession stand. My vision moved deeper, farther, pushing past people and obstacles, until I spotted the broken-down building off to the side, a small warehouse that housed tools and parts for the rides.

I stepped forward, my feet carrying me so fast that I actually felt my flip-flops leave the ground. I whipped past a group of teenagers. A collective gasp and a *Holy shit,* followed by a *What the hell?* trailed after me. I should have stopped, vamped them, and covered my tracks, but I didn't (Sorry, Ma!). I was past the point of caring. I had to move. *Now.*

I neared the building. My gaze sliced through the darkness, drinking in the row of windows that sat an inch above the ground. Each square of tinted glass measured roughly six inches by six inches. Big enough to provide light for the basement below, but small enough to prevent burglary: No one was crawling in or out.

I headed around the side of the building until I spotted the only window that sat open, the glass pushed out several inches. To my left the top portion of a carousel was visible. The lights played across the building and pushed around the pane of glass, and crept through the opening to sprinkle the cement walls inside.

My heart seemed to stall as I leaned down and peered into the opening. No snaxy bounty hunters or freaked-out kids. Just a bunch of dusty tarps, a few old carousel animals, and a giant rusted teacup.

Disappointment rushed through me, followed by a surge of panic. I started searching again. I followed the row of windows around the back, to the opposite side, peeking inside each one. My anxiety mounted and my sticky flip-flops kept sticking to the concrete.

"I could use some help here," I finally blurted when I stuck my fingers around a window to open it up, and the glass slammed shut. Two of my nails cracked and snapped. I stared down at the ruined manicure and my eyes welled. Not because I'd lost a nail (no, really), but because Ty needed me and I couldn't find him. I was close, but I wasn't there. "Please." My throat closed around the word and I swallowed, closing my eyes for a long moment to try to get a grip.

Vamps didn't cry, I told myself. They raised hell and kicked ass and they stayed strong. I gathered my courage and sniffled. "I am NOT blubbering like a baby."

"Yes, you are." The deep, familiar voice echoed through my head and my heart skipped its next beat.

"Where are you?" I murmured, and then I heard him.

"Here." The word was little more than a croak, and it didn't come from the other side of the damnable window that now owed me a manicure.

I turned and eyeballed the next building. It was a brick structure that fit halfway beneath the roller coaster. It probably housed the guts of the ride. Maybe an engine room. There were no windows, just a small section of bricks near the ground that had been pulled out of the mortar so that someone could peer in from time to time and keep an eye on what was going on below.

Because whoever had taken Ty was close by. Watching.

I glanced around, tuning my senses, searching, but I saw nothing. Felt nothing. Just the desperation that came from beyond the hole in the brick. The ride had shut down and so there was no rattling wood, no groan as the cars raced around the track.

I walked over to the building, knelt, and peered inside.

My heart lunged into my throat as I saw Ty's shivering body draped over a mortared stack of bricks. In the far corner, the young boy crouched, his face tear streaked, his eyes full of fear and worry and desperation.

I had half a notion to barge through the hole (my manicure was ruined anyway), but a crazy vampire slinging bricks was sure to attract more than just a *holy shit* or *what the hell?* On top of that, I was pressed for time. I needed to get inside and save the two people inside before their abductor came back.

Rounding the large structure, I found a door at the very back. I grabbed the padlock and twisted. The lock crumbled in my hands and the door creaked open.

The ride had shut down, but the motor still hummed. The smell of diesel surrounded me. I sent yet another thanks to Sistah Vamp in that Great Big Coffin in the Sky for the fact that I didn't need to breathe, otherwise I would have been flat on my back before I found Ty instead of after, as I'd anticipated (see life-affirming sex).

It took several minutes and a lot of stumbling before I found my way around the monstrous machines to the rickety staircase that led below. The stairs creaked and moaned, leading to a small hallway lined with doors. I filtered out all of the engine noise coming from upstairs and focused on the small ticks and creaks that surrounded me.

I turned to one specific door on the left. Another padlock barred my way, but I crushed it, splintering the pieces and letting them fall to the floor.

It had been over a month since I'd actually seen Ty, and while I could picture him clearly in my mind, seeing him in the flesh was a completely different experience. Every nerve jumped to attention. My heart paused in my chest. Awareness bubbled up my spine, followed by a rush of dread.

My gaze pored over his face, battered and bruised because he'd yet to feed and, therefore, heal. His lips were swollen. More bruises dotted his bare torso. Angry red slash marks crisscrossed his chest and I felt my own back throb. He wore a pair of jeans and nothing else, the material filthy and stained. My heart gave a painful thud and suddenly I couldn't move. Pain paralyzed me, a feeling that had nothing to do with my mental connection with him and what he was feeling, and everything to do with my own feelings for him.

"It's okay." His voice echoed through my head and zapped me back to reality.

I turned toward the small form that cowered in the corner. The boy looked to be about eight or nine. Average size with blond hair and blue eyes.

"Hey," I said when I reached him.

His eyes popped open and he stared up at me as if I were about to whack him with a ruler and haul him to the principal's office.

"It's okay," I told him. I reached for his shoulder and started to pull him forward, and he bit me. "Ouch!" I snatched my hand back and eyed the faint indentations in my skin. I contemplated biting him back for an eighth of a second, but I'd always liked a more mature flavor of blood. Something aged and mellowed, not bubbling and prepubescent.

I forced my most understanding smile. After all, he was freaked. Biting was totally understandable.

I reached out again and he kicked me. And then he pulled my hair. And then he grabbed my shirt—

"Hold it!" I gripped his shoulders and exerted enough pressure to make his eyes go wide. "I'm trying to help you, all right?" My gaze pushed into his. Calming. Entrancing.

He went limp then, and I was able to lift him and head for the door. A few seconds later, I headed around the building and started toward the small security stand that sat near the park entrance. Several yards away, I stood him on his wobbly legs and stared into his glazed eyes.

"Listen up, kid. I want you to turn and walk straight over to that security guard. Tell him your name and your mother's name and your phone number." He knew that, right? I tried to remember myself at eight, but that had been during the pre-cellphone era. In fact, we're talking pre-Morse code.

"You know your phone number?" The glazed look faded for a split-second and realization struck. He nodded.

"Good." I smiled and stared deep into his eyes.

You're going to give the guard your digits and then you're going to forget all about me. I sent the silent message. *And the bad vampire who abducted you. And the really hot, hunky vampire who suffered so that he wouldn't hurt you (awww). It was all just a bad dream thanks to too many hot dogs. You're also going to listen to your mom, clean your room, and do your best in school.*

Hey, what's the point of being a Super Vamp if you can't do something good for mankind every once in a while?

A whole list of answers rifled through my head, starting with (1) the point of being a Super Vamp is to make little Super Vamps, and (2) to bend humans to your will and feed, and the ever popular, (3) to make oodles of money so that you can support the little Super Vamps and bend humans to your will and, of course, feed.

I tuned out my vamp conscience—which sounded way too much like my mother—and turned.

One down. One to go.

I headed back inside the engine room, down below and into the basement. Crossing the concrete floor, I leaned down and touched Ty's shoulder.

"Hey. Can you hear me?"

"Yes." His lips were thick around the word.

He forced his eyelids open a fraction and I saw the deep blue of his gaze. Pain clouded the vivid color, and I felt a rush of anger. I was so going to kick someone's ass after I helped Ty to safety.

"I'm going to carry you out of here," I said and started to slide my hands beneath him.

My fingertips grazed his bruised and swollen flesh and he bucked. He caught his lips against a scream of agony and his fangs sank deep into his lower lip, drawing blood.

"I'm sorry."

"Okay," he finally managed. " . . . don't think . . . I . . . can . . . move." Each word was a struggle and my heart twisted.

He'd been starved for so long that he couldn't heal. Rather, he was one big open wound. I could move him, but it would hurt. So much that I knew I had to figure out something else.

I remembered that night at my apartment when Ty had shown up and let me drink from him that very first time. I'd gotten staked in the shoulder, and we're talking mega pain. A few sips from him and I'd felt loads better.

At the same time, that's what had linked us in the first place. I'd drank from him and bam, instant mind connection. If I let him drink from me, it would make the link that much stronger. The sharing of blood was serious business among vampires. We're talking an unbreakable bond. A serious commitment. A—

Well, you get the idea.

I was already halfway there and not liking it one bit because I knew on a realistic level that Ty and I were doomed. He wasn't my type and I wasn't his. It was a tragedy about to happen. The typical born vampire would cut her losses and head for the nearest twenty-four-hour Neiman's.

At the same time, there were no twenty-four-hour Neiman's and I was hardly the typical born vamp.

I'd drank from him. And slept with him. And I actually liked him. I couldn't NOT help. Even if it made walking away that much more difficult.

And I would walk. I had to. I had little vamps to squeeze out, after all.

But not right now.

I glanced at the inside of my own arm. Blue veins bulged just beneath the smooth, tanned surface, pulsing with life. I opened my mouth and bared my fangs. Sinking them into my own wrist, I opened a vein and held it to his lips.

The blood drip-dropped into his mouth and his Adam's apple bobbed. Once. Twice. His lips moved and his tongue lapped at my wrist. A few more seconds and his arm stirred. His hand came up, catching my wrist and holding it to his mouth as he took control.

His mouth opened. His fangs grazed my flesh and sank deep. I gasped and leaned against him. My eyes closed.

He drank for several moments, sucking so hard that I eventually felt the pull on my nipples and between my legs.

No, I told myself. This was a dire situation. Perilous. We weren't in a penthouse suite somewhere in Manhattan: No champagne chilling on the nightstand, no rose petals sprinkled on the bed, no Barry

White drifting from the speakers. But I couldn't help myself. This was Ty and I'd missed him and—*oh*. *Ohhhhhhhh* . . .

He pulled away just before the *oh* morphed into a *yesss*!

I sagged against the table and tried to gather my wits. I'd almost swept them into a nice big pile, too, when I heard the cold voice that drifted from the doorway.

"Well, well. Isn't this sweet?"

Thirty
♥ ♥ ♥

His name was Logan Drake and he was a born vampire.

The first I knew because he said, "I'm so glad we're finally getting the chance to meet, Miss Marchette. Logan Drake at your service."

The second I knew because his scent rushed at me, spiraling through my nostrils. I had an instant flashback to my childhood. Many a midnight I'd hidden in the cupboard to eavesdrop on the latest castle gossip while the human maids had gabbed and scarfed raisins and rice pudding.

I *know*.

I felt nauseous just thinking about it. Smelling it really made me want to blow chunks.

Just for the record, I'd faced off with sadistic vampires on more than one occasion—all in the past few months, as a matter of fact. First, there'd been Super Scary Vamp who'd been kidnapping girls, turning them to vamps, and leaving them for dust once the sun came up. And then Ayala, a client and born vamp princess who'd blamed me for killing her werewolf lover (a *long* story). But this guy definitely topped my list of dangerous and psychotic night stalkers.

Drake was tall, with dark hair that had been slicked back and dark brown eyes that tried to drill through me. He wore black slacks, a dark brown shirt, and enough hair gel to make even Mr. Weather look au natural. He looked as handsome as any other born vamp. Dazzling even, especially when he smiled. But his eyes were cold. Yeah, I know. That was classic vamp, too, but in a weird, twisted way that stirred a wave of dread instead of the usual *Ugh, here we go again with the snotty pretentious bullshit.*

"I see you showed up just in time for dinner." He stepped inside the room, his attention shifting, searching. "Where is our little friend? The leftovers, anyway." Another sweeping gaze and his smile died. "He isn't here."

"And the lightbulb goes off."

His gaze shifted back to me. "You got rid of him."

"I returned him." My mind raced. "Um, that is, after I ripped him to shreds." We're talking danger-ous and psychotic, which meant I needed to be equally dangerous and psychotic. At least he needed to think so, otherwise, I wasn't going to make it out of here with Ty. "And then I ate his heart," I added.

He stared at me as if I'd declared myself a Democrat. (FYI: most born vamps are card-carrying Republicans.) His expression settled into a frown and he took another step into the room. And another.

"Stop, or I'll eat yours. I swear."

He smiled this time and fear rippled up and down my spine. Crazy, I know. While I'd never actually eaten an internal organ in my entire afterlife, I could have if I'd wanted to. I'm a mad, bad vampire, after all.

I was little match for this guy. He was older. Ancient, judging by the deepness of his eyes and the confidence with which he faced me. I'd seen my father (more than eight hundred years old) face down his next-door neighbor Viola with the same look.

Of course, he usually had a power tool in hand, or a gold club, or at least some heavy-duty weed killer. But you get the idea.

"What do you say I rip out your heart?" He wiggled his eyebrows. "And, of course, we'll let Ty watch. Then again, he really isn't in much shape for a show, so he'll have to settle for a play-by-play commentary."

I spared a quick glance at Ty. The pasty white pallor of his skin had faded and slowly but surely his color was returning. But he was still bruised and battered, the welts raw and oozing. While he'd drunk his fill, he'd been starving for far too long to get his strength back any time soon. He needed to heal. To sleep.

Uh-oh.

Logan stepped toward me again and I inched away from Ty. He was still vulnerable, and I didn't want Psycho Vamp freaking out and harming him when I was the one he really wanted.

"First up, the powerful Logan Drake advances," the vampire said as if he were doing commentary at a Knicks game. "He reaches out."

I sidestepped the hands that grabbed for me and whirled.

"He advances again, going for the throat."

I ducked and twirled, stumbling in the process because he lunged again before I could get my footing.

"She's fast, boys, but Logan is faster. He goes for the arm."

I dodged his hand, which pushed me closer to the wall.

"He goes for the throat again."

I ducked to avoid the hand. But while it passed overhead, his other hand moved in from below, catching my throat in a viselike grip. The pressure cut off my blood flow and everything went hazy as he slung me around and threw me toward the opposite wall. I slammed into the wall. Cement shattered and pieces flew. Before I could open my eyes, he reached for me again, grabbing, squeezing, throwing. He tossed me around like a rag doll several more times, his voice echoing through my head.

"She's weakening, folks. Soon Logan will go for the kill. He'll rip out her jugular, feast on her blood. You hear that, Ty? She'll die by my hand. I'll take her from you just as you took Loralei from me."

Grab. Choke. Slam.

Over and over.

"I'm through playing," Logan announced, his voice barely pushing past the pounding of my heart. "I'm going to rip her apart now and bathe in her blood."

Ick. I don't *think* so.

I wasn't sure if it was the ick factor that spurred me on or the fact that I was pissed. Either way, I managed to gather my determination and get my knee up just as he reached for me again. I kicked him full in the stomach, sending him flying toward the opposite wall.

Concrete flew as he hit and I struggled to my feet. I moved fast, flying across the room and landing another vicious kick to his middle before he could get back up.

Yep, he was older, all right, which gave him the confidence advantage. But I was younger, with more to lose (my afterlife and a pair of sticky flip-flops that I was determined to salvage).

He flew at me and I met him halfway. He chomped down on my arm and I twisted at his head, fighting him off as the blood spurted and sprayed my favorite pair of Chloe's. Pain hit me hard and fast, but it was nothing compared to the anger. I was so pissed.

We're talking *Chloe's*.

A red haze washed over me, my fangs extended. My own hiss echoed through my head as I twisted him loose and shoved him backward. I lunged for his throat. My hands locked and tightened and I slammed him back against the concrete. I leaned in, his throat looming in front of me—

"No!" Ty's voice pushed past the thundering of my heart.

I wasn't sure what happened next. I just knew that one minute I was this close to sinking my fangs into Psycho Vamp and the next I was sprawled on my ass on the floor. Ty was on his feet, teetering in front of me, looking as if he might topple over at any moment.

I saw a flash of black as Psycho Vamp did a quick disappearing act through the open doorway, and then it was just the two of us.

My mind did a quick mental on what had almost happened—me plus Psycho Vamp equaled vicious murder—and a shudder ripped through me. I'd actually . . . I'd been about to . . .

"It's okay," Ty murmured before he staggered to the side and slumped against the wall.

A split-second later, Ash barreled through the doorway, his gun drawn. Hot on his heels were Zee and Moe, guns in hand. Several other men followed, a mix of vampires and weres.

"Lil?" Ash knelt in front of me and reached for my arm, which gushed blood onto the cold, concrete floor.

"He's getting away," I said, motioning toward the door.

"Who?"

"Born vamp," I gasped, pain zigzagging through my head with each word. "Ty's kidnapper."

"We didn't see anybody. We just followed the noise." Ash motioned to Zee. "Check it out."

Zee nodded and headed through the door as Ash turned back to me. "You're losing a lot of blood."

"I'm a vampire. I'm okay." Or I would be once I got cleaned up and crawled into bed to sleep and heal. But Ty . . . I motioned toward the sagging bounty hunter. "Help him."

"We are." Another nod and the handful of men surrounded Ty.

I watched as they picked him up and started from the room. Panic bolted through me and I stepped forward. "Wait a second."

I reached Ty in less than a heartbeat and touched his bruised face. The questions swirled in my head. So many. Too many. "I don't understand—," I started, but he caught my hand and held tight.

"I can't do this right now," he managed with thick lips. "But soon. I promise."

I nodded and started to move away, but he held tight to my hand, as if he never wanted to let go.

As if.

Nevertheless, his fingers stayed strong and firm around my own. His gaze held mine and I had the strange feeling that he was drawing strength from me in some way.

"You did good," he finally said, his eyes twinkling before he let go of my hand.

I stepped back as the men closed in around Ty and

then I turned to Ash. "Where are they taking him?" I finally asked.

"Someplace safe." Someplace where I obviously couldn't go, judging by the closed expression that settled over Ash's face. "He'll be all right," he added, confirming the suspicion that he wasn't going to tell me where they were taking him. "We'll get him patched up and debriefed and then he can contact you."

"What happened?"

"From the looks of this place, you kicked some royal ass."

"I mean afterward." Ty had stopped me. He'd saved his abductor for some reason that I couldn't begin to understand. Not that I was complaining. I'd felt guilty enough when I'd accidentally pushed Killer off the couch yesterday. Ripping someone to shreds— even a bad someone—wasn't something that would bode well for my conscience.

"Why did he do it?" I asked. He gave me an odd look and I realized that he hadn't even seen the psycho vamp, much less witnessed Ty's interference.

He touched my arm. "Do you want me to call someone? Your folks, maybe?"

I grimaced. "I think I'm feeling miserable enough."

His warm chuckle slid over me and the pain subsided just a fraction. "I could give you a lift home?"

"No, no. You go with Ty." The last thing, the very last thing I wanted was to have Ash in my apartment when I wasn't at my strongest. It had been during just such a weak moment that I'd fallen off the wagon and drank from Ty. I didn't even want to think about what would happen to me if I took a bite out of a demon.

"Not just any old demon," he told me as he pushed to his feet, a grin tugging at his lips. "I've got seniority."

Thirty-one
♥ ♥ ♥

"So I told her to keep the damned thing because, of course, I can more than afford to buy a gross of chainsaws if I want to. My net worth far exceeds that of some lowly werewolf."

"He didn't really say that to Viola, did he?" I asked my brother Max, who was parked next to me on the sofa.

It was Sunday night, and my mother's dinner party was in full swing. And so was my dad. He stood center stage, his favorite golf club in hand as he demonstrated his latest swing.

Max shook his head. "Not to her face. He sent a letter via Hugo." He pointed to a large, burly man who stood in the corner.

Hugo Divine was my dad's latest bodyguard/gopher. He was large and intimidating, with a wrinkled-up face, a green suit, and slicked-back hair: the human product of unprotected sex between Mrs. Shrek and Anthony Soprano.

"It's his new strategy," Max went on, "to make Viola feel inferior and vulnerable so that she'll crack under the pressure, give up the chainsaw, and worship at his feet."

"That sounds like the old strategy."

He shrugged. "You know Dad. He's set in his ways."

At least my mother was (I never thought I'd say this) slowly evolving. She was (gulp) actually being decent, maybe a tad overconcerned.

My gaze shifted from my father to my brother Jack, who sat in a nearby chair. He had his feet propped up, a glass of blood in his hand, while my mother fussed over him.

He shifted in the chair and she signaled Sally, one of her housekeepers, who rushed forward to fluff Jack's pillows.

Note: I said evolving, not deranged. She saw no reason to lift her own fingers when she had a bevy of willing humans to do any lifting for her.

Yep, she was definitely being decent. She hadn't made even one derogatory remark to Mandy.

Okay, so she hadn't actually talked to Mandy because my soon-to-be sister-in-law had gotten stuck working a double shift at the morgue and Jack had arrived solo. But I felt fairly certain that Jacqueline Marchette would have kept her digs to herself.

I'd been here all of forty-five minutes and she'd

hardly spared me a glance, much less a *When are you going to get a real job?* or a *Gruella DeMaurier has ninety-six grandchildren and I don't have a measly one.*

She hadn't even commented on my clothes. I had on a new crinkle chiffon Rebecca Taylor halter dress (I'd needed something to cheer me up after facing off with Psycho Vamp), python and leather Vivia sandals, and a Chan Luu beaded silk clutch. While I looked totally fab (as usual) and beyond reproach, my mother could always find *something*.

Not tonight.

My gaze shifted to Nina One, who stood in the far corner and laughed at something Rob had said. They were really hitting it off and I had a feeling, judging by the predatory light in Nina's eyes, that they'd be trying out my parents' hot tub before the clock struck midnight. Or the bedroom. Or the nearest closet.

All in all, the dinner party I'd been dreading wasn't turning out half bad.

I should be happy.

"Too bad Remy's mother couldn't make it," Max remarked.

Forget happy. I should be ecstatic.

My attention shifted to Remy, who stood near my father and pretended unwavering interest in his latest golf swing. The police chief looked positively yummy in dark jeans, a gray henley, and tan loafers. His blond hair was mussed, his eyes twinkling. He smelled of soap and hunky male and nothing else. No raisins and rice pudding, or anything putridly sweet that could clash with my eau de cotton candy.

We'd spent the past half hour talking about the local ins and outs of the department and my latest matchmaking coup. Word and Suze had hit it off and were planning date number two. I'd explained my Rachel the were-Chihuahua predicament and Remy, bless his undead heart, had actually given me the name of a male were-spaniel (who woulda thunk it?). The spaniel had recently given up a brief stint coaching Little League (he'd had a hell of a time during games, what with all those balls flying around) and had taken a city manager job. He was stable, nice, and ready to settle down with someone who could squeeze out a few puppies. Literally.

Yep, Remy was a good vamp. A nice vamp. The perfect vamp. And I like him. He actually made my tummy tingle.

Not the full-blown quivering that Ty produced, but enough to make me think *maybe*. Particularly since he was here and Ty wasn't.

Of course, that might not be Ty's fault. It had been almost forty-eight hours since I'd found him. The wound on my arm had completely healed, but Ty might not be as far along in the healing process, which would explain, of course, why he hadn't contacted me.

I debated calling his cell for the umpteenth time, but I wasn't sure what to say.

I'm so glad you're okay?

I miss you?

I like you?

I hope you like me?

I hope you *don't* like me because then I can tell myself what a lying, stinking rat you are and devote myself to someone who might actually be able to give me a commitment ceremony, a honeymoon in Fiji, and a half dozen baby vamps?

I shook away the nagging questions and tried to concentrate on the words coming out of Max's mouth. Something about his latest fight with a copy machine at Moe's (my bro is totally hot and totally boring). I managed to nod and make it through the next ten minutes before I had to call it quits.

I slipped outside, walked past the pool, and perched on the steps leading to a lush stretch of green grass and landscaped gardens.

I debated making a run for it and heading back to Manhattan, but we still had to hunt and I so didn't want to turn my mother from pampering parent to vengeful vamp. Better to go with the flow, count my good fortune that I was having a decent time, and make it through the rest of the evening.

Pulling out my cell phone, I punched in Esther's number to get a quick update on the wedding dress. She wasn't in and I got her machine instead. I left a message and then punched in Evie's number.

"I hope I didn't wake you up."

"I'm watching *Dog the Bounty Hunter*."

"Where's a good episode of *CSI: Miami* when you really need it?"

"Sorry." Evie had no clue about Ty's abduction. As

far as she knew, he was a conceited jerk who'd had torrid sex with me and failed to call. "I didn't mean to remind you."

"No big deal. Besides, I've got this new guy and I'm totally into him."

"You kiss him yet?"

"We're not that far along."

"Then you're not totally into him."

"Says you. Listen, I was thinking that we could match up Gwen Rowley, that amateur photographer I told you about, with Mr. Weather."

"I didn't know Mr. Weather was one of our clients."

"He isn't, but Gwen is, and since she likes taking pictures and he likes getting his picture taken, I thought we could call and see if we could set something up."

"Why in the world would he ever agree to go on a date with one of our clients?"

"Because I've got pictures." I explained the fiasco of a date, minus the part about me being a vamp and spooking the horses, of course.

"You're evil."

"Yeah, well, a girl's gotta do what a girl's gotta do. Tell him I'll give him the pictures if he agrees to a date."

"Will do." We chatted a few more minutes about various clients.

"Try to get some sleep," she finally told me.

"I will."

"I mean it. Just forget about him."

"Ty? Ty who?" I punched the off button and slid the phone into my bag. I sat there for a few seconds, awareness rippling up my spine. Geez, just talking about the guy got me worked up—

The thought stalled as my gaze snagged on the tall, dark, and delicious cowboy standing several yards away near a patch of trees.

He wore a black leather vest, no shirt, and black pants. His dark, shoulder-length hair flowed down around his broad shoulders. He still bore a few bruises, but all in all he looked as strong and muscular as ever.

"Thanks to you." His deep voice echoed in my head and awareness zipped up my spine, and suddenly he was there, standing right in front of me, so tall and powerful and healthy that my heart gave a little jerk. "And your blood," he added, saying the words aloud this time.

"Yeah, well, you were in pretty bad shape. I had to do something."

"I never did get a chance to tell you how grateful I am."

"It's okay. You weren't really in any shape to talk." I drank in his face, from his neon-blue eyes fringed with dark, sooty lashes to his perfect nose, strong jaw, sensual lips. My gaze went to the tiny scar that jagged its way through his eyebrow. It was a leftover from his human days, a reminder that he was different from me, and it should have sent a jolt of reality through me.

Made vamp. Born vamp. No dice.

Instead, my fingers itched and I barely resisted the urge to reach out.

"You look like you're feeling better," I said instead.

"Much."

We stood there for the next several minutes, eyeing each other and trying to decide what to say. Crazy, huh? I was closer to him than I'd ever been to anyone—vamp or otherwise—yet I still felt a million miles away.

"You saved him because you owe him, didn't you?" I finally asked. The scene had played over in my head many times, stirring many questions and many answers. "You took something from him, someone, and so now you owe him. That's why you saved him."

"I didn't save him." His gaze caught and held mine. "I saved you." He turned away before I could do something crazy like reach out and kiss him (which I so wanted to do). "I know what it's like to live with blood on my hands," he said, his gaze hooked on the gardens. "I didn't want you to have to do the same." He shook his head. "You're not like me, Lil."

"When did you figure that one out, Sherlock?"

He flashed a quick grin before the expression faded. "I'm not talking about males and females. Made vamps and born vamps. We're different in other ways. You're different. You've got—"

"—a big mouth?" I cut in, reminding him of what he'd told Ash.

The grin returned for a split second. "That, and you've got heart. A conscience."

"So do you."

He shook his head. "I thought so at one time, but then I did something really bad and it proved otherwise. Logan forced me to face the truth of what I'd done."

"He turned you, didn't he?"

He nodded. "Back before I was turned, I used to rob banks for a living. Trains mostly. I never hurt anyone. I just took the money and ran. But there was this one job." He took a few steps, his gaze focused on the distance. "There was only supposed to be a small crew on the train, no passengers. But when I climbed on, there was a whole car full of them. Scared. Screaming. A few of the men tried to rush me and I fired. I hit one in the knee. Another in the shoulder. Nothing deadly. But then this woman . . ." He closed his eyes. "She came at me full force, screaming and yelling, as if she wanted to rip my head off. I didn't mean to fire. I tried to hold her off, but the gun discharged and it was done. She took a bullet in the chest and she died right there. She bled all over me." He ran a hand over his face. "I turned the gun on myself and fired."

"You killed yourself?"

"I tried. I felt so much guilt. I couldn't imagine living the rest of my life like that, so I ended it. Logan found me while there were a few breaths left in my body, saw what I had done, and decided that death was too good for me. I'd killed the woman he loved, the woman he'd intended to turn and spend the rest of eternity with. He knew I was sorry. He could see it in my eyes and he decided the best way to punish me wasn't to rip out my throat. It was to turn me, to make me live with my regret forever. And that's what he did. Whenever I find a little happiness and start to forget, he reminds me. That's what the past few weeks have been about. I was doing just fine, living with my regret, feeling like shit most of the time, and then I met you. You actually made me forget about all of that for a little while. You made me laugh."

"Which is why he came after you."

He nodded. "That's why you and I . . ." He turned toward me and our gazes locked. "We can't be together."

Another black mark on the already overflowing slate of *Why Lil Marchette and Ty Bonner have no hope in hell*. "I can see your point."

"The two of us . . . It's a bad idea."

I nodded. "*Really* bad."

His eyes darkened and his gaze dropped to my mouth. "The worst," he added.

My lips tingled. "The absolute worst."

"The last thing I can ever do is get involved with someone."

"Me, too. I'm totally focused on my business right now and I certainly don't need any distractions."

"Even meaningless, heat-of-the-moment sex is a bad idea."

A memory stirred and my nipples pebbled. I nodded again. "Very bad."

"We can't see each other again. Logan's watching me. I can't risk him hurting you. I won't."

"I completely agree. Me being hurt? Not my idea of a good time." I licked my lips. "Then again, I *am* a born vampire. An equal match, as we've already seen, for this Logan guy." I was treading tentative ground, but I'd already had all my happily-ever-afters-with-Ty fantasies ruined. I wasn't giving up my life-affirming sex one, too. And while Ty was paying a lot of lip service to the whole eternally indebted thing, I knew he secretly wanted me as much as I wanted him. At least I was hoping. "I'm fully capable of taking care of myself."

He gave me a *yeah, right* look. "You're a marshmallow."

"A marshmallow who can kick ass when necessary." My gaze narrowed. "Don't make me kick your ass and prove it."

"You and what army?"

I eyed my Vivias, debated their going the way of my flip-flops. "Me and my two hot-looking friends." We faced off for a few minutes and I actually thought he might make a move. Finally, he grinned. "You're something, you know that?"

"So they tell me."

Another long, silent stretch passed before he finally licked his lips. "I should probably turn and get out of here. I'm meeting Ash on business."

"Have a nice afterlife."

"You, too."

"So go," I told him when he didn't budge. "Unless you're thinking what I'm thinking."

"Which is?"

"That maybe we should have a more meaningful goodbye. I mean, it's obvious we both need some closure, otherwise you'd be history and I'd be gulping down AB negative with the chief of the Fairfield Police Department."

His gaze narrowed and shot past me toward the house. "Remy Tremaine's in there?"

Okay, so I didn't purposely try to make Ty jealous, but I have to admit that I was sort of jazzed at the way he looked ready to rip something to shreds.

"My mother invited him," I said. "He's tonight's fix up."

He stared a few more minutes, as if fighting down the jealousy that clawed at him before finally shaking his head. "You're right. We definitely need some closure." His gaze met mine. "So what do you have in mind?" A gleam lit his eyes. "A handshake?"

"That's not exactly what I'm thinking." *Kiss me*, I sent the silent message. *Just kiss me and then you can sweep me up in your arms, we'll head for the pool house, and we won't come out until I've had a full dozen orgasms and you're so limp you can barely stand.*

A grin crooked his lips. "A kiss on the cheek."

"No." *Dumbass.*

"A wave."

"Hardly, although I am tempted to shoot you the bird right now."

"A smile?"

"*No.*"

"What then?"

What the hell? It was the twenty-first century and I certainly wasn't getting any younger. "*This.*" And then *I* kissed *him.*

We didn't end up in the pool house.

When I finally opened my eyes to come up for air after *the* best kiss of my afterlife, I found myself on a moonlit beach, sand sucking at my heels, the breeze ruffling my hair.

"What the—," I started, but Ty pressed a fingertip to my lips.

"All vampires have their specialty." He shrugged. "Mine is illusion."

Okay, so I knew all *born* vampires had a little somethin' somethin' in addition to their sweet, addictive scent. A particular power unique to that specific vamp. What I didn't know was that the Big V Upstairs had doled out a little *oomph* to made vamps, as well.

My oldest brother, Max, could summon lightning. Rob could stir up a windstorm. Jack could walk through walls. Me? I could sniff out a bargain within a ten-mile radius.

Ty's primo skill, however, had all of us beat.

I stared around, my eyes wide with amazement. Water rushed in and lapped at the shore. Palm trees swayed. The moonlight reflected off the shimmering water. White sea foam slithered around my shoes.

"I know you've got a thing for the beach." He knew this because he'd been lurking in my thoughts. And my fantasies.

I had the sudden notion that I should be properly pissed, but horny kicked righteous indignation's ass any day. I'd been waiting for this moment for far too long to ruin it by being bitchy.

I smiled. "It's perfect."

"No." His dark, smoldering gaze met mine. "Not quite."

His eyes traveled the length of my body and just like that, snaps started to pop open and buttons slid free. Material slithered and fell away until I wore nothing but my high heels and an air of impatience. My hands shook and my thighs trembled.

I wanted him to touch me. I really, *really* wanted him to touch me. His rough hands on my body. His bare skin pressed to mine. My nipples grew hard, eager, and I gasped for a decent breath to calm my pounding heart.

"There," he said after his attention swept me once, twice. "Now it's perfect."

"Says you," I managed, my voice suddenly thick. "Your turn."

I did a little effective ogling—er, I mean staring, and his leather vest slid from his broad shoulders and sinewy arms, and dropped to the sand. *Yeah, baby.* The top button on his pants popped open and the zipper started to slither down. Halfway, it stalled, unable to make it past the hard-on stretching the material tight.

I focused all of my energy. *Come on*. But the damned thing wouldn't budge.

"To hell with this," I finally blurted.

I crossed the few feet that separated us and went for it. My fingers brushed his crotch, gripped the zipper and gave it a fierce tug. The metal teeth gave and he sprang hard and hot into my hands.

I stroked his long, hard length, my fingertips tracing the head before sweeping back up and brushing the silky dark hair that surrounded the base of his shaft.

He groaned, the sound rumbling in my ears, and suddenly I couldn't wait to get him inside of me.

I finished undressing him, kicked off my own shoes, and pulled him down to the sand. I straddled him and was *this* close to sliding down onto his erection when his hands closed over my shoulders and he stopped me.

"Wait," he breathed as I stalled, my body poised over the head of his penis.

"What for?"

"This." And then he kissed me, his mouth plundering mine, his tongue plunging deep.

The kiss was endless, thorough, desperate, and I knew that he couldn't wait any more than I could.

He flipped me onto my back, settled between my legs and thrust into me.

I lifted my hips, sucking him in. I wanted to feel him deeper . . . harder . . . *there*.

Just. Like. *That*.

His groan echoed in my head and I forced my eyes

open in time to see him poised over me, his lips parted, fangs bared. His gaze drilled into mine and I caught myself arching my neck toward him.

Hello? Closure, remember?

Oh, yeah.

I closed my eyes, breaking the powerful connection of his gaze meeting mine, and concentrated on having an orgasm.

Just an orgasm. No biting. No blood drinking. No cosmic connection. No meeting of the minds. Or souls.

Ty Bonner was NOT my soul mate.

No matter how much I found myself wishing otherwise.

Even more, this was it. Our last encounter. One last hurray before he hit the road and I went back to my life. Once the sun started to creep over the horizon, that would be it. *The end.*

But until then . . .

I slid my arms around his shoulders and surrendered to the delicious sensation swamping my senses. I was going to have the wildest, hottest, most memorable night of my afterlife.

Guaranteed.

Epilogue
♥ ♥ ♥

"I'm having *so* much fun!" Mandy announced as she plopped down in the chair next to mine and took a long swig of her frosty margarita.

She wore a white, makeshift veil dotted with condom packages and a T-shirt decorated with Lifesavers and a pink glittery caption that read *Suck for a Buck*.

Um, yeah.

Needless to say, I'd steered clear of any vampire hangouts for tonight's rite of passage (otherwise referred to as a human bachelorette party). Instead, I'd herded everyone (Mandy, Evie, the Ninas, moi, a couple of Mandy's cadaver-expert sistahs from the morgue, Esther, and Shirley) into a cab bound for Night of Enchantment, the Brooklyn equivalent of Chippendale's. I, myself, had opted for an intimate dinner at Spago's, but then I'd picked up *How to Plan a Bachelorette Party She'll Never Forget* (on account of I'm a born vampire who's never actually planned such a bash). Based on the sample parties I'd read about, I'd quickly changed my mind about the five-star restaurant.

I'd needed loud. Tacky. Sweaty.

Voilà!

I eyed Nightrider, a guy decked out in a cowboy hat, boots, and a leather G-string. He strutted down the catwalk in front of our table and I barely resisted the urge to duck. Talk about a Gatorade commercial just waiting to happen.

"He's so hot," cried one of Mandy's morgue buddies. "Yoo-hoo!" She stood on her chair and waved a dollar bill. "Over here."

"Me, too." Buddy number two shot to her feet and waved a five.

"He sort of looks like Wilson when he's excited about a particular stock option," Nina Two declared, eyeing the beefcake that sauntered and shimmied our way.

Nina *Deux* is the conservative accountant half of the Ninas. She'd been happily committed to her equally conservative financial analyst since I'd hooked them up several months back.

"Not that I'd spend an entire dollar on a kiss," she added. "Think what that money could buy."

"Lighten up," Nina One told her. She wore my Hermés scarf (sniff) and a glam pink Chanel sparkle dress. "It's a party. You're supposed to get wild and crazy."

Despite her advice, I noted that she still had her own roll of ones sitting in front of her. She'd also texted four messages to my brother and was, at this moment, staring at her cell phone, a love-struck expression on her face.

My heart gave a little hitch and I smiled.

My gaze shifted to Esther and Shirley, who stood near one of the adjacent stages. They waved dollar bills at a tall, buff construction worker who went by the name Power Tool. He shook his moneymaker in front of Esther's awestruck face before plucking the dollar bill from her hand. She panted and I made a mental note to get busy on the made vampire hunt ASAP.

I owed her BIG TIME.

She'd really come through on the dress. Inadvertently, of course, but results were results.

See, she'd been in the middle of finishing up the barest of changes when disaster had struck. The name of said disaster? Miffy. The cat had resented the dress from day one (smart cat), and so when Esther had spread it out on the dining room table for the last cut, the animal had attacked.

Fab, right?

Wrong.

Miffy had done her *Fatal Attraction* imitation only eight days before the wedding and, even worse, a measly five days before the bridal-portrait sitting. I hadn't had the heart to tell Mandy, who'd already been *muy* freaked because my mother had called in the infamous doctor Pierre Claude Van Dorien to document my brother's condition.

I'd been *so* busted.

My mother (after dishing out enough guilt to get me to agree to a real date with Remy sometime in the near future) had launched a last-ditch effort to break up Jack and Mandy. She'd even hired a private investigator (the woman now hiding in the corner behind an oversized cutout of Zorro) in the frantic hope that Mandy would rip off her clothes and boink Nightrider, or do something equally atrocious. Fuel for my mother to prove to Jack that tomorrow was going to be the biggest mistake of his afterlife.

Anyhow, the dress had been ruined and we'd had only two choices. Mandy could wear one off the rack from Shirley's or Esther could attempt to make one from scratch. I'd supplied the material, a dozen bridal magazines, and a temporary home for Miffy, while the made vamp had spent the next five days cutting and sewing.

Esther had unveiled the finished product at the photographer's and I'd actually kissed her. A totally sexless, completely heartfelt gesture because, (1) I truly loved the dress and am totally heterosexual, and (2) she would now be taking Miffy home.

I already had Killer, and one snotty, pretentious, lazy-ass cat hogging the pillow was enough.

I know, I know. Shouldn't the hot, hunky bounty hunter be hogging my pillow?

If only.

Closure.

That's what we'd both said when we'd gotten jiggy in the pool house. And then back at his place. And then at my place. And then dangling over Central Park.

Talk about an extraordinary night. Our last, obviously. I wasn't his type and he wasn't my type. He'd gone back to bounty hunting and paying his debt to the deadly born vamp Logan Drake, and I'd gone back to matchmaking and fantasizing.

Over. Really.

Dead End Dating was thriving, thanks to the bump from *Manhattan's Most Wanted* (they'd aired outtakes from the mad, bad carriage ride). I wasn't too jazzed about the extra attention (I'd become somewhat of a local celebrity), but I couldn't complain about the publicity it generated for DED. I was now—drum roll, please—bringing in enough money to pay my credit card bills and, therefore, much too busy to angst over Ty.

Rather, I played it ultra cool—translation, no crying or begging—whenever we ran into each other, which turned out to be fairly often since I was still determined to land Ash Prince and his demon counterparts as clients (sexual demons meant satisfied women and easy moolah) and Ty had a close working relationship with them.

"Come on, Daddy. Give it to Big Mama!" Shirley's voice rose above the blaring lyrics of *I'm Too Sexy* and killed any and all thoughts of Ty.

Sort of.

Shirley wore red polyester pants, a flower-print smock and a cloud of Emeraude. I watched as the buxom owner of Wedding Wonderland crawled up onto the stage and started to bump and grind (which looked more like bobbing and jumping). Daddy, aka Power Tool, turned and ran for the dressing room (smart guy) and left her dancing all by her lonesome.

"We're going to get thrown out of here," Evie told me. "You know that, right?"

One could only hope.

"As long as she doesn't touch anyone, we're okay," I heard myself say. "Let her have her moment. She's just excited."

Understandably. Shirley had not only aced her first major wedding (Mandy and Jack's), but a few more as well. Word had quickly spread about her one-of-a-kind bridal gowns thanks to the photographer who'd done Mandy's wedding portrait and yours truly, who'd just so happened to mention Shirley's boutique during a radio interview regarding the *MMW* outtakes. Shirley had hired Esther to be her head designer and they were already putting together sketches for a fall collection.

"Houston, I think we have a major problem," Evie said as Shirley unbuttoned her blouse and started twirling it in the air while dozens of intoxicated women chanted *"You go, girl!"* "You don't think she'll actually—uh-oh."

Elastic snapped and the bra came off.

Evie gasped.

I screamed.

And that's all, folks . . .

Read on for a tantalizing taste of
Kimberly Raye's
Just One Bite

Being a five-hundred-year-old (and holding) born vampire, I've pretty much seen the worst of the worst.

War.

Famine.

Natural disasters.

Stock market crashes.

Powdered bob wigs (my father is *so* not living that one down).

Bottom line, there isn't much that can shock me, the Countess Lilliana Arrabella Guinevere du Marchette (aka Lil for short), Manhattan's *numero uno* when it comes to matchmakers.

Except walking into the office of my hook-up service—Dead End Dating—to find an Anthony Soprano clone holding a very lethal-looking stake.

I came to an abrupt stop in the doorway, my Constanca Basto sandals refusing to carry me the rest of the way inside.

Twisted, right? I had the whole vamp super package—HD vision, enhanced hearing, mind-reading capability—working for me. Throw in the glamour trick (aka the ability to mesmerize and persuade the opposite sex with my deep, entrancing stare), and I really had little to fear despite the nuclear toothpick in his meaty hands.

Then again, he *was* wearing a pair of pitch-black Ray Bans, which sort of put a crimp on the mind reading and the glam thing. He sat behind my desk, his feet propped on the glass and chrome. He had thinning brown hair and a recessed hairline that said he was in his late thirties, maybe early forties. A black Gucci jacket hugged his pot belly. Black slacks, argyle socks, and gleaming black loafers completed the outfit. He shuffled the stake from one hand to the other. Back and forth. And eyed me.

My heart shifted into overdrive and I drank in a deep, calming breath (so NOT a necessity for my kind, but after years of blending with humans, it's become sort of a habit).

I tamped down the urge to bolt (hey, my feet *were* frozen) and decided to go for Plan A—faking my way out of a very difficult situation. I pasted on my most mesmerizing smile. "Can I help you with something?"

"Lil Marchette?" he asked, a Bolivar cigar hanging from the corner of his mouth. He had a thick Jersey accent and the cold, emotionless tone of a hit man.

Duh.

"Um, no," I blurted. "I'm Evie. Lil's assistant. She's on vacation right now. A really long vacation."

"Evie, huh?" The Ray Bans swept over me once, twice. "Funny, but I met an Evie about an hour ago." He waved the cigar at me. "You don't look anything like her. I mean, you're both blondes, but she's short and you're tall. And a vampire."

So much for Plan A.

Enter Plan B—charming my way out.

"Nice jacket," I told the guy.

"You like? My mother bought it for me."

"She has excellent taste."

He actually smiled. "Damn straight she does. She's a saint, that woman." The Ray Bans zeroed in on my face. "Goes to mass every Saturday and Sunday. She don't like liars, and neither do I."

"I'm not really Evie," I admitted, giving him a sheepish smile. "I just thought you were another fan from *MMW* and I wanted to avoid a confrontation."

Manhattan's Most Wanted was a local reality dating

show fashioned after *The Bachelor* that paired Manhattan's hottest guys with a bevy of beautiful, buxom women. While I hadn't made the final cut for the actual show, I had made it into the outtakes that had aired a few short weeks ago.

"I saw you riding that carriage through Central Park. You're a wild one."

"That's me."

"I bet you've seen all kinds of crazies."

"There was this one guy who wanted to lick my toes and another who asked me to spit on him. But most are just desperate. And lonely. They just want a date." I eyed the stake and swallowed against the sudden lump in my throat. "There's no chance that you're here for that, is there?"

He shrugged. "Maybe. I mean, I *am* here to kill you, but I might consider a date instead."

"I'm there," I said, hope blossoming. "Just name the time and place, and you've got a deal."

"Not with you. You're not exactly my kind of woman."

True, so why did the comment make me feel so crappy? Oh, yeah. Because I was a hot, megalicious vampire usually wanted by any and all males, vamp or otherwise, and so this was a stab at my already fragile ego.

We're talking paper-thin, ultra-delicate, *this* close to snapping in two—thanks to one hot, hunky bounty hunter/made vampire. We'd had fabulous sex several times and then he'd walked.

Uh, yeah. You both agreed that there was no chance of a future, remember?

I was a born vampire (i.e I'd come into the world via eighteen hours of labor, done the toddler and adolescent thing, and had stopped aging when I'd lost my virginity) and he was made (i.e. a human who'd been bitten and turned), and the two DID NOT go together. BVs lived to make money and procreate. I was planning on doing both someday, just as soon as I paid down a monumental VISA bill and found my eternity mate (aka another born vamp with a high fertility rating—a little digit that reflected the likelihood that a male vamp could hit a bullseye when it came to procreation—and great taste in clothes). Made vampires, on the other hand, lived to drink blood and have gratuitous sex. No bullseye needed.

While Ty didn't come across as the typical MV (he seemed more interested in hunting dangerous criminals than sucking and humping any and everything with a vagina), he still wasn't the guy for me.

My head knew that, but my undead heart . . . Talk about a slow learner.

"What's your name?" I asked him.

"Vinnie Balducci."

The name echoed in my head and stirred a great big *Aha!* Suddenly, everything made sense. I'd become somewhat of a local celebrity thanks to *MMW* and I'd obviously attracted the attention of the local representative of the SOBs, short for Snipers of Otherworldly Beings. They were a worldwide organization committed to the extermination of any and all paranormal creatures. I'd heard my father mention Vinnie on occasion, along with the juicy tidbit that the man could be bought off if the price was right.

For my father, that meant a monthly delivery of free file folders and liquid paper courtesy of *Moe's* (think copy machines and office supplies and printing services and *major* boredom).

Moe's was the family business and my biggest fear should my dating service go bust. All three of my brothers managed various locations while my father oversaw things at the corporate level. I had my own stash of Moe's uniforms (beige dockers and lime green polo shirts) hanging in my closet just waiting for me to fail.

"I can get you free toner cartridges." I launched into Plan C—bribery.

"Your father already threw in a stash last month."

"Highlighters?"

He shook his head.

"Copy paper?"

"Got it."

"New business cards?"

He seemed to think before shaking his head. "No, forget it. I need kids."

O-kay. On to Plan D—more bribery. "I thought you wanted a date?"

"Well, yeah. One that's interested in kids. See, Mama wants grandchildren and it's high time I settled down and gave her a couple. Which means I need someone who can squeeze them out on account of the only thing I can squeeze out is a—"

"Gotcha," I cut in. "No need to elaborate."

He grinned. "That's where you come in. You can help me find the right broad."

"So what sort of, um, *broad* are you interested in?"

"Somebody nice. Sweet. Wholesome. Catholic. That's what Mama always says. 'You need somebody nice and sweet and wholesome and Catholic. Don't go bringing home any atheist bimbos. I don't like atheist bimbos in my house.' "

"So no atheist bimbos."

"Exactly."

"How about a Catholic bimbo?"

He shrugged. "That would work, as long as she behaves herself in public. Oh, and she ought to be demure. My mama likes demure. And she has to be Italian."

"Those sort of cancel each other out, don't you think?"

"You'd better hope not. Otherwise, you'll be getting a one-way ticket to hell along with the rest of the blood drinkers and weres and Others." He held up the stake. "Make no mistake, I know how to use this. You'll be my five thousandth kill in the born-vamp category. That's a record, you know. One whack straight into your heart, a twist to the left, one to the right. The blood spurts and runs all over the floor, and it's adios afterlife."

A major rush of ickiness went through me. FYI— while I might be a blood-drinking vamp, I don't really do the bite-and-suck part all that well. I'd rather uncork a bottle of the imported stuff in the comfort of my own living room. No spurting. No running. No *ick*.

"I take you out and I make SOB history," he added. He pushed to his feet and rounded the desk.

My feet thawed at the speed of light and I inched backward.

"Go 'head. Run. You'll get away. For now. But when you come back, I'll be waiting."

"And if I skip the country and head for Reno? Or Switzerland? Or the Bahamas?"

"You move into someone else's territory. Someone who might not have a saintly mama who wants grand-children."

Which meant I could go somewhere else and get whacked (*ick*). Or I could stay in Manhattan and eventually get whacked (*ick*). Or I could match up Vinnie with his ideal and NOT get whacked (not so *ick*).

Number three won hands down.

"Okay, I'll do it," I told him. "Just put down the stake and you've got yourself a deal."

He dropped the piece of wood on the corner of my desk and grinned. "I never had a doubt."